Antonina Irena Brzozowska was born and educated in the north-east of England.

A former teacher, her interests incorporate the Polish, Canadian and Hawaiian cultures and traditions.

Her extensive travel experiences in these countries, have provided her work with an invaluable asset to her writing.

To all who read this book.

Antonina Irena Brzozowska

The Samovar

Austin Macauley Publishers

LONDON · CAMBRIDGE · NEW YORK · SHARJAH

Copyright © Antonina Irena Brzozowska 2025

The right of Antonina Irena Brzozowska to be identified as author of this work has been asserted by the author in accordance with sections 77 and 78 of the Copyright, Designs and Patents Act 1988.

All rights reserved. No part of this publication may be reproduced, stored in a retrieval system, or transmitted in any form or by any means, electronic, mechanical, photocopying, recording, or otherwise, without the prior permission of the publishers.

Any person who commits any unauthorised act in relation to this publication may be liable to criminal prosecution and civil claims for damages.

This is a work of fiction. Names, characters, businesses, places, events, locales, and incidents are either the products of the author's imagination or used in a fictitious manner. Any resemblance to actual persons, living or dead, or actual events is purely coincidental.

A CIP catalogue record for this title is available from the British Library.

ISBN 9781035888368 (Paperback)
ISBN 9781035888375 (ePub e-book)

www.austinmacauley.com

First Published 2025
Austin Macauley Publishers Ltd®
1 Canada Square
Canary Wharf
London
E14 5AA

Thank you to all the team at Austin Macauley Publishers for all the help and support given to me.

Thank you to all those who have supported and encouraged me in any way.

Kraków, Poland
1950

Intermittent spikes of jagged lightning quivered in the semi-darkened room as the young girl, pinned down to her bed, lay trembling beneath the heavy weight on top of her. Deafening blasts of thunder drowned out her muffled screams and, with them, her hope of an imminent release. She squeezed her eyes tight to obliterate his blubbery face, as he twisted his fleshy lips on her lips; the stench of garlic, intermingled with vodka, making her stomach churn and her whole body wrench and writhe with revulsion for the monster on top of her, as he pumped on mercilessly. Hot prickly eyes strayed to a shiny silver samovar on a small round table in the corner of the room, where they witnessed a minuscule reflection of the animal on top of her, a surge of intense hatred rising within her as she silently vowed between clenched teeth, *I'll get you back for this, you pig; if it's the last thing I do!*

Chapter One
Kraków, Poland 1954

"Cholera jasna!" Elżbieta Kaminska cursed her unruly shoelace as she fell unceremoniously to the ground, her school books following suit. Bending down her eyes encountered a pair of shiny liquorice-black, tightly laced boots.

"Here, let me." Before she could object, a pair of broad hands picked up the books and handed them over to the wide-eyed teenager.

"Th… thank you," she stammered, taking the books and averting her dark eyes, abruptly turning on her heels. Taking hurried steps in the opposite direction, she fleetingly glanced back at the kind man, dressed in full military uniform, now engaging a young woman in conversation, taking her slender hand and linking it with his own protectively, as they disappeared into the motley crowd occupying the Main Square in the Old Town of Kraków. Turning, Elżbieta took quick steps to Grodzka Street where, on the corner, stood the small Romanesque Church of Saint Adalbert partly obscured by ancient trees, graciously allowing the church's patinated copper dome to remain visible. Pushing the heavy door open, she stepped into the damp coolness and eerie stillness, relieved to have reached her sanctuary; relieved to be away from her father and her brother; relieved to close her mind to Tadek Lisztek, the one human being she despised with all her heart and soul.

Closing the bulky door, she sighed deeply glad to be alone for a little while with only the presence of her God, the One Being she could depend on. She clomped her way down the aisle, her heavy brogues dully echoing her determined steps in the oppressive dusky silence. Genuflecting, she slipped into a pew and knelt on the wooden kneeler, shifting her knees as she felt the rough hardness of wood on her skin. Her eyes flitted automatically to the solid gold crucifix placed on the centre of the altar, which was covered with a pure white, stiffly starched altar cloth, adorned by blazing candles on either side softening the stark reality of death the crucifix was there to represent. Her dry lips opened and out came the string of antiquated words: "Our father, who art in heaven…" while jumbled-up thoughts and memories performed a wild, erratic dance in her head.

"Oh Lord," she sighed heavily, her stark eyes staring past the crucifix, "why do You allow these things to happen?" A swishing black soutane swept past. The figure stopped and turned.

"My, you are early, Elżbieta; trouble at home?"

Her startled eyes jumped upwards. "Father Stanisław!" Immediately, a rush of a heated hue of red rose to her pale cheeks, making her curse silently, and her heart skip a beat as the young priest, barely out of the seminary, cast his dark, curious eyes upon her. She shrugged her narrow shoulders, her mouth clamped shut. *I can't say anything, even if I want to*, she firmly told herself, *not after the last time…* Her mind wandered off to the vicious beating she had received from her father when he found out that his one and only daughter had been telling tales out of school.

Only, they were not tales. Her lips clamped into a tighter line. To this very day, her back bore the scars of his ruthless belt. It was a lesson well remembered. One does not let family secrets out, ever.

"Elżbieta, is something troubling you?" Father Stanisław laid a gentle hand on the girl's shoulder, his dark eyebrows rising in question, as a rush of genuine concern washed over him. He felt sorry for the young woman. Stories of Kaminski's harsh treatment of his daughter had circled the immediate community and inevitably had reached him, but when confronted, Elżbieta always denied it all. Only on one occasion did she succumb, and he knew secretly she had paid a heavy price.

"I am fine," Elżbieta answered firmly, looking away from the young priest's steady gaze, relieved she could hear the sound of her fellow students approach.

While Father Stanisław elaborated on the sanctity of marriage, Elżbieta silently opposed his every word. *The sanctity of marriage*, a voice in her head scoffed. *What a laugh! It's nothing but a joke; a colossal, laughable joke. Where is the sanctity in Mama and Tato's marriage? Where the honour, trust and respect? Where the love? In Tato's damned bottle and penis, that's where.*

She stared at Father Stanisław's mouth opening and shutting, his hands speaking a language of their own, his black soutane swaying gently in rhythm with his body movements. Suddenly, she rose and, roughly pushing past her friends, clambered out of the pew and, without genuflecting, stormed out of the cool church into the still-hot afternoon sunshine in time for the ritualistic, haunting sound of the bugle player. She raised her eyes to the tower of Saint Mary's Church, and there they rested, as she was gently hypnotised by the evocative notes of the Hejnał, played every hour on the hour. She'd heard it hundreds of times before, yet each time brought with it a fresh excitement, a new cry to bury the old and to herald in new hope and today was no exception. Her joy was short-lived as her rich brown eyes clouded over, and the sparkle was replaced by a deep inner pain, dark and secret.

Like the thirteenth-century Polish watchman, who sounded the alarm when he caught sight of the Tartars advancing the battlement, and whose call died in his throat when he was shot by a Tartar's arrow, but whose alarm saved the city, she too felt dead inside when Tadek Lisztek… She squeezed her eyes tightly against the black memory of it all, her lips compressed as she swallowed a hard lump of secret bitter humiliation that had risen to her throat. *There is no hope,* she told herself, *that… that animal has robbed me of the one thing I could give a man. I am nothing now.* Swiping away the hot prickly tears trickling down her flushed cheeks, she abruptly turned her back on the bugle player, and Saint Mary's tower, and hurried on in the opposite direction.

Paweł Jaroszynski's eyes followed the figure for the second time that afternoon as she disappeared behind the church, down Florianska and out of view.

Chapter Two

The pungent smell of over-boiled cabbage hit Elżbieta's nostrils before she reached the place called home. In reality, except for her mother, her home was nothing but a roof over her head, which also sheltered the two most contemptible people she hated the most in the world; the third monster was Tadek Lisztek who had brutally torn her body, heart and soul apart and left her with nothing. At the age of sixteen, with vibrant thick black curls cascading down her back and large brown eyes, with the promise of putting anyone under their spell, she was very much the beauty her mother had once been; but Elżbieta felt old, used and abused and tired of living; tired of hoping; tired of striving for a better life. All that she felt capable of doing was to survive and only that, she felt, was due to God's help.

Only, more and more she was now feeling that He too was abandoning her and leaving her to her own dismal and unavoidable fate. Trudging the flights of steps the sweet overbearing smell of cabbage became stronger making her stomach wrench. For a brief moment, her fingers lingered on the scuffed wooden doorknob, her feet yearning to run to she knew not where. Closing her eyes tight she took in a deep breath, bracing herself to the hell that was within; the hell her father and brother had created, and in which they ultimately reigned.

Her heart sank at the sight of her mother bending over a large pot of bubbling green liquid. Quickly, she rushed to the gasping, asthmatic woman stirring the nauseating mixture and steered her to her bed. Surreptitiously, she peered around the small apartment for any sign of the men folk, switched off the stove and, with a deep sigh, seated herself on the edge of the bed, taking her mother's thin hand into her own.

"Have you taken the pills the doctor has given you, Mama?"

Krystyna nodded her head avoiding her daughter's questioning glare.

Yes, I bet you have, thought Elżbieta despondently, deciding to let the matter drop this time. "I told you I would make the soup, Mama. You know you are not well enough."

"And... and you know your father. He wants it on the table when..." she paused and took a deep gasp of air.

"Yes, I know my father," interrupted Elżbieta, a wave of pure hatred surging through her young body at the mere sound of his name. "Where is he?"

"At work."

"With his so-called friends, pouring vodka down his throat, more like. Should I go and get him, Mama?"

"No... no... No..." Krystyna's eyes stared starkly at her daughter, her hand grasping tightly Elżbieta's arm. "You know that would only cause more trouble."

Elżbieta nodded. *Undisturbed shit doesn't smell*, she silently concluded, a saying she often secretly referred to when thinking of her father. "I'll get you a bowl of soup, Mama." She rose from the creaking bed.

Raucous laughter, intermingled with a spattering of curses and swearing, preceded Wojtek and his son, Jan's, entrance. Two pairs of eyes flitted nervously to the opening door, while hearts beat rapidly beneath trembling exteriors.

"Ah, look, son, no manners, no etiquette, and my beloved wife always claims she comes from higher stock." Casting contemptible eyes at Krystyna's frail figure, he snarled, showing his yellowed teeth, "Can't be bothered to wait for us; too busy gorging your own upper-class face, eh?" He approached the bed with his heavy dirty boots, casting a disdainful look at his wife, his red blotched eyes darting and resting on Elżbieta.

"We waited for you, Tato," Elżbieta lied, trembling visibly. "Mama has not been feeling well." She stated in as calm a voice as she could manage, avoiding her father's angry glare.

He turned his twisted face on his son, his bulging eyes almost popping out of his bloated face. "No cholerine manners, eh son?" Abruptly he turned his whole bulk around and, with one ferocious swipe of his hand, knocked the bowl of soup from Elżbieta's hand, causing her to yelp out in pain as the boiling liquid splattered onto her hand. He ignored her cries swearing, "You cholerine bitches; you good-for-nothing whores..." His gnarled hand poised in mid-air, and flaring eyes staring through Elżbieta, he took a wobbly step forward.

"Go on, Tato, hit me, if you must," she encouraged. "But don't you dare lay a finger on Mama. She's ill." Elżbieta glared at her father her heart racing, her guts twisting and churning, her young body taut and ready for the onslaught. She would sacrifice herself for the sake of her mother, the only real friend she had in the world; she would do all for her, just as they had done for each other in the past. Eyes stared at eyes. Elżbieta's heart thumped as she kept silently saying over and over again, *and, this too shall pass*. His hand came slowly down.

Jan posed menacingly in front of his sister, shaking his head in utter disbelief, sniggering, "My father seems to be losing his touch but don't you worry, my dear Elżbieta, I haven't. I will let you off this time, my dear." His grin broke into raucous laughter as he headed for the stove, leaving the two women trembling inwardly in his wake.

From the safety of her bed, Elżbieta watched as the two men slurped their soup, roughly tearing their bread rolls apart and stuffing them in their greedy mouths, a half-filled bottle, in pride of place, in the middle of the scuffed table. *It's going to be another long night*, she thought, *unless they drink themselves into oblivion and allow Mama and myself to have some peace*. The two women were trapped; there was no way out; there was no way of escape. They were both locked in a prison of mental and physical torture, and there was nothing they could do about it.

Unless… Elżbieta stared at the fast dwindling liquid in the bottle, wobbling precariously in her father's tremulous hand, as he poured the last of the clear substance down his glutinous throat. *Yes, there is one thing I can do, and it just might work*. Her heart beat wildly at the anticipation of it all. *I just have to have the guts to do it*, she told herself determinedly, the ghost of a smile playing on her lips.

Chapter Three

Sleep eluded Elżbieta that night for fear of losing consciousness before her father and brother lost theirs and of a fearful dread of what they might do if they didn't lose consciousness. Multitudinous thoughts and ideas concerning her mighty plan added to her anxiety. Finally, after watching and waiting for hours, she heard their alcohol-induced snores as her eyes strayed to the two bulks, their drunken heads resting on their grubby elbows on the table, empty bottles strewn between them. She threw off her bedcovers and rose to sit by the grubby window, as the first signs of daylight began to break. Never had she been up so early, and it both thrilled and amazed her to see the birth of a glorious dawn, as a milky whiteness turned gradually into a splendid pink and then gold.

The blaze of every vestige of colour, silent and totally serene, spread creating a mosaic of colour as it softened the walls and the roof of the grey oppressive building in front of her. Her eyes averted from the window and flitted across to the larger of the two heaving bulks, as her face twisted into a scornful, pitiless mask of disgust. *They are nothing more than animals, just like Tadek Lisztek; three of a kind.* She shuddered at the memory she had so desperately tried to bury and forget but was unable to lay to rest, for it tortured her during her waking hours, and haunted her dreams and nightmares. *Yes*, she decided firmly, her eyes stuck on her father, *he was going to pay*.

Her tired itchy eyes switched to her mother's frail body, beneath the threadbare blanket, as it gently rose and fell. *She doesn't deserve this*. Scanning the sparsely furnished room her eyes rested again on Wojtek. *He has robbed Mama of everything*, she grimly concluded: *her wealth, beauty, dignity and, above all, her respect, and left her a shell of the fine woman she once was.* Lithely, she rose and scrambled under the large bed, her eager fingers searching for and withdrawing a small wooden box from under her parents' bed.

Cautiously, opening the lid, her fingers flicking through an assortment of old addressed envelopes, notes, receipts and photographs her eyes and fingers froze. *It was still here!* She heaved a deep sigh of relief and carefully withdrew the item to view it fully. It was old and the colour had faded, but she could still make out two smiling happy figures.

She brought the photograph up closer and peered intently, thinking, *this man with his arm around Mama's waist was not Wojtek Kaminski. Without a doubt he was a fine figure of a man, who knew Mama well, but who on earth was he; a former beau of Mama's? No, Mama had never mentioned any men in her life before Tato, but that doesn't mean to say… A brother? There was only one uncle, and he had died at sea.* She peered closer, her eyes becoming mere slits. *Who is he? Could he be the means of our escape and Tato's ultimate downfall?* She asked herself over and over again and as always, when she had the photograph in her hands, she was denied the answer.

Her ears pricked to the stir at the table. Quickly, she stuffed the photograph back into the box and shoved it in its hiding place. Her mind switched to her cousin Zosia's forthcoming wedding. When it was over it would, she decided, be the right time to look for answers.

At twenty-five, Zosia Koperkowa was already deemed, by most, to be an old maid. She was Elżbieta's beloved cousin, loyal friend and role model; a strikingly beautiful young woman who was tall in stature, of slim build with fair cropped hair, which showed off her perfect bone structure and complexion. Her eyes were cornflower blue with a hypnotising effect on anyone they rested on, especially the likes of Wojtek Kaminski who thought that a woman, any woman, but especially a beautiful woman, was either to be used and abused or had already been used and abused and was, therefore, a good-for-nothing tart.

People were drawn to Zosia's softly spoken voice and gentle nature. Not Wojtek Kaminski. He despised her for she was his best friend, Lisztek's, potential tart that got away. But he knew that sooner or later, married or single, he himself would have her. *Yes*, he vowed silently as he leered at her, across the table at the last family gathering, *I'll fuck that bitch*. He would not rest until his fantasy was accomplished.

Knocking impatiently on the brown peeling paintwork of the grubby door, Elżbieta's young heart pounded in her chest for the long-awaited day was almost upon them, and today was the day of the final dress fitting. The two girls hugged tightly, Elżbieta spotting her beaming auntie from the corner of her eye.

"Am I too old for a hug, my dear?" Mania Koperkowa extended her plump arms and approached Elżbieta. "Now then, how is my favourite niece, eh?" After long seconds, she withdrew from their tight embrace and scrutinised her niece fondly, stroking her black curls. "You are more beautiful each time I see you. And how is your mother?" she asked, the twinkle in her eyes disappearing and her blue eyes clouding over, for she dearly loved her one and only sister, but she knew full well the predicament Krystyna endured.

"All right," Elżbieta lied changing the subject. "How are the wedding preparations getting on?"

"Oh coming along, coming along. Everybody is giving a hand. Piotr's parents are good people. They are…"

"I am sorry we can't help more," interrupted Elżbieta, a look of concern, mixed with genuine regret, shadowing her young eyes.

Mania took the girl's hand and patted it gently. "Ssh, you and your mother have done enough." Her blue eyes scanned her niece's drawn, pinched face. "You've lost weight, eh, Elżbieta." Her wise eyes took on a look of grave concern as she added in a low, determined voice, "You must not let him get the better of you; you know that, don't you, Elżbieta."

Mania peered deeper into the young eyes as if trying to see into her very soul, secretly warning her, reassuring her, giving her one and only niece her full support. Elżbieta dropped her eyes to the dull threadbare carpet below, her eyes stuck on a pinkish faded rose pattern, noticing that the petals of the flower had disintegrated with age and constant wear. Mania's words had touched a painful spot, bringing with them a bitter lump to her throat. She managed a vague smile.

"Everything is fine, Ciocia Mania… really." Her flickering, glassy eyes rose to meet those of her auntie's and quickly she looked away lest her secret sorrow should be revealed. And, that wouldn't do, for Mania Koperkowa had also suffered much at the hands of her ruthless, overbearing, violent and now dead husband. Elżbieta's trembling hands reached out for the delicate fabric covering the back of the bulky armchair. "May I try it on?" she asked in as excited a voice as she could manage, forcing a smile.

Mania gazed at her niece in total admiration, the corners of her eyes crinkling with pure affection. *To have suffered at the hands of a brute; to have lived through years of cruelty, humiliation and misery and still be able to smile took an exceptionally strong person, like Elżbieta. But…*her heart sank; *there is only so much a person can cope with. One day*, she silently determined, *my niece will learn the whole truth. One day when she can carry the burden, but not today.* She pinned a smile on her lips, patting Elżbieta gently on the shoulder.

"Come, let's get you into that dress, Elżbieta, and see what needs altering."

Chapter Four

The day of Zosia and Piotr's wedding was a glorious hot June day. The church of Saint Adalbert was well attended by well-wishers and local gossip, witnessing for themselves what the likes of Mania Koperkowa would provide. Most were pleasantly surprised, some shocked and a few disappointed for there was nothing to criticise. Mania did her one and only daughter proud, pulling out all the stops, using all her savings apart from keeping back some money for her own burial.

As Zosia, dressed in a full-length gown of white organdie with a long veil to match, walked elegantly down the narrow aisle on the arm of her soon-to-be husband, a pair of bloodshot eyes glared lustfully from beneath heavy lids, a thick tongue licking dry lips in eager anticipation of what would be in the future. Krystyna Kaminska stood beside her robust husband, gripping tightly the wooden pew lest her legs would fail her, and she should cause a scene. Her eyes were not following the bride, they were fixed on her daughter she so wanted to marry off, before the good Lord took her, and she would be forced to leave Elżbieta to the cruel intentions of her so-called father. Swallowing a hard lump she secretly determined: *It is my duty, as her mother, to find my daughter a husband, and time is of the essence.*

Elżbieta's young heart beat wildly as she walked down the aisle with Stach, a friend of the groom's and her escort. Though they were one of four pairs she felt all eyes were upon her as if she was the bride; for a few treasured moments the sins of her past had miraculously evaporated away and all was fresh, unsullied, innocent; for a few happy seconds, she dared to feel she had a future despite her tarnished past. The smile on her face died a sudden death as she caught sight of her father leering glutinously at her before his red drunken eyes rested once more on his more valuable prize. Elżbieta quivered, her guts churning mercilessly, her only hope and prayer that her father would not cause a scene on Zosia's special day. Deep inside, she feared this was too much to ask.

Father Stanisław beamed at the happy couple before commencing the solemn proceedings, thrusting Elżbieta into a black well of negativity. She had long ago discarded the solemnity of marriage, viewing the present ceremony as a farce in the eyes of humanity. *Still*, she sighed inwardly as she stared at the solid gold crucifix before her eyes, *it has to be done. And, one day*. she told herself, *I, no doubt, will be standing in this very spot, uttering the same vows. It's expected; there is no way out.*

She breathed a loud exasperated sigh causing Stach to cast a concerned look. Their eyes met and locked. Abruptly, Elżbieta looked away, a flush of red rising to her cheeks, the lingering stare of a man immediately making her tremble, bringing her past to the forefront; her half-naked body, Lisztek's bulk on top of her, his rough fat fingers on her young breasts, his hard tongue in her mouth, his large penis inside her thrusting, pushing, hurting; robbing her of the one gift she could give her husband on their wedding day, and leaving her with nothing. A silent teardrop fell onto her open prayer book. She raised her watery eyes as Father Stanisław's mouth continued to open and shut, emitting meaningless words.

It's all a cholerny joke, she silently cursed, *a damn, despicable joke.* Her eyes flitted to Zosia as she willed her feet to root to the spot. *For, to run out on Zosia today would break both their hearts.*

The happy couple strode out into the glorious sunshine followed by four bridesmaids and their escorts, in turn, followed by the rest of the congregation. Abandoning the horse and carriage, decked in white ribbons and fresh-scented jasmine, Zosia and Piotr decided to walk the two-kilometre walk to Piotrs parent's house, the rest of the gathering following closely behind. Stach engaged Elżbieta in casual chit-chat; he failed to engage her heart. That was stone-cold. It had been frozen with iced emotions for years.

The lively band, consisting of two fiddlers, two cymbal players and an accordion player were playing a polka with enthusiastic vim and gusto, as merry guests joined the bride and groom in the energetic dancing. In the corner of the room, Elżbieta sat alone and looked on, her eyes flitting from Zosia and Piotr and resting on her parents sitting together, emotionally poles apart. *They might as well be complete strangers*, she thought, her eyes fixed on her drunken father. *He is a mess*, she grimly concluded, *and a bully.* Her eyes followed him as he rose from his chair on his wobbly feet, roughly grabbed his wife by her thin bare arm and unceremoniously slumped to the floor, causing a mound of half-filled glasses, a splattering of beer and a cold roasted chicken leg to fall on top of him.

In her mind, she heard him spew a barrage of curses at his wife and anyone else who happened to be in his way. "He is despicable," she stated aloud to herself. "And the sooner I get out of his house the better." There was one major stumbling block to her plan. She could not leave her mother with this monster. Her eyes instinctively rose to a shadow of a tall figure looming over her, as she focused on his warm smile and broad hands outstretched inviting her to dance.

"Would you do me the honour?" He cocked his thick eyebrows in question.

She glared at him as one would look at a worm crawling out of a carefully prepared salad. "I don't dance," she stated coldly, heavy finality edging her voice.

His smiling mouth changed into laughter. "What do you mean, you don't dance? Everyone dances. Come on, Elżbieta," he urged as he grabbed her by the arm forcing her to stand up, while her eyes spewed out venom and her guts wrenched at his touch.

"I said I don't dance, Stach. Now, please let go of my arm," she stated through clenched teeth as she roughly snatched her hand back.

"I don't think so, my dear Elżbieta. Not before you dance with me." His playful chuckling resumed.

"Let go!" she insisted raising her voice, her eyes narrowing to mere slits.

"I don't think so." He smirked, placing a firm hand around her slim waist.

"Let go!" she demanded, her voice becoming ever shriller, making people around turn and watch the proceedings with avid interest.

The sudden slap on his cheek turned his twinkling eyes to cold steel, his grin into a twisted form. "There's something very wrong with you, Elżbieta Kaminska. You need seeing to," he sneered.

His cruel words ripped through her like a jagged blunt blade for she knew they were true. Quickly, picking up the train of her white dress she pushed her way through the dancers and headed to the safety of her mother, and the bloodshot eyes of her father staring angrily at her. She dropped her eyes to the floor.

"Just like her father, violent and unruly." A plump woman shook her head in disapproval.

"I have heard that Wojtek Kaminski has done certain things to that poor girl, that would send anyone over the edge," muttered another gossip.

Both women now glared and shook their heads at Kaminski. Wojtek ignored their stares and turned his red glassy eyes on his daughter's bowed head, wagging his thick forefinger as he tried to formulate a sentence. Krystyna sighed inwardly and braced herself for what was to come, hoping against hope she would not have to witness a public showdown between her drunken husband and beloved daughter. Her silent prayer went unanswered as she watched Wojtek's twisted mouth pouring out spits of saliva, intermingled with a barrage of curses and ominous threats.

"H…how dare y…you em…embarrass me…me, your f…father, in public, you c…cunt?" He snarled with his crooked mouth, his glazed drunken eyes fixed firmly on Elżbieta. "How d…dare you, y…you…, you good-for-nothing t…tart?" He raised his voice for all to hear as his fat, tremulous hand snatched and pulled a generous handful of Elżbieta's hair, forcibly raising her head until her eyes met his. Like a frightened rabbit, at the hands of a treacherous poacher, she stared wide-eyed at him as if hypnotised.

"P…please, Tato, not here," she pleaded, her voice barely audible, acutely aware that many sets of eyes were upon her; aware that once again she was being humiliated in public, becoming the centre of attention for all the wrong reasons.

"Wojtek," whispered Krystyna, bestowing a gentle gnarled hand on her husband's thick arm. "Let it be. Please, let it be."

Roughly, he snatched away his arm from his wife's gentle touch, throwing her a scathing look, muttering loud enough for Krystyna to hear. "G…go and f…fuck yourself, w…woman and leave m…me alone." He turned his contemptuous, glaring eyes at his daughter. "W…who the h…h…hell do you th…think you are? When a man a…asks y…you to d…dance y…you jump, you y…you f…fucking well jump to at…atten…ion and fucking well dance."

His angry words boomed in the young girl's head, making her feel dizzy. She turned her eyes away not able to look at his blubbery twisted face any longer; closing her eyes tightly against the raw pain and bitter silent humiliation, as he grasped her hair tightly, twisting it tighter around and around in his bulbous fingers, making her eyes water.

"P…please, Tato," she yelped.

He brought his bloated face as close as he could get to his daughter, making her guts wrench as she inhaled the stench of vodka fumes from his opened carnivorous mouth "Y…you're spoilt goods, g…girl, used and soiled. Y…you're damned we…well lucky if a man l…looks at you, n…never mind i…if he as…asks y…you to d…dance. Next time y…you d…dance. Do y…you he…hear me, you good-for-nothing tart? You d…dance!"

Elżbieta nodded her head feeling a vicious pull, her eyes soft and imploring silently begging her father's mercy, as his bitter words echoed relentlessly in her aching head. *I know I am rubbish*, she desperately wanted to say. *I know I am good-for-nothing, but don't humiliate me in this way, in front of all our friends and neighbours.* He tightened his grip further as she closed her eyes abandoning herself to his will, as she always did.

"Good evening."

The greeting was soft but firm. Two pairs of eyes shot to identify the source, Kaminski releasing his captive hold over his daughter. Elżbieta's eyes scanned the tall, well-built body, the attractive face, the hair of shining jet with speckles of silver and the darkest eyes she had ever seen. She stared, her mouth slightly open and speechless, her body still quivering inside from her father's onslaught. The stranger's lips broke out into a generous smile, making the corners of his eyes crinkle into a fan of creases as he looked down at the young woman; *young enough*, he surmised, *to be his daughter*; the woman he had come to rescue from her father's clutches. His eyes flitted to Kaminski and rested on Elżbieta.

"You will do me a great honour if you will dance with me," he said, his soft gentle voice allowing the young girl to feel a strange warmth exuding from this stranger. Her eyes darted nervously to her father, who was staring unflinchingly back at her. She had learned her lesson.

"Y…yes, yes, I will dance with you," she stammered fumbling, with trembling fingers, for the loop of her train.

Krystyna's heart pounded with a mix of silent relief and inner dread, as the middle-aged man led her daughter onto the makeshift dance floor.

"Isn't that Ch…mielowski?" asked Wojtek catching his wife's eye.

"Yes," she answered in a whisper looking away, not able to hold her husband's gaze, her heart thudding.

"He o…owns that l…and up Kosćiòszko's way, eh?"

"Yes," Krystyna answered softly, knowing only too well what was going through her husband's mind.

"That t…tart is lucky he l…looked at h…her, never m…mind…"

Krystyna was deaf to his words. A teetotaller through and through, she picked up her husband's vodka glass and downed the potent liquid in one go, instantly making her whole body tremble, and an open-mouthed Wojtek to stare at his wife in total disbelief. Immediately, it soothed, leaving her oblivious to her husband's lashing tongue, for a few moments making her feel totally free; free of Wojtek Kaminski, the man she hated and feared; the man she wanted, above all else, to protect her daughter from. She caught a glimpse of Elżbieta and Zygmunt Chmielowski as they twirled around the floor to the sound of a flowing melodious waltz. *He is*, she thought, *the perfect gentleman; rich and handsome and looking for a wife. Yet*, she shook her head vehemently, *this could never, ever be. Never!*

Elżbieta wished the dance to be over; wished the wedding party to be over so that she could crawl back under her stone and be left alone. As the band stopped playing, Zygmunt took her right hand and brought it up to his soft lips bestowing on it a light kiss, making her whole body quiver, her sheer inner panic only taking its leave when he led her back to her parents and released her hand. For a lingering moment, he gazed into her innocent face, his dark eyes glittering like pieces of coal. He smiled and left her presence as Wojtek Kaminski watched the proceedings with immense interest.

Elżbieta's eyes dropped to the floor, her heart and mind in a whirl as she desperately tried to get a hold of her feelings. When she finally looked up her heart sank as, with horror, she watched her father approach Zygmunt and engage him in deep conversation. Abruptly, her puzzled eyes turned to her mother, whose eyes were firmly fixed on the two men, a look of grave concern etched on her thin face.

"Why is Tato talking to that man?" Elżbieta asked nervously, a thousand possible scenarios flashing through her head.

Krystyna's mouth remained clamped as her eyes remained fixed, one thought driving all others away: *This liaison with Zygmunt Chmielowski cannot be, under any circumstances. It must stop.*

Chapter Five

The days following Zosia and Piotr's wedding were somewhat of an anti-climax for Elżbieta, for there was nothing on the horizon to look forward to except her father's incessant drinking and her brother's harsh tongue; however, she was thoroughly shocked and pleasantly surprised, when only a moderate amount of drinking took place and when, on one occasion, Jan lashed out at his sister for overheating the potato soup, Wojtek severely and most uncharacteristically admonished his son.

Deep in her heart, Elżbieta knew this genial behaviour was too good to be true. *It was only a matter of time*, she told herself, *until the bubble bursts. But* she asked herself, *why this sudden change? What is Wojtek Kaminski up to?* For she knew, without a shadow of a doubt, that he was up to something, and this something would not be to her advantage. On the unaccustomed occasion, one morning, of sitting down to breakfast together, a piece of scrambled egg resting precariously on the precipice of her fork, her heart racing, she narrowed her eyes and cocked her head in question.

"Mama, is something going on?" She asked in a quiet voice, afraid of what she might hear for fear of bursting the magic bubble.

Krystyna raised her eyebrows. "What on earth do you mean, Elżbieta?" She flicked her eyes from daughter to husband, and back to daughter.

"You and Father are acting very strangely just lately. I thought…"

"Eat your breakfast," retorted Wojtek fixing his stern eyes on his daughter.

"I… I…"

"Nothing is going on," responded Krystyna, catching her daughter's eye and silently begging her to leave it be.

"Are you sure?" Elżbieta's eyes flitted from one parent to the other before a loud scream emitted from her mouth, allowing a piece of chewed-up rye bread to fall onto the starched white tablecloth. She focused her vicious eyes on her brother, the source of the savage kick on her leg.

"Cholera jasna! What is this?" Wojtek demanded, the fire in his blood sending a flush of deep red to his angry face. "Can't a man eat his breakfast in peace at the family table? You," he focused his angry eyes on Elżbieta, "get out of here before I…"

"I am sorry, Tato," she mumbled timorously, her nervous eyes on Wojtek.

"Get out!" he roared with the ferocity of an angry lion roaring at an early Christian. "Get out!"

Rapidly, Elżbieta stuffed the last remnants of dry rye bread into her mouth, picked up her coat and ran for the door.

"Wait!" bellowed Wojtek turning his bulky body, his eyes fixed firmly on his daughter and waving his fork at her. "Tonight, I want you looking your best. Do you hear?" He grinned showing his stained yellowed teeth. "Your very best," he emphasised. "Do not disappoint me, Elżbieta." He sneered a wicked smile playing on his thick lips, happy in the knowledge that his plan was now firmly set in motion.

"Elżbieta, for goodness sake, pay attention, girl," yelled her teacher throwing a blackboard rubber in her direction, missing her and hitting a highly strung boy sitting on the bench behind; as he continued to rumble out the dates and conquests of Lech, Czech and Russ. *Why have I got to look my best tonight?* She asked herself repeatedly. *It was not a special day; no one's name day, no holy day of obligation, no anniversary of any importance. Why, even if it was, what's new? They were never remembered, never celebrated.* Her father's strict command played on her mind throughout the day, giving her no respite. She was no wiser when, still mulling it all over she bumped into Father Stanisław in Kraków Square on her way home from school, forcing her to snap out of her muddled reverie.

"Oh, I'm… I'm sorry, Father." She forced a smile, her feet itching to run so as not to be confronted by any awkward questions. She turned.

"Hey…hey…what's the rush, Elżbieta. Where's the fire?" He looked at the figure before him, a look of concern lacing his kind eyes.

"No fire. It's…it's just that Tato wants me home spick and span, looking my very best for tea tonight." The words rushed out, her eyes fixed on the ground below.

"Special occasion?" Father Stanisław raised a black eyebrow in question.

"No… yes… I don't know. I wish I did know. Something is going on for sure, and I don't know what it is." She spurted out the words rapidly in bursts, causing the young priest to shake his head in amusement, and bestow an irrepressible smile on the girl before him.

"I think I can put you out of your misery as long, that is, if I don't put my foot in it and spoil a family secret."

Elżbieta's eyes shot upwards and locked with the young man's twinkling eyes, making her tremble inwardly. "Well? Tell me please, Father Stanisław. Tell me." She pleaded, hoping to God the priest would not notice the tremor in her voice.

He did notice, but she wasn't the first girl to tremble in his presence. "It's your cousin, Zosia. Your mother was telling me this morning that after Mass, she is coming home soon and that she has something special planned."

"That's it! That's it, Father!" She exclaimed joyously and, without thinking, perched on her toes and gave him a peck on the cheek, turned and merged with the crowd and vanished out of his sight.

"That girl!" he exclaimed, his smile widening, "needs a good man to marry."

Hot and flushed, her heart beating wildly, Elżbieta ran down the maze of narrow streets leading home. *Zosia was coming tonight. What joy! What bliss! There would be so much to discuss: the wedding, the honeymoon in Zakopane with its majestic Tartas and Swiss-style chalets dotted about the mountainous landscape. Zakopane… what must it be like? But then*, she mused, *there could be nowhere else in the entire world which could match enchanting Kraków.* For, without being anywhere out of Kraków, she decided, it was the best place on earth possessing: the Wisła, the dreamy cathedral spires and church domes, Wawel Hill and, her favourite place of all, the Sukiennice constructed during the fourteenth century.

It was a place which at first served merchants who came to Kraków to trade their wares, at that time mainly woollen cloth. Now, it was still a place of trade where Elżbieta loved to walk through the arcades, watching the buyers barter to secure a bargain. Her mind wandered to a happier time when her mother had taken her out for the day:

Their precious time together began at Wawel Castle of the Polish kings. How they had admired the arras tapestries, which were one of the greatest treasures of Wawel. How her eyes were entranced by the szczerbiec, a thirteenth-century sword used since 1320 as the coronation sword of the kings of Poland. The other weapons on display she didn't much like, and shuddered inwardly at the mere thought of the harm they could, and did, inflict on the enemy. She remembered well Wawel Cathedral, the place of coronations, and the resting place of the kings.

She had nightmares after visiting the nave and the sarcophagi of Polish kings, sculpted in expensive marble and surrounded by grand and impressive Gothic, Renaissance and Baroque chapels. She found the Sigismund Chapel, built between 1519 and 1539 the most magnificent, especially its breathtaking golden dome. That night she dreamt her father was raping her under the gilded dome.

Most especially, she remembered the little Krakowianka doll her mother had bought her, that day on their visit to the Sukiennice. The doll with long plaits framing a beautiful face, wearing a black velvet bodice colourfully sequined with ribbons flowing from one shoulder, a long red satin skirt with colourful ribbons *around the bottom and red boots. On her head, she wore a flowered headdress with ribbons on both sides. To this very day, the doll was her most treasured possession, for it was always a reminder of the best day of her life.*

Abruptly, she snapped out of her magical reverie as she found herself outside her door. Curling her fingers around the gnarled door knob, she inhaled deeply the appetisingly delicious smell of fried kotlety, intermingled with the warm and comforting aroma of a cinnamon and almond cake her mother baked on special occasions, as she walked inside. *My favourite; and Zosia's too*, she smiled as she inhaled deeply once more, savouring each delicious moment. *What an evening this is going to be; one to remember, that's for sure! Immediately*, her eyes opened wider to a sight she had never witnessed before: her father clean shaven with sleek combed back hair, attired in his one and only suit. Her eyes flitted to his pristine shirt sporting a neat black bow tie.

He was sitting at a laden table of: śledzie, roast pieces of cold chicken, and an assortment of bread, sausages and salads, smoking his rolled-up cigarette, his eyes engrossed in the *Dziennik*. He raised his eyes to his daughter, his twisted mouth betraying his otherwise calm exterior. "I told you to look your best, girl," he shouted, his eyes piercing into Elżbieta's very soul. "Now, go and get some decent clothes on and put some of that… that stuff to make your cheeks look more alive. You look like a damned corpse. I want you to look your best. Do you hear me, girl; your best!"

A wave of puzzlement swept over Elżbieta's face, her wary eyes flitting across to her mother who, in her best pink flowered dress, was stirring barszcz at the stove. She gave her daughter a fleeting glance returning her eyes to the deep red liquid, with thin strips of beetroot, bubbling away in the large pan below. "Do what your father tells you, Elżbieta," she said softly.

"But… but it's only Zosia who is coming. We never made such a fuss of her before."

"Go… Now!" roared Wojtek, the flimsy newspaper shaking in his tremulous hand, as he stubbed out his roll-up with the other.

Elżbieta disappeared into her room, her young heart thumping with euphoric anticipation, a smile dancing on her lips. *Soon,* she mused, *my cousin Zosia will be here and that's all that matters.* Her smile died. *But why is Tato going to the trouble of staying sober and dressing up for the occasion?* She shook her head taking out her best white dress, laying it on her bed and admiring it. It had been shortened since the wedding just to below the knees, but it was the only nice dress she owned, and she wanted to look her very best for her cousin.

"What the hell is taking you so long?" Her father's gruff voice, intermingled with a bout of ferocious banging on her door, made her jump.

"I… I'm sorry, Tato, I'm almost ready." She quickly slipped into her dress tying the sash around her slender waist, with trembling excited fingers she undid her braids and vigorously brushed her hair, remade her plaits and secured them around her head, with two sturdy pins, forming a neat crown, making her look younger than her sixteen years. She wanted to look young that day. Once before she witnessed Zosia's fiancé admiring her in an appreciating way. It was harmless, but how she had blushed outwardly and squirmed inwardly. She dabbed a little scent behind her ears, took a hasty look at her reflection in the cracked stained mirror and walked out of her room. Krystyna cast an approving look at her daughter and gave her an appreciating smile.

"She looks like a damned ghost," snapped Wojtek staring at Elżbieta. "I thought I told you to…"

"I don't have anything to put on my cheeks or lips, Tato," she cut in, her own sentence interrupted by three firm knocks on the door. "It's Zosia!" she exclaimed running to the door, sheer excitement overtaking her whole body.

"Elżbieta, sit down!" demanded Wojtek. His command went unheard as the door opened and Elżbieta's eyes fell wide open, as did her mouth. She stood on the spot, rigid, her fingers clamping tight the doorknob, making her knuckles white; the fingers of her free hand digging deep crescents into her palm as she stood in frozen silence, her lips tightly pressed into a thin line, her eyes wide and stark at the looming figure standing before her.

"Good evening, Miss Elżbieta." The deep warm voice resounded in her ears, her insides twisting ruthlessly as he took her free trembling hand and brought it up to his lips kissing it softly. Their eyes met. She looked away.

"It's not often I get such a greeting from a young lady." He smiled genially.

"I… I was expecting someone else," confessed Elżbieta, her wild excitement now turning into churning dread as a strange inexplicable sense of foreboding descended upon her.

"I am sorry to have disappointed you. Perhaps," he paused, withdrawing from behind his back a large box decorated with a blue silk bow, "this might help to ease your regret."

"Chocolates!" she exclaimed unable to contain her rising excitement, her eyes wavering with disbelief, as this was indeed a rare treat.

His dark eyes flitted to Krystyna. Eyes locked with eyes. Abruptly, she looked away. Cautiously, he took steps towards her. "For you, Pani Kaminska." She took the bouquet of colourful roses, her heart thudding, avoiding his eyes, wishing to God this evening was at an end.

"Come… come, Zygmunt." Wojtek approached the door extending his hand to this most important guest. "Come into my humble abode. Sit down, my good friend, and have a sample of this finest of spirits." He clicked his fingers. "Krystyna; glasses."

Casting a surreptitious glance at the two men sitting at the table, glasses in hand, Elżbieta closed her eyes for a moment to the scenario unravelling before her, disappointment churning away in the depths of her heart. Taking her mother's roses she escaped to the sink. The shrill shriek forced both men, glasses raised, to look around.

"You stupid bitch!" exclaimed Wojtek unable to restrain his rising hot anger, his face twisted cruelly. "Can't you do one thing right, girl?"

"Let it be, Pan Kaminski. I am sure it was an accident; young women are sometimes preoccupied," stated Zygmunt in a gentle, steady voice.

"A little preoccupied! This girl's head is stuck in the cholerine clouds," snapped Wojtek, immediately cursing himself for putting down his daughter in the presence of this great man, lest he believed his words and turned his attention elsewhere. "Yes... yes... maybe a little preoccupied," he muttered, making a hasty U-turn.

Zygmunt averted his eyes focusing his attention on his glass.

Elżbieta stared down at the damp patch on her dress and thought: *At least this Zygmunt fellow had the decency to look away from my embarrassment.* Her mind drifted back to the dance they shared at Zosia and Piotr's wedding: *How gentle he had been; how so unlike Tato. Maybe, this man is not that bad*, she mused arranging carefully the last rose in the large crystal vase and placing it on the dingy sideboard, instantly brightening the dim, pokey room. She escaped back into the small kitchen where she could see the three of them making awkward, polite conversation, a deep feeling of betrayal gnawing away at her. She stared at her parents in turn.

How could they? She asked herself over and over again, her eyes now riveted on her mother's black head of hair. *How could she? How could my own mother, the one person in the world I trust, do this to me? To betray Father Stanisław, or was he in the act too?* Cold undiluted anger swept and settled over her like a dark heavy blanket, overwhelming her whole senses, making her head spin as she stared at her mother's hands adjusting the side dish of butter on the laden table, her pink flowered dress brushing against Zygmunt's chair. *How could she?*

"Elżbieta, dear, come to the table," Krystyna said softly, her softly spoken words making the young woman's guts writhe.

Begrudgingly, with slow steps, she approached the table, her eyes set firmly on a vacant chair. "Where is Jan?" she asked in a clipped tone, her eyes avoiding all others.

Wojtek shrugged his shoulders, his greedy eyes fixed firmly on the red-hot soup before him, tearing a chunk of rye bread in two before stuffing it into his mouth.

"Jan?" Zygmunt asked pointedly arching his eyebrows in question.

"The black sheep of the family," muttered Elżbieta her dark eyes dancing with sudden mischief, capturing Zygmunt's heart.

"Silence!" roared Wojtek, as pure wrath fulminated inside him at his daughter's stupidity, of showing herself and her family up in front of this most distinguished guest. "Silence!" He banged his metal spoon on the table, causing a strip of beetroot to slither down from its shiny surface onto his wrist, and a nearby pepper pot to fall onto its side, causing Zygmunt Chmielowski to stare incredulously at his host.

"Janusz is our son, Pan Chmielowski." Krystyna stated avoiding his eyes. "He has gone to a friend's poprawiny and, as you know, these parties can go on for days." Her grey eyes firmly fixed on her own bowl of barszcz, she desperately hoped she had quelled the potential catastrophe of raising her husband's fierce temper.

"Indeed… indeed," Zygmunt nodded his head raising a glass. "And now, may I propose a toast to the two most beautiful ladies my eyes have ever had the pleasure to behold?" His eyes flitted from Krystyna and lingered on Elżbieta, and he smiled.

Unblinkingly, she stared at Zygmunt through her thick lashes musing: *This man is old enough to be my father but… but…* Something, she knew not what was inexplicably drawing her towards him; something dark and mysterious; something that, at the same time, was urging her to run and hide away from him. She sat, as if transfixed, staring at his deep-set black eyes under heavy brows, his sleek black hair speckled with silver and combed to one side and his warm smile. His eyes caught her eyes. Without warning, and to her innermost utter humiliation, she felt a fiery flush rise in her neck, suffusing her face with a scarlet veil, as she felt the uncomfortable prickly heat rise to the root of her tightly braided head.

Zygmunt'e eyes watched Elżbieta's every move, as she helped Krystyna to clear away the soup bowls. His eyes followed her slim hands as they placed, on the table, a side dish of fresh forest mushrooms mixed with sour cream and chopped onions, and another containing mizeria, consisting of fresh cucumber thinly sliced mixed with sour cream and fresh dill. Krystyna followed close behind, carrying a large serving plate on which lay a succulent roast chicken. *A far cry*, he thought, *from the roast quail pigeon or venison his own discerning palate was used to, but*, he wryly concluded, *it's probably all these folks can afford, and his host had obviously gone without a few vodkas to be able to create such a laden table.*

He had discerned, from the moment he had walked into their tiny apartment, that Wojtek Kaminski had not ventured far from his peasant origin; he also knew why Wojtek had invited him to this get-together, for he had heard talk about this man, and what he had heard he did not like. His eyes flitted back to Elżbieta's hands: small hands, young hands already reddened and chapped and the nails, he noticed, bitten so badly. His eyes rose from her hands and thin wrists to her bare thin forearms, where he noticed small dark hairs. His eyes rose further to her upper arms and shoulders covered by the white fabric of her dress; he could only wonder what hidden delights lay beneath, waiting to be touched and caressed by a man.

"Pan Chmielowski, perhaps another drink?" Krystyna attempted to interrupt his secret reverie for the second time, a wave of concern rushing over her lest their guest was becoming bored. *Her secret*, she firmly concluded, *had to remain a secret a little longer, for her daughter's sake. She had to play it slowly; she had to play it cool*, she determined, *for if Wojtek got a whiff of anything all hell would be let loose, and their lives would certainly not be worth living.* Without waiting for his response she fled the table and a few minutes later reappeared, planting on the crowded table a bottle of the finest of Polish spirits.

"Pani Kaminska, you will be getting us all drunk!" exclaimed Zygmunt.

"How many more bottles have you got hidden away, woman?" Wojtek cast his accusing eyes on his wife, narrowing them in a menacing manner; then, pointing his fork laden with potato and chicken at his guest he stated, "Women are never to be trusted, my dear friend; no…" He shook his head vigorously from side to side, shoving the food into his mouth. "Never, ever trust a woman," he repeated slowly emphasising each word, while his partly chewed-up food rolled around his mouth. "Women are good for two things; and two things only: the kitchen and the bed. Why…?" he pointed his fork at Krystyna, "My good wife here; my loving wife before we were married was…"

"Wojtek!" exclaimed Krystyna so loudly Wojtek's mouth opened wide, allowing a gnawed-up morsel of chicken to fall back onto his plate.

"What?" he snarled staring fixedly, and with pure disdain at his wife. "What's up with you, woman?"

"Not here. Not in front of our guest." Her eyes bored into her husband's eyes, flitted to Elżbieta and back to him, hoping to God he would understand the unspoken message. He understood the message, for before his eyes flashed what would be lost if he let certain things slip. *For as day follows night, we'll never again find such another golden goose; never!* He silently concluded coughing hard to clear his throat and directing his full attention on his esteemed guest. "Of course, my daughter Elżbieta here is not like her mother; oh no, no, no."

He shook his head vehemently resting his eyes on his new victim. "Elżbieta takes after her grandmother, my dear mother, God rest her soul. She was a God-fearing woman, Pan Chmielowski. Oh yes." His glassy eyes darted to and penetrated Zygmunt's pensive gaze as he continued, "Do you know, Pan Chmielowski, my dear man, my daughter is a virgin and as pure as the virgin snow? Never has a man so much as touched her; never has a man…"

"Tato!" shrieked Elżbieta throwing her knife and fork onto the plate, shooting rigidly to her feet and staring piercingly at the man she called her father, as she tried desperately to blink back the surge of hot prickly tears welling up in her eyes. "Tato… please…" she pleaded.

"I know your daughter is a good girl, Pan Kaminski; I know," Zygmunt stated in a quiet voice raising his warm eyes to Elżbieta, a benign smile on his lips hoping to disarm her fear, if only temporarily.

All eyes focused on Elżbieta. Slowly, she sat down picking up her discarded cutlery; feeling comforted by Zygmunt's reassuring smile and his kind words, as her large brown eyes stared at him intensely. *Maybe*, she thought, *I could trust him; just maybe.*

The two men monopolised the dinner conversation. Elżbieta noticed how the composed Zygmunt Chmielowski gradually took control of every subject with his eloquent, well-accomplished lines of repartee. She was mesmerised by it all, taking a small delight in her father's discomfort in his lack of knowledge in the more important topics, her brown eyes burning with intense animosity as she watched Wojtek shrink beneath the weight of his inadequacies, of being unable to hold a conversation with someone far above his intellectual status, without being able to drip out his usual venom. Her eyes flitted to Zygmunt: *a true gentleman*, she mused, her eyes darting back to her father: *a filthy, disgusting, good-for-nothing piece of shit*, she concluded, *whose stench could be smelt anywhere he went.*

A sudden inexplicable urge took over her whole body making her want to: stand up, scream, shout and lash out at her father, her mother, Tadek Lisztek, herself and the entire world. She snapped her eyes shut biting her bottom lip hard. *For God's sake, control yourself, girl*, she severely scolded herself. Abruptly, she left the table and joined her mother in the kitchen. Taking a plate of royal mazurek in one hand, and another plate stacked high with sweet chrusty in another, she placed the plates back onto the table and faced her pale-faced mother.

"Mama, are you all right?" she asked her heart skipping a beat.

Krystyna waved her skinny hand dismissively. "I am all right. I am all right." She retorted harshly turning away, unable to conceal the pain in her eyes. "Go and see to the needs of the men folk."

Elżbieta did not expect what was to follow; neither did Zygmunt, Wojtek and Krystyna. As Elżbieta placed the plates of cake and sweet pastries on to the table, she felt the touch of a hand. Violently, she turned eyes of fire on her captor as fear, anger and resentment surged through her entire body making her lash out in the only way she knew how. The hard blow on Zygmunt's cheek made him instantly release his hold on Elżbieta. Her body taut; full of bitter contempt for her father, her brother, Tadek Lisztek all men she squeezed her eyes tightly obliterating them all. *Please, Boże, allow a deep pit to swallow me up!* She silently begged. Finally, she managed to force the words out of her dry mouth.

"I'm... I'm sorry, Pan Chmielowski. I didn't m...mean to..."

He chuckled softly running his fingers through his thick hair. "I was only going to reprimand your mother and yourself for spending so many hours in the kitchen, and to thank you for these delicious culinary delights."

Immediately, she felt the familiar flush rising uncontrollably to her face. "I am sorry," she repeated almost in a whisper, her eyes on the floor.

"You will be when I'm done with you!" roared Wojtek rising to his feet, his fists waving wildly in the air, his face as red as the royal mazurek on his plate below. "You will be more than sorry, my girl, when I get my hands on you. Nobody; nobody treats a guest the way you have... nobody! You... you..." He pushed his enormous bulk past the table, causing a dirty fork to slide off his plate and onto his burial trousers, and his mouth to spew out a barrage of curses.

"Stop it! Stop it!" Krystyna shouted her whole body shaking, her eyes firmly focused on her husband, flitting to Zygmunt without holding their gaze, "I am so sorry, Pan Chmielowski. Would you care for a small glass of krupnik to go with your mazurek?"

"No thank you," he smiled genially, "however, I would like to propose a walk after this sumptuous feast."

Elżbieta breathed a sigh of relief staring at her father, who downed his krupnik in one swallow, for she was certain he would decline the invitation.

"Pan Kaminski?" Zygmunt's eyes darted to Wojtek.

"What I want is another drink," snapped Wojtek lurching forward to retrieve the fast fading liqueur. "Forget about the walk, my friend, have another drink." He waved the bottle at Zygmunt.

"Pani Kaminska?" Zygmunt persisted in his line of enquiry.

Krystyna shook her head. "I am a little tired."

"I will go with you." The words rushed out before she could stop them as eyes darted to the clamped-lipped, stark-eyed young woman.

Zygmunt broke the ice turning to Wojtek. "If your father and mother will allow, it will be an honour to escort you." He smiled at Elżbieta, making something inside her stir with a strange unfamiliar excitement.

"Go." Wojtek waved a dismissive hand.

"Only for half an hour, Pan Chmielowski," stated Krystyna, "Elżbieta needs to help me with the clearing up."

He turned his full attention on Elżbieta. "Shall we?" He looped his arm, and she looped her arm through his as butterflies fluttered in her stomach, head and heart.

Though Elżbieta had lived in the same apartment for the whole of her sixteen years of life, she felt totally disorientated walking down the familiar streets of her neighbourhood.

Vegetable sellers hooted the horns of their carts, cyclists sped past, pedestrians walked on by, children tugged at their mothers' skirts, and trams weaved their way around them; all making her feel like an alien in a foreign world. Casting a sideways, surreptitious glance at the confident-looking Chmielowski she wondered: *Who is this stranger? Why is he spending his time with me? What does he want in return from me?* Like a trapped bird in an invisible cage, she tried to wriggle away her arm, as it was sliding away he secured it firmly with his free hand.

In a busy kawiarnia in Kraków Square, he ordered her a glass of lemon tea and himself a black coffee. Sitting opposite with his hands around the cup, he narrowed his black eyes making his thick brows above come together and scrutinised his young companion. "So, Elżbieta, am I right in thinking you finish school this year?"

She took a sip of her lemon tea avoiding his inquisitive eyes. "Yes."

"And then?"

"And then?"

"And then, what do you propose to do with your life?"

She giggled nervously her eyes on the amber liquid in her glass.

"You find my question funny?" he asked in a serious tone raising one dark eyebrow.

"No… no… it's… it's just that nobody has ever asked me what I am going to do after I finish school." Fleetingly, she glanced at him before returning her eyes to the steaming tea. "I suppose I shall have to marry and have babies; or, I can be an old maid and be frowned upon and pitied by the whole of Kraków."

His roaring laughter forced her to drag her eyes away from her glass and meet his dark laughing eyes. He leaned back in his chair, his loud laughter descending into a light-hearted chuckle, as his keen eyes rested on the mysterious girl sitting in front of him; narrowing his eyes to mere slits he loudly surmised, "Now, let me see, an old maid you will never be. You will never qualify for you will never be grumpy, uninteresting, ugly or unloved. So, I guess, it will be a choice between marriage and education."

"No." She shook her head adamantly. "There will be no choice involved here. My family will never be able to afford further education. So there is only one thing for me to do, I will have to find myself a husband, won't I?" she asked rhetorically.

"Will you?" A mischievous smile flickered on Zygmunt's lips. *This conversation*, he thought, *was growing more interesting by the second.*

"I will." Her eyes looked into his warm honest eyes. "The… the trouble is I… I don't trust men."

"All men?" he asked in mild surprise.

"Every single one of them," she stated resolutely.

"Does that include me?" His penetrating eyes looked deep into her eyes.

"Yes… no… I don't know." She closed her eyes tight as she took a gulp of her tea.

"My, my, for such a young lady to have such mistrust is…"

"Let's go back," she interrupted his flow of words rising lithely to her feet. "My mother needs me to help her."

"Of course, yes, we must go." Lightly, he placed his broad hand on her bare arm, sending a tingle up and down her spine, "Elżbieta, will you do me the honour of spending Sunday afternoon with me? I'd like very much for us to be friends."

"Yes, yes," she replied avidly without giving his request a second thought. "Now, let's go home."

After the door was firmly closed behind Zygmunt, Wojtek raised his drunken head from the table and his body, suffused with alcohol, from the chair swaying, his bloodshot eyes trying to focus, his wobbly legs giving way causing his body to slump to the floor, his trembling hands catching the linen cloth dragging it, and a plate of gherkins, to fall on to his best trousers.

"Cholera jasna!" he cursed throwing the gherkins one by one onto the table, his raucous laughter making Elżbieta feel sick to the stomach. "Ha…d a go…od f-fuck, d ….aughter of mi …ne? D…id he gi …ve you a go…od un?" He slurred the filthy words out, his glassy red eyes fixed on his daughter, his fat forefinger waving unsteadily about in front of his bulbous nose.

Elżbieta stood silent, rigid, inwardly quivering with hot undiluted hatred for this man she was forced to call her father. Her eyes flew to her mother, the only true friend she had in her life. *But even Mama*, she silently admitted, *has betrayed me today, sided with my father and abandoned me.*

"Y…yo…u h…have not an…sw…ered my qu…est…ion, you c…cunt." Wojtek glared at his daughter, his hands shaking uncontrollably as they held on to the empty krupnik bottle. "I… I a…as…ked you wh…whether you…"

"I heard you," shouted Elżbieta. "I heard your disgusting filthy words, and do you know, Tato, you make me sick! You make me sick!" She approached her father and stared eyeball to eyeball. "You have destroyed everything. You are no father of mine!"

"W…hy you… you…" Wojtek staggered towards his daughter and grabbing the nearest object from the sideboard, he hurled it with an almighty force at Elżbieta.

She stared at the small crumpled bundle on the floor. "My Krakowianka," she whispered, eyes of icy hatred darting to her father.

"Leave the animal," ordered Krystyna, turning back to the dirty plates in the sink.

That night Elżbieta sat curled up tightly on her bed, her broken Krakowianka doll tightly clamped in her hands, as bitter salty tears fell silently down her cheeks onto the coarse grey blanket covering her knees, as she listened to the drunken curses coming from her parents' bedroom; her father exploding into a venomous, crude, full-blown confrontation determined, above all else, to open every familiar wound he could remember in his befuddled mind, and belittle his wife in any way he could. Elżbieta shivered uncontrollably bringing her trembling hands to her ears, pressing them as hard as she could to block it all out;

not wanting or allowing herself to hear or feel what her mother was hearing and feeling; not wanting to know, to feel, to live.

Vigorously, she rubbed her sore eyes with the palms of her cold hands and rose from the bed, her whole body flinching as she caught sight of her reflection in the cracked mirror. *Who was this frightened, damaged, young woman staring back at her? Who was this young woman whose life had finished before it had begun?* For long minutes, she stared intently at the red watery eyes, the pale goose-pimpled skin and the tight-set lips; the strange woman standing before her.

The stranger stared back at her. She snapped her eyes shut screwing them tighter screwing all the muscles tight, tighter still. *Is this what a prune feels like?* She asked herself as she gradually released the tension in her face. Taking a handkerchief from her drawer she sat on her bed, blew her nose hard, and stared at the peeling plaster on the wall.

What on earth did Pan Chmielowski mean when he said, I have a choice? She wondered as her mind drifted off into his world; a world where a person could choose, and she imagined herself in this strange world, his world, and it felt good, very good as she drifted off into a deep sleep clutching the broken Krakowianka doll.

Chapter Six

The first Sunday of July was hot and overbearing. Elżbieta sat on a three-legged rickety stool on the balcony, seeking relief from the oppressive heat inside. Surreptitiously, peering over the wrought iron parapet she saw him before he saw her, as he walked briskly towards the block of apartments, a bouquet of white and pink roses held proudly in one hand, clutching a bulky brown paper parcel in another, as the strong afternoon sunlight cast highlights of fire-red and silver through his black hair.

He glanced upwards, an amused smile playing on his lips, as he witnessed Elżbieta's fast-disappearing retreat into the dim room. She had been caught out in the act of anticipating and awaiting his arrival and both of them knew it, much to the young woman's chagrin and Zygmunt Chmielowski's secret amusement. He mounted the stone steps and disappeared through the dimly lit entrance.

Elżbieta felt sure her mother could hear her fast pounding heart, for it seemed to thud louder with each passing second; feeling as if it was about to explode when three firm knocks were bestowed on the door, making her feel as if her heart had stopped altogether. She froze clutching her hands so tightly her fingers dug visible crescents into her sweaty palms, her wide expectant eyes were glued fixedly to the closed door, not able to move a centimetre. Inside she felt sick, the vomit rising to her parched throat where it stuck only, she feared, to spew out in an inappropriate moment onto her cotton dress. She closed her eyes scrunching them tight, wishing to never open them again, willing the floor with its dingy threadbare carpet to swallow her up and relieve her of this unbearable torture.

For, in the last few days, she had had time to think and had come to the conclusion that Zygmunt Chmielowski was the last man, apart from Tadek Lisztek, she wanted to see in this life or the next. *Why*, she told herself, *he is old enough to be my father; and one father in a lifetime is quite enough. After today*, she firmly resolved, *I shall never see him again. Never!* In her reverie, she did not hear the door open and was unconscious to the sound of footsteps walking in.

"Good evening, Elżbieta." His warm voice propelled her eyes into opening, as her hands automatically reached out for the bouquet in his hand. Suddenly, her ears pricked at the sound of an involuntary sigh and dropping the bouquet on the table she rushed to the kitchen.

"Mama, are you all right? Mama…"

"Allow me." Zygmunt held out his strong hand of support, as Krystyna begrudgingly leaned on him, and he slowly guided her to the sofa. As he began to release his hold, their eyes met, suffusing into a union making her heart beat wildly, her eyes showing a mixture of acute pain and immeasurable sorrow. Roughly, she thrust his hand away.

"I can manage," she snapped easing herself onto the sofa.

Wide-eyed Elżbieta stared at her mother, shocked by her uncharacteristic rudeness. *But then again*, she concluded, *pain does not oblige etiquette*.

"Perhaps we should call for the doctor," suggested Zygmunt, glancing back at the drunken unresponsive Wojtek.

"No," Krystyna stated firmly avoiding Zygmunt's eyes. "No!"

Elżbieta's eyes wandered to the drunken lump on the bed and scanned his tattered and torn clothes, his greasy ruffled hair, the stubble on his face, smelling his *stench* from where she stood. *No effort made this time*, she dismally concluded, *to impress the esteemed Pan Chmielowski*. Loud grunts spasmodically emitted from his misshapen gaping mouth, an empty bottle, like some rare jewel, secured protectively in his grubby hand. *Some father*, she thought. *Why couldn't Mama have married someone like Chmielowski? Why? Why? Why?* Her eyes flitted to Zygmunt, "Thank you for my flowers. I better put them in a vase before they start to wilt." She turned.

"Actually, Elżbieta, the flowers are for your mother."

She stopped and closed her eyes tight, thankful he could not see her face; the familiar heat rising and suffusing it with a red sheen. *Oh Boże*, she silently admonished herself, *why can't I get one thing right? Tato is right. I am stupid.* "Of course, how silly of me," she said almost in a whisper. His next words made her heart skip a beat.

"I have something else for you, Elżbieta." She turned her eyes dropping to his empty hands. "To be given to you when the time is right," he added turning his full attention on Krystyna.

"She needs a doctor, her chest pains are becoming more frequent," stated Elżbieta, concern clouding her eyes.

"Pani Kaminska…" urged Zygmunt.

"No more, Pan Chmielowski." Krystyna severely admonished as with trembling hands she gripped the side of the sofa and laboriously got onto her feet. Turning her back on her daughter and the man she was about to date, she slowly walked towards the kitchen, her heart full to the brim with dread and woe.

They walked in complete silence heading for the castle of the Polish kings. Elżbieta looked straight ahead, her troubled eyes fixed and unseeing; he now and again glanced at the young woman walking beside him young enough to be his daughter, though wise enough and mature enough in years to be his wife. Time for him was of the essence; a son and heir was needed to one day take over his land, and now was the time to take things into his hands and find himself a wife. His mind wandered back to the past… back to Krystyna…

As they left the Market Place and entered the limestone Wawel Hill, they were welcomed at the Wladyslaw IV bastion by the equestrian bronze statue of Tadeusz Kościuszko, Poland's great hero. Elżbieta's eyes scanned the multitude of tourists. *Surprisingly*, she thought, *they're not really looking at us. Perhaps they think I am here with my father.* Her thoughts drifted to Wojtek; *my father, what a laugh; Father in name only. You'd have to bribe him with a barrel of vodka before he would take the slightest interest in his family, let alone take me on a sightseeing tour*, she grimly concluded. Zygmunt's voice boomed in her head.

"And do you know, Elżbieta, in Poland this here Wawel Castle is the most popular museum? Apparently, there are seventy-one rooms of the most magnificent stature and a few thousand invaluable works of art here on display."

"Really, that's amazing." She tried desperately to sound interested.

He detected a note of apathy, deciding to let it be, as they walked silently through the hall vaulted gate and into the Renaissance arcaded castle courtyard. "Elżbieta, did you know, this is where knights tournaments, colourful pageants and dances took place?" Glancing sideways at her pale emotionless face, he continued his lecture. "I have read somewhere that the arras tapestries here are the most valuable of the entire works of art in the Wawel collection. Indeed," he enthused, "the city of Kraków owes the existence of this rich artistic legacy to King Sigismund Augustus I. It was he who commissioned the very best of Flemish weavers for the work, and personally supervised it during the course of twenty years. Of all the tapestries, I believe, there were over three hundred and fifty at the time of the king's death, unfortunately, only about a third of them have survived. Isn't that a great shame, Elżbieta?"

"Oh yes... yes... yes, a great shame." She tried desperately to quell the rising urge to run, to get away from this man, while her confused head fought in a desperate war of wills: *stay... run... stay... run... stay...* Her eyes opened to his soft eyes gazing upon her. *A kind man*, she thought, *who has taken time out to spend with a nobody.* "Yes," she nodded her head, "he was indeed a great king," she stated with forced enthusiasm.

They passed into the Crown Treasury, Zygmunt continuing his lecture. "Apparently, the Crown Treasury, ravaged as it frequently was over the centuries, doesn't contain all the treasures it used to house years ago. One of the items which managed to escape the destruction and devastating turmoil of the wars, I find most interesting, and I would like you to see is the szczerbiec."

Her heart stopped.

"It's a sword, I believe dating back to the thirteenth century used as..." His words were a mere echo in her pounding head, the lustre of the treasures on display causing shards of a fragmented, distorted nightmare to crash into her consciousness... the szczerbiec... a shiny surface... a samovar... Tadek Lisztek on top of her... their tiny reflection in the shiny surface of the samovar... "Elżbieta..." He tugged gently at her arm. "I am boring you. I am sorry, I have no manners. You must know the history of Kraków by heart. Who am I to..."

She felt herself drowning in his dark seductive eyes. "It's... it's all right, I know very little. Please, do go on."

He obliged. She didn't hear a word.

Sharing a coffee in a small kawiarnia off Market Place, Elżbieta's fingers played nervously with the fringes of her white crocheted shawl, her eyes fixed firmly on the black liquid in her cup, lips tightly clamped, stomach tight as a ball wishing she was anywhere but sitting here with Zygmunt Chmielowski. In the distance, she could hear the bugle player play his hypnotic notes. *Today*, she thought, *he doesn't bring hope.* Inexplicable despair was scratching at her heart giving her no respite, gnawing in the depths of her invisible soul.

Why? she asked herself, slowly raising her eyes to the man sitting opposite; *a kind gentleman, everything Tato is not; a handsome man, financially secure; a pillar of the community, a good man and yet... There was something about him... a mystery shrouding his mere presence.* She cast her mind back to the look exchanged between him and Krystyna, she had witnessed earlier. *Zygmunt Chmielowski has something to do with Mama's past*, she silently concluded.

"A grosz for your thoughts." Zygmunt smiled softly, a tinge of sadness lacing his eyes.

"They're not worth that much." A wan smile wavered on her lips as eyes locked with eyes and, there in his eyes, all became clear. *The photograph!*

Chapter Seven

Her feet pounded the streets and did not stop running until they reached the scuffed door; only when she was on the other side did her heart stop thudding. Casting her surreptitious eyes on her father slumped on the table, and no sign of her mother's presence, she scrambled under her parents' bed and hurriedly withdrew her mother's secret. With trembling fingers she lifted the lid and rummaged through papers and receipts and stopped, her eyes glued on the photograph. It was faded, but she managed to see the man standing beside her mother with his arm around her waist and recognised him to be Zygmunt Chmielowski. "Mama and Zygmunt Chmielowski," she muttered her eyes staring, glaring, riveted on the two images before her until they glassed over, and became one watery undistinguished and unrecognisable watery mass.

Opening her eyes, they were still there. *They had been there, together*, she mused, *all these years. Mama and Zygmunt Chmielowski. But where was Tato?* A thousand possible scenarios flew erratically around her head. She brought the photograph up closer and peered intently, staring at the protective arm around Krystyna's waist. *Was he an acquaintance? No… no, too close to be a mere acquaintance; a friend? Possibly, but still too close; a lover? A lover… Oh Boże, a lover…*

The scuffle at the door made her heart race. Quickly, stuffing the photograph, with the rest of the contents, back into the box she shoved it under the bed, breathing a sigh of relief as the door opened and Krystyna, carrying two bulky grocery bags, walked in.

"Elżbieta, you're home!" exclaimed Krystyna secretly relieved. "I… I wasn't expecting you quite so soon. How was…"

"It was all right," Elżbieta interrupted watching her mother unpack the rye bread and place it into the crock, the clanking of the lid breaking the impregnated silence. Her eyes continued to follow Krystyna as she put away the rest of the groceries in the thick heavy silence. "Mama, I need to ask you something." Krystyna unwrapped the pungent-smelling herrings from the newspaper and placed them in a bowl of cold water, her hands delving back into the grocery bag. Elżbieta walked over to her mother and placed her young hands over her mother's gnarled hands, preventing her from continuing her task. "Come; let us sit on the bed for a few moments, Mama."

"I am not in pain, Elżbieta." She thrust her daughter's hand away, avoiding her eyes.

"Please, Mama," she directed her mother to the bed. The second Elżbieta dropped to her knees and withdrew the box, Krystyna knew her dark secret was out, and it was the beginning of the end. She sat rigid on the bed her heart racing, her eyes staring into the past. "This is Zygmunt Chmielowski isn't it, Mama?" The stark words crashed and reverberated in Krystyna's head as her heart turned to frozen ice. "This is Zygmunt Chmielowski isn't it, Mama," she repeated the words slowly, pronouncing each word clearly and concisely.

For long moments, Krystyna stared into space; finally, her eyes dropped to the floor. Elżbieta raised her hands to her mother's arms and shook her gently. "Mama, I need to know. Is this man standing next to you in this photograph Pan Chmielowski?"

Krystyna raised her head slowly, her eyes staring deep into her daughter's eyes. Rising to her tired feet she said in a low voice, "I need to prepare your father's tea."

"Mama… please…"

Elżbieta was met with a cold stony stare.

Chapter Eight

Zygmunt briskly set off on his three-kilometre walk. It had been two weeks since Elżbieta ran out on him, and he had thought of little else since. Always a level headed focused man, he had never allowed the slightest indecision to play a role in his life; sorting the problem out there and then or soon after. During the last fourteen days, his private world was turned upside down; one moment he had made up his mind to call on the Kaminskis; the next moment rubbishing the idea as being totally ludicrous; no sooner had he dismissed the absurd thought from his intelligent mind, when it came crashing to the forefront of his thoughts giving him no peace, no respite, no sleep or appetite.

In his forty-six years, he had never felt so confused and out of control, so in love except for… He shook his head vigorously. This was different in so many ways yet very much the same, for Elżbieta Kaminska was so very much like his first love so many years ago. *That was then*, he told himself; *this is now. That love was forbidden, both parties vowing they would never bring the subject up in any shape or form; this time it was encouraged, at least by Wojtek Kaminski. Elżbieta herself was too young and innocent to know about true love and Krystyna…* He quickened his pace.

The three knocks on the door involuntarily forced Wojtek to stir from his alcoholic slumber. "O…pen th…e da…mned th…ing," he slurred cocking a bloodshot eye at Elżbieta pouring over her Polish grammar books. The young girl leapt to her feet and opened the door, an uncontrolled gasp escaping from her lips.

"W…who th…e ch…ole…rny h…ell is it?" Wojtek grabbed the bottle of clear liquid from the table and attempted to pour the contents into his glass, spilling most of it on to the table. "Cho…lera j…a…sna!" he cursed between tightly clenched lips, his voice raising an octave. "I… I sa…id who the ch…ol…erny he…ll is i…t?" He turned his glassy eyes and squinted at the partly opened door trying to focus. The image which formulated before his eyes forced him to laboriously haul himself into a sitting position, a crooked grin spreading on his twisted mouth. "Come… co…me in m…y g…ood f…frie…nd. What b…rings yo…u he…er to us?" He turned his fierce eyes on Elżbieta. "W…wh…ere a…re y…ou…r ma…nn…ers g…i…rl?"

Her body was tight as a ball, lips firmly compressed, she motioned Zygmunt inside, her heart pounding as she reached for a chair for their special guest.

"Thank you, thank you, but I am not staying. I am on my way to see Father Stanisław," he lied turning his attention to Wojtek. "I am here, Pan Kaminski, to ask for your permission to invite Elżbieta to the Dożynki dance."

A wide satisfied grin on Wojtek's stubbly face was confirmation of his answer. "Of co…ur…se m…y fr…iend," he slurred offering his fast-diminishing bottle to Zygmunt.

"No thank you, Pan Kaminski, I really must be on my way." With a curt nod to Wojtek, and a warm smile to Elżbieta, he was out the door leaving Wojtek to his bottle, and the young woman's heart and head in a whirl.

Her stomach in multiple knots she approached her father, "May I take a look at the invitation please, Tato?"

He stuffed the printed, golden patterned edged, invitation into his trouser pocket. "Y…you're g…oi…ng to th…at d…ance, g…irl, wh…th…er y…ou w…an.t to or n…ot." He dropped his greasy head back onto the table and, in a few seconds, was back in his alcoholic stupor.

As the evening of the Dożynki dance approached, both women in the Kaminski household were in their own private hell. The gentle objections Krystyna posed were to no avail. Wojtek was having none of it. Elżbieta couldn't get a word in edgeways. Wojtek Kaminski was going to have his own way, and nobody was going to stop him. According to Kaminski, his daughter was going to the Dożynki, and Zygmunt Chmielowski would have eyes for no other. *All stops would have to be pulled out, his wallet opened*, Wojtek grimly decided.

Wojtek Kaminski raised his eyes to the image standing before him. Decked in a dark brown full-length evening dress made of taffeta, shoes and a clutch bag to match, Elżbieta felt very much the princess; a sacrificial princess who had no say in her fate.

"You look beautiful," Krystyna said in a soft voice, inside her guts twisting mercilessly for she knew this should not be happening.

"Tato?" Elżbieta slowly twirled around, eyes on her father desperately searching for his approval.

He leered at her his eyes on her flushed face, rising to her black curls interlaced with small silk flowers. *She looks so innocent*, he thought; *spoilt goods*, he miserably surmised turning away. "You'll do," he hissed opening his crumpled newspaper, willing Zygmunt and Elżbieta to be on their way so that he could stop performing and get back to his drinking.

Elżbieta paced the small room her cold hands clenching and unclenching, her lips in a tight line, her eyes fixed on the closed door. The three gentle knocks on the door made all three raise their anxious eyes.

"Well, open the damned door," Kaminski demanded impatiently. "Who do you think you are, girl, keeping a man waiting?"

Slowly, Elżbieta approached the closed door, feeling as if she was about to go to the scaffold. *Perhaps it would be better to die now*, she mused gloomily, as her fingers curled around the doorknob and turned it open. Their eyes met his dark and trusting; her eyes wavering and unsure.

"For you." Zygmunt handed her over a corn dolly broach. Her eyes dropped to his checked blue and white shirt, blue neckerchief and black corduroy trousers, ashamedly aware of the unsuitability of her own attire, feeling a deep red heat rising to her face and suffusing it with colour, abruptly making her look away. *Oh Boże, how could Tato do this to me? How could he embarrass me in this way? He knew I would stand out from everybody else, from all the other girls. How could he?* She raised her disdainful eyes and glared at her father, boiling anger surging through her shaking body. *He knew how I would feel. But... never mind as long as he got what he wanted. How could he? How could he? How could he?* She closed her eyes tight obliterating his image; her ears acutely attuned to his jovial laughter as he engaged Zygmunt in his trivial talk.

"Go and get changed, Elżbieta," Krystyna ordered her heart to hurt at her daughter's distress.

"Don't you dare, girl?" Wojtek darted his angry eyes at his wife and snarled. "She stays in the dress."

"Get changed into something more appropriate for Dożynki," contradicted Krystyna.

"No!" Wojtek roared thumping his fists vehemently on the table, his face and neck flushing an ugly red.

Cautiously, Zygmunt stepped forward locking eyes with Wojtek. "Pan Kaminski, I fear this is my fault. I failed to inform you of the dress code. Perhaps, it would be wiser for a change of clothes."

Beneath tired eyelids, Kaminski surveyed his golden goose. "Naturally."

Ten minutes later Elżbieta reappeared wearing a white blouse sporting Zygmunt's corn dolly broach, black slacks and black flat shoes, her hair in a ponytail.

"Delightful. You have a beautiful daughter, drodzy państwo," commented Zygmunt making Krystyna's guts writhe and Wojtek to declare silently, *Beautiful, but still used goods.*

Zygmunt and Elżbieta followed the trail of revellers. The cool autumnal evening breeze was refreshing after the recent Indian summer. This year the Dożynki were taking place in a large barn on the outskirts of Kraków. Elżbieta and Zygmunt travelled by horse and cart, though Elżbieta secretly wished they were walking in the very midst of the excited crowd. She hated the thought of being viewed as one of the rich kids, attending the harvest celebrations with her father f*or that*, she surmised, *is what they surely must all think.*

Casting Elżbieta a sideway glance he took in her drawn face, her eyes staring starkly ahead and hands tightly clenched together, and knew women well enough to know she was extremely nervous and ill at ease. "It will be all right." He tapped her hand softly sending tiny electric shocks up and down her spine. "Everything will be all right."

The revellers young and not so young were happy; some drunk, others tipsy, most looking forward to a joyous evening with friends. There was excitement in the air; expectations and dreams waiting to be fulfilled, broken hearts hoping to be mended and some waiting to be captured. Elżbieta wished the evening to be over and done with so that she could go home and forget about this Zygmunt Chmielowski, and his secret.

He was, she silently concluded, *too old, too serious and too intelligent for her liking. She wanted someone her own age, someone she could talk to; laugh, dance and cry with. Not this old dinosaur; perhaps, someone like… like Stach.* She thought back to Zosia's wedding. *No, not like Stach, he is so immature; maybe someone else.* But when her mind flicked over boys her own age, they all seemed too immature, childish; needing someone to look after them, pamper to their every whim. Surreptitiously, she glanced at the man sitting next to her. "No one could ever accuse you of being childish, Zygmunt Chmielowski." The words escaped her mouth.

"Pardon Elżbieta?"

She stared at him open-mouthed, hoping he could not see the heat rising to her cheeks.

"Did you say something?"

"No, no." She clamped her mouth shut tight. Out of nowhere an image of Tadek Lisztek crashed into her mind. *I want no man*, she silently stated.

The Dożynki were in full flow when Zygmunt and Elżbieta arrived. The large barn had been miraculously transformed into a heaven of harvest delight. Bales of hay were positioned here and there, corn dollies and straw pictures of skilled intricacy decorated the walls; straw was strewn on tables and heavily covered the floor, and small candles flickered giving the barn a subdued golden glow. Elżbieta inhaled deeply the powdery, sweet smell of dried grains, autumnal leaves and fruits. *How wonderful it must be*, she mused, *to live in the country*. As her inquisitive eyes roamed around the barn, Zygmunt patted her on the shoulder. "I'll be back in a moment."

"Where are you going?" she asked warily.

He was out of earshot, leaving her a solitary figure, perched timidly on a bale of hay, staring at his fast-disappearing figure as he vanished into the crowd. Her eyes wandered to a group of young men and women dressed in Polish national costumes, talking and laughing together. Her eyes scanned the men's crisp white shirts with red neckerchiefs, the red and white thinly striped baggy trousers, and long navy blue waistcoats decorated with tassels at the sides, fastened only by a wide black leather belt. On one side of the belt, there was an array of shiny metal discs, causing a delightful jingling sound with the tiniest movement. On their heads, they wore red triangular hats, trimmed with grey fur, with a large peacock feather proudly displayed on one side.

The Krakowianki, she noticed, were wearing white silky blouses with colourful glass beads around their necks, red knee-length skirts decorated with thin coloured ribbon around the bottom, elaborately sequined waistcoats sparkling every time they moved, with a spray of colourful ribbons attached to the shoulder of their waistcoats, red leather knee-high boots on their feet, and on their neatly plaited heads, beautiful flower headdresses with bright ribbons flowing from both sides. *They look*, she mused, *just like the Krakowianka doll Mama had bought me on our special day in Kraków oh, so very long ago now, but never to be forgotten.* Her daydream came to a sudden end when Zygmunt reappeared.

"I nearly forgot," he chuckled. From behind his back, he withdrew two straw hats; one plain, the other was an elaborately woven straw hat with a red silk ribbon around its middle, he placed them carefully into his own and Elżbieta's head.

"Thank you!" she exclaimed excitedly, immediately taking it off to inspect it before she placed it back onto her head. "Thank you." Impulsively, she rose and planted a kiss on his cheek. Never before in her life had she behaved so spontaneously, apart from Father Stanisław. *But he didn't count*, she concluded, *he was a catholic priest.*

He smiled, his eyes twinkling. "You like your hat?"

"I love it!" she exclaimed, her heart dancing.

"It's the present I wanted to give you at the kawiarnia, before you ran away."

"I am sorry." Her smile died.

"Actually," his smile widened, "the hat is a more appropriate gift today."

They exchanged smiles.

The music was lively and the makeshift dance floor was packed with a motley mix of dancers: young, middle-aged, elderly, brilliant dancers and dancers with two left feet. Nobody cared; everyone was happy for the harvest had been good this year, and tonight was a night for celebration. Elżbieta was caught up with the mood of the moment, tapping her toes on the straw beneath, her fingers tapping the table while her body, perched on the bale, swayed to the energetic rhythm of the polka.

"Come, let's dance." Zygmunt extended his broad hands in invitation. The lively dance was a feat in itself, and they both rose to the challenge with zest and vim; being jostled, nudged, poked and pushed was all part of the fun and nobody complained. When the dance came to a sudden stop Elżbieta felt a tap on her shoulder.

"Stach! What are you doing here?"

He lowered his head to her ear and whispered, "I've come to rescue you from this old codger." He cocked a disdainful eye at Zygmunt as a surge of boiling anger shot through her at Stach, who had dared to cast derogatory dispersions at the kind gentleman she was with.

"How dare you?" She squeezed her eyes to mere slits of utter contempt. "How…"

"Remember, you owe me a dance, kochana."

"Don't you kochana me you... you..." The scene of Zosia's wedding reception ploughed into her mind: *Stach refusing her decline of his invitation to dance, then stubbornly having to concede to her rejection of him, Wojtek's angry eyes, his brutal attack on her hair.* Squeezing her eyes tightly, she tried desperately to obliterate the haunting memory. As if her father was present, she heard herself say, "All right I will dance with you, Stach."

Zygmunt watched Elżbieta as she stiffly placed her hand onto Stach's shoulder. *There is something*, he thought, *troubling that girl... something...* He watched the young couple and his heart sank as stark reality hit him. *Yes, they are more compatible in age, experiences...* His brow furrowed, and his lips tightened as he watched the young woman wriggle away from Stach's tight hold on her. Rising from his chair, he sat back down again. *To be overprotective*, he surmised, *would damage any respect they had for each other.*

He sat, glared and silently cursed Stach for putting Elżbieta into this awkward situation. The hard slap on Stach's cheek widened Zygmunt's eyes, as a flushed Elżbieta stomped off the dance floor, ignored Zygmunt's concerned look and made for the door.

For long minutes, she stood rigidly still, goose-pimpled arms tightly folded, staring out into the dark space of a newly harvested field, seeing nothing but her past. Zygmunt took slow steps towards her and stood a few paces back, allowing her precious time to think; to get back to the present; to get back to him; to them. Slowly, as if coming out of a dream, she felt his presence.

"I am sorry, Pan Chmielowski," she whispered a sorrowful smile touching her lips, "I am truly sorry."

He approached her placing his gentle hands on her shoulders, as they both looked out into the darkness. "You will be sorry," he said in a stern voice. Abruptly, she turned to face him, her wary eyes looking into his dark mysterious eyes. "You will be sorry, young lady, if you keep calling me Pan Chmielowski."

"I should not have stormed ou..."

"I understand. You had every right," he intervened. "No man, under any circumstances, must ever take a woman for granted."

If only he did truly understand, he would run as fast as his legs would carry him; he would never want anything more to do with me, she grimly concluded.

They walked back into the lively smoke-filled barn, and immediately, he left her side and returned with two small liqueur glasses. "A little wiśniówka, for you Elżbieta."

"But… but I don't… I can't drink."

"A little drop will do you no harm, I promise." He smiled.

She smiled taking the liqueur glass to her lips, the red sweet liquid immediately infusing her entire body with warmth that made her skin tingle. Casting a scornful eye at Stach she silently declared, *who cares about that idiot anyway? as she* edged herself a little closer to Zygmunt.

The band stopped playing. A middle-aged man in a checked shirt and dungarees, himself the worse for wear, took the microphone and announced the dancing trope was about to perform. Electrical lights were switched on, a hush descended on the barn, and the colourful dancing group walked confidently onto the edge of the dance floor. Excitement stirred in Elżbieta's soul, as the band started to play the lively Mazur. The troupe ran onto the dance floor in time with the music, and in rhythm with each other, and the dance started. Elżbieta stared unblinkingly, her eyes dancing and shining with happiness, feeling as if her heart was about to dance out of her chest. *Oh, how I wish…*

The dance finished amidst hearty applause and the dancers rearranged themselves for the Oberek a more romantic, evocative dance with nostalgic undertones. For Elżbieta, it represented things lost, never to be regained. Her young eyes were riveted on the dancers weaving in and out of each other, and slowly she became mesmerised by its spell, as it seemed to weave a magic of its own around her. She felt young, free and alive with all her life before her. All too soon the performance was over, the spell broken, the magic evaporating before her eyes.

The evening rapidly raced on, much to Elżbieta's consternation. What she had dreaded to be a long, boring, tedious evening, in the company of a man old enough to be her father, had turned out to be an evening of immense pleasure, in which every fibre of her body tingled with the joy of living. When Zygmunt extended his hands for an invitation, for yet another dance, she leapt to her feet and instantly regretted her spontaneity. The rhythm was slow. Zygmunt held her closer than any man had held her, making her heart beat erratically, the mere touch of his hand on her waist sending an electrifying assault of inexplicable excitement surge through her body. Totally, awash in a sea of mixed-up emotions she missed a step, their eyes locked; their fate sealed.

From a partially opened curtain, from the window above Krystyna watched, her heart thudding, as the horse and cart came into view and the clip-clopping stopped. Lithely, Zygmunt jumped down, briskly took steps to the other side, and escorted Elżbieta down and to the door of the block of apartments. Krystyna edged closer to the window her eyes glassing over, feeling her heart was about to explode, as her worst fears were coming to fruition before her very eyes. Hot prickly tears spilt onto her drawn face and her vision further blurred, as she swiftly wiped them away. Horror widened her eyes and made her thumping heart turn to ice, as Zygmunt took her daughter in his strong arms and kissed her on the lips. Turning her back to the scene she rushed to the living room and hastily scribbled a note.

As Zygmunt said his goodbyes to the Kaminskis, Krystyna secretly thrust a note into his hand.

Chapter Nine

The clock on the mantelpiece struck twice as Zygmunt finally arrived home to his dark and desolate farmhouse. The note in his pocket had haunted his mind during the entire course of his three-kilometre journey and, in the light of a table lamp, a small measure of vodka in his hand, he unfolded the paper, his eyes glued to the brief message:

We must meet tomorrow, at 2.30, at the Mazurka Kawiarnia.
Tell no one.

He read it over and over again, in between taking sips of the potent liquid. *What could it mean? What did it mean?*

Sleep avoided him. Thoughts invaded him. Memories came back to him; long, forgotten memories of Krystyna and their time together happy times, sad times; times they had both cast into the recesses of the past away from view, never to be resurrected. But time, as Zygmunt and Krystyna had experienced in the past few weeks, had a strange way of dealing with the past. He stared at the words. *Yes*, he stated aloud, *I must meet her.*

The knot inside her stomach seemed to grow and become tighter by the second as Krystyna clock watched, in between scanning the kawiarnia window and door. Her tired eyes flitted back to the clock. *Twenty-five past two. He is not coming*, she grimly surmised rising to her feet, her heart skipping a beat as he strode into view.

"Krystyna." He nodded his head a faint smile wavering on his lips.

"Zygmunt. Th…thank you for coming." She avoided his eyes her heart beating mercilessly.

He walked over to the counter and ordered two coffees and two makowce.

"You remembered," she said softly looking down at the poppy seed cakes.

They sat in silence her fingers playing with the teaspoon; he looking at a lost love, his smile vanishing, wondering why on earth he was summoned. Krystyna felt the vomit rise to her dry throat, desperately needing to say what she had come here to say, opening her mouth and closing it again. Finally, after long minutes of impregnated silence, she began. "Z…Zygmunt. It is about Elżbieta."

He watched as her mouth shut, clamped tight, as her mind struggled with the appropriate words; his eyes dropped to the spoon performing a merry dance in her restless fingers. He placed his broad hands over hers, quelling all movement, sending a cold shiver up and down her spine as he looked into her watery eyes. His soft words came out slowly.

"I know what you are going to say, Krystyna." He paused trying, and failing, to capture her eyes. "I am perfectly aware that I am too old for Elżbieta." He smiled sadly. "Why, I am old enough to be her father, but…"

"You are… you are…" Abruptly, she rose to her feet and dashed out of the kawiarnia, oblivious to the stares in her wake.

He stayed in his chair and stared at the fast-retreating figure. He had got his answer to the mystery. *Yes*, he told himself, *I am too old. But… what is age? What is it but a mere number of years? Krystyna has no further objections. It is just my age.* His heart danced as he brought his coffee cup to his lips. There was hope.

She was seen. It was reported to him by his faithful friend, Tadek Lisztek, and now she was being punished, for no wife of Wojtek Kaminski was going to go behind his back, and be seen in the company of another man, whoever he may be. His fists did not stop where she could hide the brutal evidence, for he lashed out at her upper and lower arms, her chest, face and anywhere he could bestow a blow, and with added force the raw alcohol inside him propelled his anger to a wild, dangerous pinnacle. She ran and crouched behind the sofa, but she could not hide away or escape from her vicious perpetrator. He was out to give her a good thrashing, and a good thrashing she would get.

"H…ow d…are you go ru…nn.ing to Chmielowski be…hind my ba…ck, you wh.o…re; you de…cei…ving, cho…lerna whore! I am go…in.g to give you a be…ati…ng you will ne.v.er fo…r…get." He snarled grabbing hold of a tuft of her hair, twisting it round and round, tighter and tighter as he punched her in the face with his free hand, narrowly missing an eye.

She did not retaliate. After all these years, she knew her place well. He continued his merciless beating, curses spewing out his contorted mouth, his eyes aflame. His ears pricked at the click of the opening door. He paused lest it should be someone of importance on the other side.

Elżbieta walked in and his beating recommenced, his ears deaf to his daughter's frantic objections. She ran to Krystyna's crouching side, trying to shield her mother's body with her own from her father's ferocious and unceasing attack. She glared at him like a rabbit glaring at a treacherous poacher. *He is*, she surmised, *like something possessed, a demon. It is as if all the black evil, the poisonous venom within him, is coming out of him; as if he finds some kind of relief when he is lashing out, hurting, destroying someone else.*

"Y…ou wh…o…re. Y…ou des…pi…cable, v…ile wh…ore." He spat, missing Krystyna, the bubbling spittle landing on Elżbieta's arm.

"Tato… why?" Elżbieta raised her eyes to his. "Why are you doing this, Tato?" she asked again and again knowing full well she would get no answer.

He stood rigid as if some form of paralysis had struck him. Without warning the assault resumed, his bloodshot eyes boring into his daughter's eyes, making her blink and turn her gaze and full attention to her mother, her ears finely tuned to the verbal abuse spewing out of his venomous mouth. "Ne…ver m…ind th…that c…unt of a mo…th…er," he sneered. "I do…n't bl…ame you, g…i…rl for be…ing the way y…ou are. It's h…er…, she's to bl…ame." He pointed his fat finger at Krystyna, his eyes staring disdainfully at the crumpled mass on the floor. "Th…that lo.v.i…ng mo…ther of your's h…as gone be…hind y…our back and had a li…aison with y…ou…r bo…yf.riend, Zygmunt Ch…mie…low.ski."

"No… no," whimpered Krystyna attempting, without success, to raise her frail body from the floor.

"Sh…shu.t up! Sh…ut up wh…o.re!" he roared switching his red eyes on his daughter. "Th…tha.t wo…ma.n wan…ted to ru…in thin.gs fo.r you; she wa…nted t…o…de…str.oy…"

"N… no," whispered Krystyna her voice barely audible, her body trembling violently.

"Tato… please… please…"

"Th… at slut, be…fo.re you we were ma…rrr.ie.d, was…"

Krystyna took a deep breath, and with all the strength she could sum up in her weak body shouted, "Shut up! Shut up, Wojtek! Elżbieta…"

Wojtek's eyes darted to Elżbieta, and at that moment, a cold realisation swept over him for he realised, that if all was revealed now, there would be no hope of a liaison between his daughter and the wealthy Pan Chmielowski. He lowered his hand. Turning away from the scene of the crime he grabbed his grubby jacket off the chair. "I ne …ed a ch…ol…ery d…drink," he snarled as he slammed the door behind him, leaving echoes of his words in his wake.

Chapter Ten

Father Stanisław espied the young woman as she weaved her way through the crowded market. "May I?" He reached for the cloth bag and relieved Elżbieta of the bag of cabbages and carrots.

Her heart skipped a beat as an unwanted flush rose to her cheeks. "Father Stanisław! What a surprise."

"The pleasant surprise is all mine; now, young Elżbieta, how is your mother? I haven't seen her at Mass for a while." Her glassy eyes told him all he needed to know. "I shall come over this evening after Majòwka. I need to speak to your father."

"W…what about?" Her worried eyes silently questioned him.

His steady eyes levelled with the young woman. "Your future education."

Heart thudding she pleaded, "Oh no, Father Stanisław, don't approach my father. He…" Her words fell on deaf ears as he turned and walked briskly on, his black soutane swaying in rhythm with his purposeful steps.

"Truly Elżbieta, your common sense is somewhere in the clouds these days," Krystyna stated between bouts of shortness of breath. "So you allowed Father Stanisław to walk off with our vegetables. What will your father have to say when…" Clutching her chest with one hand, the other grabbed a chair as she slumped down gasping for air. As the pain gradually eased, Krystyna continued, "Elżbieta, I do not know what has come over you just lately."

She shook her head from side to side, knowing deep inside what was happening and knowing it had to stop. She rose from her chair, put on her raincoat, and strode to the door. "Make sure your father gets his tea, with or without the vegetables."

"Where are you going, Mama?"

The door closed firmly behind Krystyna.

Zygmunt Chmielowski's brow lifted as he opened the door. "Krystyna! Come… please come in."

Surreptitiously, her eyes glanced backwards for any sign of busybodies, as it would be truly catastrophic to be seen in Chmielowski's company again.

They sat at opposite sides of a large table; Krystyna's eyes on the table, Zygmunt's eyes staring directly at the woman he once loved. As the clock on the mantelpiece ticked away the minutes, time hung heavily suspended around them; lips firmly closed as both waited for the other to break the ominous silence.

"Perhaps a glass of lemon tea?" Zygmunt suggested lifting a dark eyebrow.

Krystyna slowly raised her eyes to meet those of the man she once loved. "I have not come here to drink lemon tea." She clamped her lips tight, silently admonishing her impoliteness, her fingers dancing nervously on the bare wood of the table, her well-rehearsed speech failing to materialise. She opened her mouth and closed it again, her eyes dropping to her fingers, her guts wrenching. "Zygmunt…" Their eyes locked. "Zygmunt, I… I have come to ask you a very big request."

A ghost of a smile flickered on his lips as he exuded a silent sigh of relief. "Anything, just ask Krystyna."

"You must never ever see Elżbieta again." She looked deeper into his eyes, failing to see the smile vanishing from his lips, or the sharp blade thrusting through his heart, as he swallowed a hard lump lodged in his throat, his eyes not leaving the stark eyes before him.

"Why?"

The ticking of the clock was deafening to them both, as the large room seemed to be closing in around them, as they were trapped in a dark bubble of their own creation and neither could escape its invisible boundary. She stared into his dark eyes, now devoid of any sparkle, as he was fast losing hope of all that he held dear.

"Why?" he repeated his eyes glazing over, as the colour drained from his taut face.

Her heart pounded, and her body froze like a solidified sitting statue: silent, still, numb, cold; feeling nothing, wanting only to run as far away as possible she knew not where, cared not where.

"Why?" He raised his voice inwardly knowing the answer.

"Because… b…because…" She stammered her fists clenching into tight fists, her guts silently crying out for mercy, "because…"

"Because I am too old for Elżbieta," he interrupted.

"Because… you are her father." The words rushed out.

The world stopped still. The room spun around. One heart raced, the other felt it had stopped beating altogether. Eyes stared at eyes as silence spread around them like a heavy blanket. Krystyna felt a tidal wave of relief wash over her; Zygmunt felt he was drowning in a sea of despair.

For the first time in his life, he was speechless, helpless and hopeless for in that moment he had just lost everything. They sat motionless eyes averted, each in their own private hell as a mass of confusing thoughts whirled around their heads, unable to formulate one logical thought or phrase to soothe the other's despair; both locked in the past without a way of escape. Their sins had caught up with them, and there was to be no redemption. Slowly, he raised his puzzled eyes.

"What do you mean I am Elżbieta's father?"

"Exactly that," she whispered unable to raise her eyes to his. "You are Elżbieta's father."

You are Elżbieta's father… You are Elżbieta's father… You are Elżbieta's father… The words echoed relentlessly in his aching head. Abruptly, he stood up accidentally tossing his chair to the floor, his fingers clamping tightly at the edge of the table, his eyes peering down at the pale-faced woman before him.

"Are you completely crazy, Krystyna?" he asked his tone incredulous. In his heart of hearts, he knew the answer; knew the woman before him to be completely sane; knew that she would only ever speak the truth. Picking up his discarded chair, he slumped onto it, his body suddenly feeling a hundred years of age, as thick cold realisation swept over him. "Elżbieta is my daughter." His own soft words hit him like a thunderbolt; his stark eyes stared into the distance seeing nothing.

"Elżbieta is your daughter, Zygmunt." Krystyna's quietly spoken words gave a loud and clear finality to all his doubts and dreams.

"I am a father," he whispered.

"Yes, you are a father, Zygmunt. You are Elżbieta's father," Krystyna stated in a soft voice, daring at last to raise her eyes to his clouded eyes.

He broke the heavy silence, "You did not think to tell me years ago, Krystyna?" His silent dark eyes questioned her.

"I… I was afraid, Zygmunt. Wojtek was already in my life."

"And you thought it best to pass my daughter on to him as his own flesh and blood."

"Yes… yes…"

After a prolonged silence, Zygmunt spoke, with an edge of finality in his softly spoken voice. "Then, no more is to be said on the subject, Krystyna. Do not fear, I will keep my distance."

She rose from the chair, placing a gentle hand on his arm as she walked to the door, glancing back at the slumped dejected man she still loved. She walked out the door leaving him with his thoughts.

Chapter Eleven

Wojtek Kaminski stared with disdain at the young man standing before him and sneered, "And so you think you can fool me, pretending you are on an errand bringing me a bag of useless vegetables, so you can sneak into my home and discuss my daughter's education. Do you think I'm made of money, you stupid imbecile?"

"But please, Pan Kaminski, let us discuss this like two intelligent adults. There are ways around financing education." Father Stanisław slid his foot over the threshold. "Please, let…"

"Get out and stay out!" roared Wojtek snatching the bag of cabbages and carrots, and slamming the door in the young priest's face.

"Was that Father Stanisław?" Elżbieta peered out of her room, witnessing the residue of anger on her father's red blotched face.

"You cunt," snarled Wojtek lifting his fist, realising at once the consequences a lashing could cause, on his daughter's future with Zygmunt Chmielowski. Lowering his hand he grunted, "You better get yourself tarted up girl, if you're thinking of ever getting yourself an education. Chmielowski won't even spit on a scrawny scrubber like you."

She swallowed hard the bitter bile rising to her throat, blinked back the scorching tears of reality, and made her way back into her room, taking solace in the fact that this evening she would be in the company of a real gentleman. *Perhaps, tonight we may exchange a kiss*, she mused, catching her wan reflection in the cracked mirror.

The minutes ticked laboriously away as Elżbieta sat rigid, hands held tightly on her lap, watching her mother bustling about in the kitchen, her eyes darting to her father engrossed in the *Dziennik*, as she waited for her distinguished guest to arrive. The door remained firmly closed. Krystyna cast surreptitious glances at Elżbieta, her heart grieving for her daughter's fate, as the young woman's eyes remained glued to the door. *Ignorance is indeed bliss*, conceded Krystyna, *for Elżbieta must never, ever learn the truth. It shall go with me to my grave*, she determined, knowing full well that Zygmunt Chmielowski would reveal nothing to no one. *His promise*, she concluded, *is his word.*

"Mama, he is late." Elżbieta's eyes darted to the slow-moving hands of the clock.

"And I thought he was a cholerny gentleman," hissed Wojtek peering over the newspaper at his wife.

Krystyna's lips remained firmly clamped, her eyes avoiding the man she loathed.

The minutes ticked on.

"The bastard is not coming," snarled Kaminski casting a contemptuous look at his daughter. "And, I'm not fucking well surprised." Vehemently, he spat out a mouthful of spittle onto the floor and poured himself a generous glass of vodka.

"I think he may have had an accident." Elżbieta cast a worrying glance at her mother.

"I think you better get changed and help me with supper," replied Krystyna avoiding her daughter's eyes.

The night was black and stark as Elżbieta tossed and turned, stared wide-eyed at the cold blackness around, and asked herself a thousand questions, finally arriving at one grim conclusion: *He is just like all the others, never to be trusted.* "Never again," she stated aloud, "will I ever trust another man; never!"

By dawn, Zygmunt had downed a bottle of vodka. Never drink more than a measure of alcohol at any one time, his head was pounding; portraying an uncharacteristic portrait of himself with his dark hair standing up in tufts, stubble on his chin and bloodshot eyes. Nausea plagued him, but it was the thought of never seeing Elżbieta again that was the worst punishment of all: *Elżbieta… my prospective wife and lover; Elżbieta, my daughter… my daughter… my daughter…* The thought haunted him, stayed with him, giving him no respite; like a train on a one-way track to Siberia, he felt he was on his own one-way journey to hell.

Krystyna's mouth remained clamped all day her mind, like a black cauldron, was suffused with a lethal mixture of regrets, wishing, wanting and resigning herself to her dismal fate. Robotically, she prepared the meals, cleaned, scrubbed the floors, bought supplies at the local market and darned Wojtek's socks; inwardly a frozen blade had lodged in her heart, and she knew, without a doubt, it would be in residence until the day she died, for she had changed the future lives of four people, and for that she would never forgive herself.

Wojtek Kaminski was none the wiser: *Chmielowski had declined a date, so what? That was a man's prerogative and a woman's lot in life. He would be back. Yes*, he smirked taking a gulp of vodka, *Zygmunt Chmielowski is our golden goose, a future husband for my tart of a daughter, a financer of her damned education and a provider of my nest egg.* He wiped his lips on his sleeve and laid his contented head on the table.

Chapter Twelve

The pain of bitter rejection sliced through Elżbieta's young heart, staying with her day and night and bringing with it heartache, mistrust and a deep sense of failure. The image of Zygmunt Chmielowski haunted her: his strength, gentleness, kindness; all the qualities of a man her father did not possess. *But* she asked herself as stark reality lodged in her mind, *what man in his right mind would want to be with me, let alone marry me? Tato is right. I am nothing but a good-for-nothing piece of rubbish.* With a heavy heart, she cleared the dirty dishes from the table.

"Ciocia Mania, Zosia and her new husband will be coming for tea tonight," announced Krystyna.

The words were an instant soothing balm for Elżbieta's tortured soul, her heart skipping a beat, a smile dancing on her lips placing heartache on the back burner for a while. There was much to be done, for Krystyna was not feeling so well and needed frequent rest breaks. Elżbieta cleaned the apartment, baked, cooked and prepared the table; realising there was more to life than thinking about Zygmunt Chmielowski, and his rejection of her. *Yes*, she thought as she waited with eager anticipation for her kin to arrive, *I have wasted enough time on Zygmunt Chmielowski. He is not worth my energy.*

Amidst the babel of excited voices Wojtek's twisted mouth remained firmly shut, his bloodshot eyes leering on the object of his desire; the woman he was going to have at any cost. He gawped at her generous mouth: opening, closing, laughing, retelling snippets of honeymoon news; the outline of her breasts just visible beneath her white blouse. *Soon, very soon*, he thought lasciviously licking his lips. Eyes locked with eyes. The laughing stopped. Sharply, Zosia looked away focusing her attention on her new husband. He saw everything.

As the evening drew to a close, Piotr's eyes and feet followed Wojtek onto the small balcony, where the older man was enjoying a roll-up. Wojtek's bloodshot eyes flitted to the newly-wed. "H…ey Pi…o.tr, had a go…od ho.ney…mo.on?" He laughed raucously showing his yellow teeth. "If y…ou k…n …ow what I me…an…" he attempted to wink and failed miserably in the process.

Piotr took a step towards the older man, his face taut and stern, eyes stark and focused, as he wagged his finger in front of Wojtek's bulbous nose. "If you dare look at my wife in that way again you are dead, old man." He moved a step closer until he was almost on top of him hissing, "Do you hear me; dead?" He walked away leaving Wojtek chuckling aloud as he took another drag on his cigarette.

In the passing days, Krystyna's health deteriorated further leaving her bedridden. Wojtek cursed unashamedly when meals were not on the table on time, or not to his liking; throwing plates, with hardly eaten food, to the floor, thumping tables and walls, drinking and falling into long drunken stupors. Jan had disappeared, gone presumably to look for casual work to fund his drinking. No one but Krystyna cared, and she was beyond doing anything about it. Elżbieta spent most of her time caring for her mother or engaged in household chores, but her education was neglected. *There was no time, or need, for education*, she concluded regretfully. A sudden burst of loud knocking brought her out of her glum reverie, and her feet to the door.

"Ciocia Mania! What a lovely surprise." She peered round the door. "No Zosia?"

"No, no." The plump woman walked inside, cast a disgusted look at her brother-in-law, and headed towards her sister's bed. "How are you, Krystyna?" She perched on the bed taking her sister's skinny hand into her own, her concerned eyes scanning her drawn-thin face. Her eyes flitted to her niece. "Koteczku, could you nip to the chemist and get me something for my throat? It's so tight I can barely swallow," she lied.

Making sure her niece was out the door and Wojtek deep in slumber, she focused her eyes on her sister, taking both her hands into her own; her heart fragmenting as she felt the bones beneath the paper-thin skin. She watched as her small breasts rose and fell in rhythm with her laborious breathing. *She is half the woman she once was*, she sadly concluded. *Time is of the essence. "Krystyna… Krystyna."* Eyes flickered, desperately trying to focus. "Krystyna… have… have you told Elżbieta? Does she know about… about Zygmunt?"

A heavy oppressive blanket of silence enveloped the two sisters; one locked in her private hell of misery and pain; the other desperately trying to unlock the past and set her sister free, before it was too late. The long deathly seconds dragged into minutes. Heavy lids closed. "Krystyna…" Mania gently shook her beloved sister's shoulders. "Krystyna…" She urged in the lowest voice she could manage. "Krystyna…" Slowly, laboriously heavy lids opened and wavered, trying hard to focus. "Krystyna… you must tell Elżbieta. It's… it's time."

Suspended silent minutes hung in the heavy air. "Krystyna, you know your daughter has a right to know the truth. She must know the identity of her biological father." Her mouth curved into a smile, as her eyes saw Krystyna's head bow in a silent nod.

She let her sleep, walked over to the bedraggled bundle half sprawled on the table and poked him stiffly in the ribs. "Zosia needs a wardrobe moving. Piotr is away looking for a job. Can you do it?"

A ghastly grin, she did not see, spread over his lascivious mouth. "Oh y…e …s I can d…o it," he mumbled returning back to his induced slumber.

Chapter Thirteen

The breathing had stopped before Elżbieta returned with her auntie's medicine; a blanket of heavy trepidation overpowering her entire body, as she opened the door to Mania's heart-wrenching cries of loss. Slumping to the floor she grasped her mother's scrawny lifeless hand, still warm to the touch, and brought it up to her trembling lips kissing it over and over again, taking it to her bosom and bringing it to her lips again, her tear-filled eyes not leaving Krystyna's pinched face, now in eternal peace where Wojtek could never touch her. Her glassy eyes flitted to her slumbering father, as his bulk heaved up and down in rhythm to his loud snores, at peace in his blissful ignorance.

Her insides wrenched with a twisting, sickly, empty rage against her father, her mother, her brother, Ciocia Mania, Zosia, Piotr, Father Stanisław, Stach, Zygmunt Chmielowski, Tadek Lisztek, God, the whole world and everybody in it, but most of all her own stupid self. Squeezing her eyes tight, till there was only blackness, she rocked back and forth, back and forth, her mother's cooling hand imprisoned in her tight grasp, not letting go; not ever wanting to let it go for well she knew that with her mother went all the stability of her own world, and what was now to come she could not bear to contemplate.

The day after the funeral Wojtek Kaminski was banging his fist on his niece's door.

"Ah, Wujek Wojtek! Please come in." Zosia extended her door, secretly fighting an inner dread rising in the depths of her guts.

He barged through ignoring all pleasantries, making her squirm inwardly as he cast his lustful eyes over her entire body, before storming into her bedroom.

Her guts writhed with fear of her own flesh and blood as she fixed her eyes firmly on the dishes she was washing, her back to him for she had witnessed the way he had looked at her; like a piece of meat. Her heart thudded for here she was alone in her home with the one man she most dreaded to be left alone with, and there was nothing she could do about it. His words from her bedroom boomed in her head.

"I need your help here, Zosia."

She stood rigid, dirty plate in hand, her feet glued to the spot, her still body solidified as her eyes unseeingly glared out the window.

"Cholera jasna! I need your help. I'm not Samson, woman." He hollered, his gruff voice reverberating through the small apartment, making her slim body shudder involuntarily. She opened her mouth to silent words.

"For God's sake, I need some help here. Are you there, Zośka?" His brusque tone penetrated through her, making her legs wobble and her shaking hands grip the edge of the sink, allowing a cup to fall and break into pieces; her eyes stark, transfixed at a single yellow leaf fluttering down.

"Zośka, the damned wardrobe is going to fall!"

Snapping out of her reverie, her heavy feet took steps towards the one man she desperately yearned to run away from, her heart hammering. Her eyes met an angry, red, twisted face with bulging eyes of venomous fire glaring behind a precariously tilted massive bulk of wood. "For God's sake, grab the end, woman," he hissed as between them they balanced the wardrobe laboriously manoeuvring it to the other side of the room. Slumping to the bed his chest heaving as he tried to grasp his breath, he grabbed Zosia and brought her down onto the bed, clambering on top of her, muffling her desperate cries with his fat grubby hand. Hopelessly, she tried to wriggle away from his enormous bulk. He pinned her down firmly with his strong hands, trapping her legs with his own, forcing his blubbery lips on her, lifting her blouse and stuffing his hand under her bra.

"Wujek please... please... I'm..."

His hand pressed firmly down on her mouth; his other hand lifted her skirt, pulling her pants down, forcing his way in, pumping... mercilessly pumping... grunting... pumping... She protested no more. Nobody was listening.

Finally, he crawled off her still body. "Cover yourself," he snarled, eyes of disgust flashing at her nakedness.

"I am pregnant with Piotr's baby, Wujek," she managed to gasp before clamping her mouth shut tight.

The words struck him like a thunderbolt. Abruptly, he turned, the wildfire flaring in his angry eyes as he roughly pulled her off the bed, glaring at her still stark eyes, her body rigid in his blubbery arms. "You're pregnant!" He roared with cold revulsion, glaring unblinkingly as he brought his tightly clenched fist onto her face. "You're nothing but a dirty whore. Now get dressed, you fucking tramp." He released his hold on her and, like a rag doll, she fell onto the bed where she lay still, empty, used and abused; her ears tuned to her rapist's footsteps walking towards the door. Her eyes closed as the door opened.

The fierce blow coming from behind forced Kaminski to fall to the floor.

"Piotr!" Zosia managed to gasp.

Piotr continued his merciless attack thrashing his victim in the head, his legs, torso, anywhere he could bestow a hefty blow. Finally, he grabbed Wojtek by his shoulders, hauled him out of the door, and gave him a thorough kicking which landed him in hospital securing, in turn, a temporary safe home for Elżbieta with her Ciocia Mania; days later news reverberated that Kaminski had discharged himself from hospital and was back on the booze. No one cared.

On occasion, Mania found her withdrawn niece sobbing though she knew that, apart from her grief, Elżbieta was experiencing a security and peace which was totally alien to her.

Mania was far from being at peace, her head whirling with a mass of contradictory thoughts. Taking an old family Bible from a drawer she flicked through the flimsy pages, her fingers stopping as she reached an old tattered photograph of two young girls, dressed in knee-length pinafore dresses and tightly laced black boots, their hair in two long plaits; her eyes glassing over and blurring the image before her. *Oh, Krystyna, why did you have to leave us? Why?* Tears fell onto the faded image. *Why did you have to take your secret with you to your grave?* She dropped her head into her hands and sobbed loudly and uncontrollably, her whole body shuddering, until her eyes were as dry as bones.

Opening the door to her niece's room, she stood staring at the young woman. "Elżbieta," she said softly, "I have something to tell you."

Chapter Fourteen

Elżbieta felt her heart stop and, with it, her world. Fingers curled around the barrel of a fountain pen poised and still, unseeing eyes stark and still stared at the older woman, her head swimming with distorted images of black and grey nothingness. Nothing was real. Nothing felt real. Her body was floating somewhere in space, in a vast special nothingness. She was nothing. The syllables of her name echoed louder and louder from somewhere, she knew not where. Slowly, a distorted black shadow was rearranged into some kind of shape.

Chapter Fifteen

1956

Elżbieta Kaminska walked hand in hand with the man she loved, a thousand excited butterflies fluttering in her stomach for she had exciting news; news that would certainly delight the man walking beside her down the rustling carpet of yellow, red and brown leaves. Kicking a colourful array of foliage she giggled like a child, as they formed a magical spray of colour in the air before they lay to rest on the damp ground once more. She smiled, her rich brown eyes twinkling, as she glanced surreptitiously at the attractive face beside her.

His mouth broke into a warm confident smile, as he felt her eyes watching him. "What is it, Elżbieta? I know you have something to tell me." He looked down at the woman he loved and cocked his head sideways in question.

The butterflies in her stomach vanished and in their place grew a heavy dread: *For, what if this news was not good news? What if this news was actually a betrayal, a knock in the teeth for everything this man had done for her?* Her nervous eyes flitted back to Zygmunt, the colour rapidly disappearing from her face. "Tato, I... I have a friend, a boyfriend, I would like you to meet. I thought it would be nice if he joined us in the kawiarnia." She blurted out the words, fearing that if she paused they would be trapped forever. She cast her eyes to the colourful blanket below, feeling a sudden autumnal chill in the air.

The silence filling the stillness filled her soul, as they continued to walk hand in hand. He stopped, turned, looked directly into her eyes and chuckled, sending the young woman's heart soaring to the highest heavens. "That's wonderful news, Elżbicta. I can't wait to meet him." They quickened their steps.

The small kawiarnia, just off the Market Place, was warm, cosy and full of students, shoppers and tourists. Above the hubbub rose the rich aroma of freshly ground coffee, mixed with the pungent smell of tobacco smoke. Elżbieta sat, pastry fork in hand, picking at her makowiec, the butterflies back in her stomach, her eyes flitting nervously to the door at regular intervals.

"He will come." Zygmunt smiled faintly; inwardly, desperately hoping this boy would come for his beloved daughter's sake.

Her eyes darted to the clock on the wall. "He's late… half an hour late," she stated, her lips set in a firm line as she continued to pick at her poppy seed cake.

Sipping his second cup of black coffee Zygmunt surreptitiously glanced at the clock wall. *This girl*, he told himself determinedly, *is not going to be let down by any man again. I will not let it happen.* "Come, Elżbieta." He stood up, carefully folded his napkin, and placed it on the table. "There's a delightful operetta…"

"He's here! He's here!" She shrieked unable to control the excitement in her voice, as she rushed across to meet him. Returning, she looked fondly at both men in turn. "This is Lukasz Chopinski. Lukasz, this is my father, Zygmunt Chmielowski."

A fresh round of coffee was ordered. From beneath heavy brows, Zygmunt observed the young couple, secretly scrutinising Lukasz as his roving eyes flitted from one female student to the next. *Not a one-woman man*, he quickly surmised.

Elżbieta saw only the two men she loved most in the world: Zygmunt, her father, who in coalition with Father Stanisław, had provided her with the opportunity and means of university education, loved and supported her in all she undertook; Lukasz, her lover. *Who could ask for more?* She asked herself.

That night Zygmunt tossed and turned; Lukasz and Elżbieta made passionate love.

Chapter Sixteen

They sat at opposite ends of the kitchen table, yet they might as well have been worlds apart. During the last few weeks, Elżbieta and her father had drifted apart. Neither felt comfortable in the other's presence; neither could, or would, accept the other's opinion. Lukasz Chopinski occupied his position between father and daughter causing a deep, involuntary rift between them. Once more, Zygmunt stated his feelings on the subject; Elżbieta did not like, did not agree and would not listen to his protestations. Avoiding her father's eyes she stared at the cold black liquid in her cup, wishing to God she was back in the apartment with Lukasz, preferably in bed. Casting a sideways glance at his daughter a heavy, exasperated sigh emitted from his mouth.

"You know, Elżbieta, I am not going to change my mind about him. Lukasz Chopinski is not good enough for you."

Fleetingly, she looked up and caught his eye, saying softly, "Nobody will ever be good enough for me in your eyes, Tato."

Clearing his throat, he added, "He is a womaniser. I have seen it with my own eyes on several occasions. He wants your money, your… body." Their eyes locked as clearly and concisely he continued, "He will use and abuse you, Elżbieta, and then he will toss you aside. He is that kind of a man."

"You mean, the kind of man you were with Mama," she stated harshly, instantly feeling a heavy veil of remorse descend over her. Avoiding his eyes, her heart thudding, she rose from the table, grabbed her coat and vanished out the door, leaving her father with his past.

Zygmunt sat rigid, like a statue, listening to the clock ticking away the heavy minutes; more minutes added to his lonely existence. *Yes*, he sadly concluded, *I have provided well for my future. I will never want for anything.* Emotionally, he felt robbed of the only woman he ever truly loved. Closing his eyes he peeled back the years when he was a young man dating his first love.

Oh, how beautiful she was with her long black hair and her sparkling eyes. Through consensual love, he had inadvertently robbed her of her virginity;

wanted to marry her but was denied all access to her by her overprotective family. They had made it known to him that he was not good enough: too poor and unsophisticated. She was expected to marry a man with status, a pillar of the community. She gave birth, Zygmunt grimly concluded, *to a bastard and married the good-for-nothing Wojtek Kaminski.*

His head shook from side to side as he muttered, "What a complete and utter waste." His thoughts drifted to Elżbieta, and he closed his eyes. "Oh Boże, I am treating her beau in exactly the same way I was treated."

Abruptly, he rose from his chair snatching his coat from its hook. He slowly sat back down again. *This is different*, he told himself; *very different. Lukasz Chopinski is out for all that he can get, and Elżbieta is blind to it all. She has to open her eyes in her own good time*, he decided.

Days matured into weeks. Elżbieta was on the point of calling on Zygmunt on a few occasions, only to decide against it. Days of study were lost as morning sickness took over. Lonely days and evenings were spent in the apartment thinking, hoping and dreaming. Lukasz came home late or not at all. Past memories, good and bad, became her constant companions. Gradually, her days rolled into one long stretch of drudgery.

On a bright *spring* day, in a bleak hospital room, she gave birth to a baby boy, Jakub Kaminski; her one glimmer of hope.

Chapter Seventeen

Young Jakub Kaminski became the centre of Elżbieta's universe. Lukasz had called once, cast eyes of disdain on his son and left. She never saw him again. Secretly, she was grateful to Zygmunt for financing the completion of her education. Contact between them remained severed.

Her sole concern was Jakub caring, protecting, providing and loving him as best as she could. He was her whole world, and she neither had nor needed anybody else in her life. She lived with her son in a tiny two-roomed apartment, taking in tailoring to make ends meet. One morning, helping Jakub with his school tie, an unexpected knock on the door forced her to abandon her task.

"Ciocia Mania! What on earth brings you here?" Her smile faded as her eyes saw unmistakable sadness etched on her beloved aunt's face.

Placing her plump gloved hand on her niece's arm she met Elżbieta's puzzled eyes. "It's Zygmunt, you're father…"

Elżbieta instantly felt her whole world crashing in around her, forcing her to slump down onto Jakub's bed. "Oh Boże… oh… no…" She shook her head, swallowing a hard lump, staring starkly at the whitewashed wall opposite, while a mass of confused scenarios swam madly in her head. "He can't be…"

Mania sat beside her niece, bringing a wide-eyed Jakub to herself, laying a gentle hand on Elżbieta's lap as she looked into her glassy eyes. "He is gravely ill, Elżbieta."

The black blanket of desperation and loss lifted a little. "Ill, but not… not… dead?" Her heart started to resume its normal beat as a flicker of hope touched her eyes.

"Not dead, Elżbieta, but I think you ought to pay him a visit, let bygones be bygones before…"

She did not hear the rest, did not want to hear the rest; closed her ears as she sat entombed in her own silence as dredged-up thoughts from the past whirled around her head: Krystyna dead; Wojtek Kaminski, her stepfather and good-for-nothing drunk, still causing havoc and misery wherever he went; Jan, no one knew where he was these days; Zosia, raped by Wojtek, beaten and he black and blue by her husband, hidden somewhere in a sanatorium; Zygmunt Chmielowski, her estranged biological father, dying; a kind-hearted responsible pillar of the community, who had been right all along about Lukasz Chopinski. *If only I had taken his advice*, she shook her head; *if only…*

The figure of the man opening the door was a mere shell of his former self. Her heart turning to stone, she stared at flesh and bones standing before her, as she surveyed the loose grey cardigan hanging over baggy trousers, supported by a tightly drawn belt. She scanned his face pinched, drawn and pale in pallor, highlighted with deep-set wrinkles etched on his brow and around his mouth and eyes, his cheeks sunken. She raised her tearful eyes to his sunken eyes, the sparkle long gone but the kindness, she noticed, was still there in abundance. He smiled. She smiled back.

"Oh Tato…" She fell into his open arms, so thin but still strong in their embrace. They stood taking each other in as the lost years rushed by, united in their grief.

They talked and talked about everything and nothing, both deeply aware of the precious time slipping away.

Elżbieta stared at the casket below. *It could*, she thought, *have been so different; so very, very different.*

Taking his mother's strong hand, Jakub raised his eyes. "Is Dziadek with Babcia in heaven?"

"Yes," she smiled, "he probably is, son."

Chapter Eighteen

As news of Elżbieta's wealth spread, many suitors came to her door. She treated them all with courtesy and respect; all had to gain Jakub's respect before having any hope of further liaisons with his mother. None, so far, had passed the young boy's approval. Jakub now eight years of age, was Elżbieta's world, her pride and joy, excelling at school and a credit to all who met him. He was her rock, her future; her everything.

The seventeenth of June started off much the same as any other day. Jakub set off for school with a bunch of wild jasmine to delight his teacher, while Elżbieta set off for a day's work at the museum. The day seemed long, and she was restless, her eyes flitting to the clock every few minutes, each minute dragging on laboriously and, it seemed, endlessly. Although she had a mound of work to do she found herself perched on a stool, twiddling her thumbs, willing the unbearable day to end.

As she sat staring into space, an inexplicable and uncharacteristic yearning to see Jakub took over her whole body until she could think of nothing else. His image, clear as day, came crashing into her mind: his fair curly hair, brown twinkling eyes, and those delightful freckles across the bridge of his nose were so very clear, forcing her to reach out her hand and grasp a handful of air. She closed her eyes and the image vanished.

"For God's sake, what is wrong with you today?" asked Małgorzata, a younger work colleague chuckling. "I thought you'd dropped off."

"Nothing… nothing, I'm just tired," lied Elżbieta her guts writhing, for deep inside she knew something was not quite right.

At home, her eyes flew between the window and the clock, as the hands of time ticked arduously on. She peered out the window, her heart thumping, as from afar she spotted two moving images on the dirt track. Running outside she beamed, her heart dancing with joy; her son was home.

"Mamusia, may I play for a while with Wałodzia?" His voice was full of eager anticipation, as he held out a bunch of wild jasmine for his mother, lest she feel he favoured his teacher.

Their eyes locked; mother and son.

Don't go with Wałodzia and stay with me, she silently begged. The edges of her eyes crinkled, a smile dancing on her lips, her heart fragmenting. "Just for an hour while I prepare the supper."

"Thank you, thank you, Mamusia." He hugged her tightly and ran off with his friend.

"Don't I get a kiss?"

He ran back, pecked his mother on her cheek and returned to Wałodzia, their young excited voices echoing back to Elżbieta, making her smile.

She prepared the supper of kotlety, mashed potatoes and carrots; Jakub's favourite. Placing the dried breadcrumbs into a small bowl of milk to soak, she glanced at the clock; rolling the minced meat, fried onions, garlic and parsley mixture into round shapes her mind drifted. *By now, Jakub and Wałodzia were probably climbing trees, getting their knees grazed, or collecting some revolting insects.* "Probably to scare the life out of me," she stated aloud to the raw kotlety on the plate, a smile playing on her lips as she shook her head from side to side. Hurriedly, she washed her hands and placed the best crystal vase she possessed, containing Jakub's flowers, onto the table, her eyes darting to the clock.

"How the time is dragging today," she sighed heavily.

The potatoes and carrots were almost ready, the kotlety sizzling in the large pan, the smell of home cooking suffusing the kitchen. She peered out the window and poked her head out the door, to the sound of a buzzing bee which had lodged itself in a sweet fragranced rose. Glancing down at her watch she frowned. "It's not like Jakub to be late," she mumbled to herself.

Biting her lower lip, she returned to the pan and turned over the kotlety once more. *Already too brown*, she silently admitted. *But Jakub won't say anything, even if they were burnt to a crisp. Where on earth is he?* She switched off the stove and walked out the door. With her hand above her eyes, to obscure the strong afternoon sun, she scanned the periphery; her heart racing she took quick steps down the dirt track, the muscles of her stomach tightening with every second. *Any time now*, she told herself, *he will come running, another bunch of wildflowers in his hand, uncharacteristically oblivious of the time.*

Turning the bend, edged on both sides with clusters of tall conifers, she briskly walked out of the boundary of her land. "What are they up to?" The words became a recurring litany on her lips.

Her feet stopped, and her heart skipped a beat as she spotted a young boy running towards her. *Jakub… no… no, it's Wałodzia*, she surmised and thought, *Jakub cannot be far behind.* Each ran towards the other as fast as their legs could carry them. Elżbieta panted, "Wałodzia… wh.where is Jakub? Where is he?" Her wide stark eyes stared directly at the young boy, black trepidation suffusing her fast-beating heart. "Where is Jakub, Wałodzia?" she demanded as vomit rose to her parched throat, her stomach in tight twisted knots, tears spilling onto her face.

"Pani Kaminska… Pani Chmielowski," he gulped trying, in between gasps, to catch his breath, staring behind, raising his forefinger in the direction of the river. "He's… he's fallen in. He's in… in the river. I… I couldn't reach him."

Her body froze; her heavy feet glued to the ground and like a solidified figure she stood unable to move, not wanting to move, not wanting to know what was beyond her immediate line of vision. She heard voices… Suddenly, she was going round and round on a carousel: trees, barley fields, red poppies and wild daisies were spinning… spinning out of focus. Wałodzia was spinning… *Where was Jakub? Where was her son?*

"Pani Chmielowski… Pani Chmielowski…" She felt the rough tugging on her sleeve. Slowly, her eyes lowered and focused on her son's friend, stark reality slicing through her unreality.

"Go and get help, Wałodzia," she urged grabbing him by the arms, digging her nails into his flesh making him flinch, staring into his frightened innocent eyes. "Go to the Kwiatowskis and tell them to bring Doctor Uralski. Quickly; Wałodzia go!"

Quickly, she ran in the direction of the river bank, scanning all directions and seeing only the desolate slow flowing water. *So placid, so welcoming*, she thought. A balm of soothing stillness shrouded her like a cosy warm blanket and, for a few glorious moments, she was at perfect peace. *Jakub was safe. Why*, she told herself, *even if he had fallen into the river, he would have climbed out. He is not stupid. And, anyway*, she comforted herself, *he can swim.*

She walked slowly down the grassy bank of the meandering river, her eyes scanning the calm water. *Jakub is probably at home now, tucking into his favourite meal*, she thought. *He's not here.*

Excited voices in the far distance propelled her to look back as the Kwiatowskis, with Doctor Uralski in tow, were running towards her as fast as their middle-aged legs would allow.

"The others are on their way, my dear." Pani Kwiatowska placed a comforting hand on Elżbieta's goose-pimpled arm.

"Others?" Elżbieta queried in a dream-like trance.

"The others," repeated Katarzyna Kwiatowska. "The search party; everyone is willing to help. Our neighbours are good people, Elżbieta." She smiled encouragingly.

"There is no need." Elżbieta shook her head. "Jakub is at home."

A heavy silence shrouded the two women. Kind, concerned eyes focused on the younger woman. "I suggest you go home, Pani Chmielowska," urged the doctor, "in case your son makes his way home."

The aroma of the heavily spiced kotlety hit Elżbieta as she walked through the door making her nauseous; an eerie stillness shrouding her. "Jakub! Jakub!" She shouted at the top of her voice, as she rushed from one still room to another. "Jakub!" The ghostly silence grew like a malignant cancer, overpowering her; already she felt dead inside.

Cold, still, rigid she sat at the table staring into space. Her long silent vigil was broken by a gentle knocking on the door. She stirred, silently scolding herself for sitting there when there were a thousand chores to be done. A further bout of knocking roused her to her feet and to the door. "Doctor Uralski, what are you doing here?"

His stern serious eyes looked down on her as he gently took her by the arm. "Pani Kaminska, I think it would be better if you sat down."

"*Jakub… drowned… body… Jakub… drowned… body…*" The disjointed words whirled round and round in her dizzy pounding head, making no sense at all. "He can't be, Doctor Uralski, his favourite meal is ready."

The following days were a blur to Elżbieta, as she had retreated into a state of total oblivion. The Kwiatowskis took her in and were there for her day and night. Robotically, she ate and helped with the daily chores. Inside, she was an empty shell, feeling nothing.

The small white coffin, a spray of wild jasmine on the lid, was brought to Saint Peter's Church by kindly neighbours. That morning the small church was full to capacity, for everyone seemed to have known the young boy, with freckles across his nose and a cheeky grin; everyone wanted to say goodbye and share in his mother's grief. Tears were abundant, many loud and uncontrollable. Elżbieta's eyes were bone dry. She stood rigid, decked from head to foot in black, staring at the gold crucifix on the altar surrounded by white lilies; the sweet smell of incense suffusing the church, as the priest swung the censer over the casket.

As the organist began to play the opening notes of *Zdrowaś Maria*, a fresh bout of cries reached the front pews. Elżbieta stood immune staring silently ahead, not once glancing at her son's coffin.

Jakub was lowered carefully into the cold dark earth to join his grandfather, Zygmunt, beneath. Elżbieta threw a handful of earth onto the box and walked silently away.

Chapter Nineteen

Placing the raspberry cheesecake onto the kitchen table, Katarzyna Kwiatowska sat down on a chair and focused her attention on her neighbour, a look of grave concern clouding her kind eyes. Taking Elżbieta's hands into her own she softly announced, "It is time, my dear." Together they slowly stepped into Jakub's room, which had been disturbed only once since his untimely death, to retrieve his First Holy Communion suit for his burial. The room was stifling as Katarzyna stuffed an assortment of shirts, trousers, shorts and jumpers into a large bag as Elżbieta looked on, seeing nothing. Finally, the older woman perched beside her friend and patted her hand. "Now, my dear," she stated, "with God's help, you will be able to move on."

As the door closed on her neighbour, Elżbieta took slow, measured steps into her son's room. Robotically, she untied the string of the first bag, took out the neatly folded clothes and placed them back on their hangers; the second bag was untied, and books and puzzles were taken out and put back on their shelves and into cupboards. Closing the door quietly behind her, she cut herself a piece of raspberry cheesecake and made herself a lemon tea.

The next morning, she found herself on a bus in the city of Kraków wondering, as she looked out the grimy window, what on earth had possessed her to take the unplanned journey. As she looked at the passing buildings and pedestrians, a multitude of memories bombarded her mind: *memories of Wojtek beating the hell out of her mother, his evil tongue lashing out at both of them, swilling anything potent that came out of a bottle before crashing out in an alcoholic slumber; memories of his bloodshot eyes lusting after Zosia; memories of her mother giving up on life; memories of dear Zygmunt, the only real father she ever had; memories of Tadek Lisztek, Wojtek's friend and her nemesis. She wondered if Tadek and Wojtek were still alive; she hoped, with all her heart, they were dead.*

Stepping into the cool interior of Saint Adalbert's Church she noticed a small wedding taking place. Not wishing to intrude, she genuflected and sat down at the back of the church. Straining her eyes to the altar she wondered if Father Stanisław was presiding over the ceremony. The voice filtering down to her told her it was not, propelling her into wondering what had become of her old friend.

The organ's happy, melodious tune cued the happy couple to take their leave and start their future together. *Oh, how happy they must be!* Elżbieta mused as the couple walked towards her. *How beautiful*, she thought, *the bride looked decked in a long fitted, white satin gown, a delicate veil framing her radiant face, her eyes so happy.* Elżbieta's eyes flitted to the groom. Eyes locked. At that moment, the fate of Elżbieta Chmielowska and Andrzej Jaroszynski was sealed.

Chapter Twenty

She wore black. She grew thinner. She did not wish to see anyone, nor did she encourage visitors. All farm work was undertaken by local farmhands, any financial business was in the hands of her trusted solicitor. Outwardly, she seemed to have no worries; inwardly, she was dying a secret death.

Memories of her mother, Zygmunt and Jakub bombarded her mind. She lived and breathed in their memory, and they had become her silent and constant companions. Sometimes, she felt their calming presence, heard their soothing voices and caught herself talking aloud to them. They were in her world, and she felt she was already in theirs. Thoughts of joining them became more frequent until she found herself thinking of her own release, and consequently planning it in some detail became a daily exercise. On one such morning, unscrewing the top of a bottle of sleeping pills, she jumped at the unexpected knock at the door.

"Ciocia!" she exclaimed stuffing the small bottle deep into the pocket of her skirt, as she wondered what on earth had brought her auntie out all this way, silently cursing her for her trouble. "Come in… come in." Scanning Mania's unusually drawn pale face she braced herself for the onslaught of bad news. "Is it Zosia? Is she all right at the sanatorium?" she asked with heavy trepidation.

"It's Wojtek," she stated blandly. "He's dead. He died last night. I thought you should be informed." Avoiding her niece's eyes, for fear of what she may see, she buried her plump hand into her canvas grocery bag and extracted a large covered dish. "Gołąbki. I heard you're not eating well, my dear. Wojtek's funeral will take place next Monday, at eleven o'clock. Zosia is not doing well at the sanatorium. She has totally withdrawn into herself. She will speak to no one. I can't get through to her. I wondered, Elżbieta…"

"I will go and visit her," interrupted Elżbieta.

The bus journey to the sanatorium was long and uncomfortable; made more torturous by uninvited memories of Wojtek crashing into Elżbieta's mind: *his cruel fists thumping… thumping… thumping her mother's ribs, his vicious tongue spewing out his cruel words of condemnation… You are nothing… just like your mother... nothing... nothing... nothing... Indeed*, she silently agreed, nodding, her eyes looking out the window seeing a good-for-nothing tart. *I am nothing. He was right. I am nothing; disowned for years by my biological father, abandoned in death by my mother and son, hated by my stepfather and rejected by my lover. He was right... he was right... he was right...*

With a heavy heart, and feet like lead, she stepped off the bus, unsure and frightened of what was to come. As she approached her destination, her eyes widened, an involuntary sigh emitting from her mouth, for this was not the kind of place she was expecting to see. Rigid, she stood in front of the large foreboding building, hopeless scattered thoughts flashing through her mind. *This is no sanatorium, this is a mental institution*, she grimly concluded as a ferocious tsunami wave of bitter anger washed over her against Mania for her grave misinformation.

As her feet slowly walked on, a calm sea of forgiveness overtook the sea of anger. "Ciocia Mania couldn't accept the truth," she said aloud and, taking a sharp intake of breath, she walked into the dark shadows of the ominous building.

Her eyes flitted nervously around the cold and dark waiting room. The high grey ceiling matched perfectly the dull grey peeling walls, with only a small single window well above the span of vision. "This is a prison," she stated grimly as her eyes darted to the opening door.

"Pani Kaminska?" The lips of the approaching woman were set into a thin line, her small eyes scrutinising Elżbieta from head to foot.

"Actually, it's Pani Chmielowska now." Elżbieta extended her hand.

"Pani Chmielowska." The woman's eyes rested firmly on Elżbieta's face as she continued. "I must warn you that Zosia is seriously ill. You may not get a word out of her; believe me, we have tried, using many different methods without a grain of success." She paused before adding, "It will not be in your cousin's interest to persist. I will allow you ten minutes."

"Ten minutes!"

"Ten minutes," the nurse repeated, finality etching her words.

Ten minutes, Elżbieta silently repeated, *when we used to talk for hours.*

The brisk walk down the long, dimly lit corridor seemed to last forever. Abruptly, Elżbieta's feet stopped, and her heart froze as her ears pricked to sudden frantic cries and screams, followed by a barrage of stern authoritative words escaping through a firmly closed door. *This is indeed prison,* she concluded, drawing in a deep breath as she walked through an assigned door.

Elżbieta's eyes shot to a painfully thin, pale-faced young woman who lay uncomfortably rigid on a hard mattress. Hands stiffly by her side, legs together, stark and unlinking eyes staring at the ceiling, the patient was unaware of her cousin looking down on a living corpse. Elżbieta took slow steps towards the bed, her heart beating out of sync.

"Ten minutes," stated the nurse, closing the door behind her.

For long minutes, Elżbieta perched on the bed staring down at her beloved Zosia, her heart slicing in two for the shell of a woman who used to be so full of life, laughter and hope. Suddenly, aware of the precious time slipping away, she took her cousin's limp hand into her own shocked by its coldness, its lifelessness. "Zosia," she whispered. "Zosia…" Gingerly, she ran her fingers through her cousin's greasy and uncombed hair *which*, she reflected, *used to be so immaculately groomed.* She kissed her softly on the forehead, as the young woman beneath continued staring into oblivion. *Time was of the essence*, she silently stated, her heart beating faster as she tried desperately to find the right words before it was too late, and she was ushered out.

"Zosia…" Out of the corner of her eye she saw the slight movement of a forefinger, her eyes shot to her cousin's eyes where she saw a tiny flicker. She dropped her eyes, Zosia's body was still rigid. "He is dead," Elżbieta stated clearly and concisely. "Wojtek Kaminski is dead. You are free. You are free, Zosia." Eyes rapidly flickered and snapped shut. The door opened. The ten minutes were up.

Dressed in a straight black dress, coat to match, a single strand of pearls around her neck, Elżbieta pinned up her glossy black hair into a large pearl clasp, slipped on her black patent shoes and grabbed her black patent clutch bag. Knots tightened into tighter balls in the pit of her stomach, her heart beat rapidly as she held her head high and walked through the church door and sat in the back pew. The service was simple and short. She stared as Wojtek Kaminski's casket was lowered into the dark damp hole. *Good riddance to bad rubbish*, she silently stated. As she raised her head, her eyes looked straight into the stark eyes of her nemesis.

Chapter Twenty-One

She stared with eyes of ice at the vermin standing on the other side of the grave; the vile animal who had snatched away her innocence and left her broken—a nothing. She stared unblinkingly as his body visibly flinched, a sickly grin on his mouth. He lowered his glassy eyes to his friend's casket.

"He can't help you now," Elżbieta stated in icy cold words, her eyes firmly glued on the creature who had robbed her of her innocence.

Slowly, he raised his eyes to meet her dark, still eyes. "Elżbieta…"

She stood unmoving, staring fixedly at the man before her, feeling him writhe beneath his now puny exterior; feeling him squirm as she abruptly turned her back on him, and began her confident walk out of the cemetery, her ears pricking to the gravel crunching behind her. She turned, venom weaving into her icy eyes as she felt a tug on her coat sleeve and focused her unwavering eyes on Tadek Lisztek, taking in his pitiful skeletal face; secretly delighting that she was staring into the eyes of a dying man. Her cold controlled eyes continued to stare at him as if surveying a despicable creature, which had crawled out from beneath its rock.

Immediately, the years rolled back as… *intermittent spikes of jagged lightning quivered in the semi-darkened room as the young girl, pinned down to her bed, lay quivering beneath the heavy weight on top of her. Deafening blasts of thunder drowned the muffled screams and, with them, her hope of imminent release. She squeezed her eyes tight to obliterate his blubbery face as he forced his twisted fleshy lips on hers, the stench of garlic and vodka made her stomach churn, her whole body wrench with revulsion for the monster on top of her as he pumped mercilessly. Her hot prickly tears strayed to a shiny silver samovar on a small round table in the corner of the room, where she witnessed a minuscule reflection of the monster on top of her. Intense hatred rose to the surface of her being as she vowed silently between clenched teeth: I'll get you back for this you animal. If it's the last thing I do. You will pay!*

"E-Elżbieta…forgive me… please," he rasped.

Is that it, instant forgiveness? She asked silently as her lips remained firmly clamped, her stark unblinking eyes staring into the depths of his black soul.

"I... I have lost everything, Elżbieta; my wife, my child. Please—please—forgive me. I have lost everything."

She stared at the quivering self-pitying wreck before her as pure incredulity rushed in angry waves through her entire body. "I will meet you tomorrow in Kraków Square. Eleven o'clock," she stated; her words clipped and cold as she turned her back on him and walked briskly away.

The next morning, she woke up with a strong sense of urgency surrounding her every move. Staring at her pale reflection in the mirror she vigorously brushed her long hair till it gleamed. "Today," she stated at the woman staring back at her, "is the day of retribution."

Dressed entirely in black, her hair secured at the back with an ebony clasp, she carefully retrieved a cumbersome bulk hidden away in the depths of her wardrobe. Diligently, scrutinising every centimetre of it, making sure every piece was intact she placed it into a large cloth bag. Taking a final look in the cheval mirror she took a deep breath, picked up her bag and walked out of the house. The mist in the surrounding fields was lifting. *It was going to be a fine day*, she smiled.

Elżbieta sat grim-faced, with both hands firmly gripping her precious cargo perched on her lap. Unseeingly, she stared out the window; the journey was taking forever. Finally, she disembarked and took swift steps along Franciszkanska, made a left turn onto Bracka and on to the Rynek Główny where she stood in front of the façade of the Church of Saint Mary, which dominated the Square. Focusing her eyes on the old Gothic landmark, she scanned the aged brick structure raising her eyes to the tips of its spires. Entranced by a blackbird gracefully balancing on one of the spires, as if performing some daring acrobatic act, she sighed heavily, *Oh, if only I was that bird, I'd fly away and never come back.*

"Pani Elżbieta." The quiet, almost inaudible, voice instantly made her insides freeze, a gush of blood rushing to her head making the old church swim before her eyes. Turning slowly she stared at his cream-coloured shirt, his cream and black diamond patterned tie, and the lapels of his well-worn leather jacket; her eyes slowly rising and fixing on the eyes of her perpetrator; old eyes silently begging for a grain of forgiveness as they stared into the eyes of the woman he raped. Eyes locked with eyes; soul with soul *as they were back in the dingy room as intermittent spikes of jagged lightning quivered in the semi-darkness.* "Pani Elżbieta."

A gentle tug on the sleeve of her coat dragged the young girl out of the semi-darkened room; dragged the mature woman out of the black nightmare, her eyes staring directly at the brutal evidence of her past, as she took in his sunken eyes and drawn face. *He looks ill*, she thought, feeling nothing. "Pani Elżbieta, you wanted to see me. Perhaps—perhaps, there is some hope of mercy?"

Shut up you despicable, vile old man, she yearned to shout, as she snapped her eyes shut to obliterate his contemptible image; the brief moment of blackness was a welcome barrier between them. She stood rigid, her eyes as black as the coat she wore. "Not here," she stated coldly.

"May I suggest the Kawiarnia Marianska?" He smiled showing his tobacco-stained teeth.

She stared at his sickly grin. "We will go to the Wawelska," she stated with cold authority in her voice.

Side by side, they walked in stony silence turning their backs on the Rynek Główny and walking on to Bracka. Placing the cloth bag under the table, well out of sight, she waited for him to place the order. Her eyes scanned the busy coffee shop, a smile dancing on her lips. *The place was full of regulars and tourists; a first-class setting*, she decided, her eyes flitting to the walking corpse, grasping nearby tables to regain his balance, as he cautiously approached the counter on his wobbly feet, his jacket and trousers hanging off his scrawny body. She watched his every move as, with trembling hands, he placed the coffees on the table, her mouth set in a firm line.

"You have spilt coffee onto the saucers," she stated icily, her own body feeling as if it was corroding with pure hate.

"I'm sorry—I'm sorry—" He glanced up at her as she unblinkingly stared as he mopped up the coffee spills. With each sip of her coffee, the soothing liquid brought a comforting warmth, as she stared silently at the old man sitting opposite, her free hand reassuringly patting the content of her bag, a smile flickering on her lips.

He saw a glimmer of hope in her smile as he raised his sunken eyes to her dark, unyielding, unforgiving eyes; his trembling lips opening, opening wider as they failed to emit words of contrition, as he silently begged the young woman to come to his aid, to help him in his hour of need. Outwardly, she sat unmoved;

inwardly, her guts wrenched at the vile creature before her grovelling for mercy; her mercy.

Time ebbed away. Finally, from somewhere in the depths of his being, he summoned the words he thought would save him. "I am dying, Pani Elżbieta."

After long silent minutes, she uttered, "I know."

His eyes dropped to the black liquid in his cup, his spirit deflated. She stared at her nemesis, her heart dancing.

"I've brought you a gift, Pan Lisztek; something for you to remember me by," she said, trying desperately to hide the tremor in her voice.

He raised his flickering eyes to her. "So... so, you forgive me, Pani Elżbieta?" he asked in a quavering voice, hope entering his dying heart.

She rested her still eyes on his. Slowly, her words came out, "I forgive you, Pan Lisztek, but I don't want you to forget me."

"Forget you? Never... never, Pani Elżbieta; I will never forget you!" He exclaimed, his heart dancing for now he could die in peace. His wizened eyes puzzled over as the cumbersome package was placed on the table, causing inquisitive diners to cast surreptitious glances at the large mysterious bulk.

"Open it, Pan Lisztek. It's yours." She enthused as her eyes scrutinised him intently, watching his every laborious move as he carefully, with trembling fingers, untied the string securing the package and carefully lifted out the heavy bulk, placing it back on the table, wondering what on earth this was doing here.

"Do you remember it?"

His eyes peered curiously at the item slowly registering its owner's identity. "Yes... yes... it's your mother's samovar."

"Yes, it was my mother's samovar. Pan Lisztek, do you remember where it stood?"

Lisztek vigorously scratched the side of his head. "Why yes, yes, it stood, as I remember, on a table in the corner of the room."

"Yes it did," she agreed vehemently her voice rising, causing others to look on, as she placed her hands around the base of the samovar, and moved it towards the one human being she hated above all others. "This is a gift from me to you. In your dying days, it will remind you of the day you robbed me of my innocence; robbed me of the only gift I could give to a man; robbed me of me. This samovar was a witness to it all. When you look at it, as you are gasping for your final breath, may you see our reflection; may that be your punishment."

That afternoon, retrieving a large pair of scissors, she cut her black attire into shreds. As she watched the burning flames, for the first time in her life, she felt alive.

Chapter Twenty-Two

After sorting out Jakub's possessions, Elżbieta replaced her black mourning clothes with colourful blouses, dresses and skirts. She began to take more care with her appearance outlining her eyebrows in black pencil, popping on a spot of blusher or a subtle shade of lipstick; she started visiting old friends and took more pride in her house and in her work at the museum. She started to smile again; to feel once more. Suitable suitors came and went; she gave her heart to no one. She looked forward to her daily visits to the cemetery; there she talked to those she loved: Jakub, Krystyna, Zygmunt; laughing and sharing her joys and woes. She needed nothing, and nobody else.

As always, the autumn days brought with them a tinge of sadness, and as she walked through the melange of yellow, cinnamon, olive, rusty red, brown and gold leaves, her heart died a little. Taking off her leather gloves, her forefinger traced the gold tone letters spelling, *Jakub Chmielowski.* She continued to trace the letters: *Aged eight. In God's tender care...* as salty tears spilt down her checks. Raising her eyes to the sullen sky she asked over and over again, "Why Lord? Why?" Swallowing the hard lump in her throat, swiftly wiping away the tears from her face, she cleaned the graves and placed a large bunch of gold chrysanthemums on each, in preparation for tomorrow's big day.

"Actually, maybe I shall give it a miss this year," Elżbieta said nonchalantly.

Katarzyna and her husband were having none of it, for in their minds Elżbieta had to live through this day, and all its sadness, to move on a step further. All Saints Day was the most important day remembering the dead in the Polish calendar, and there was no way Elżbieta was going to miss it. She was going to the cemetery whether she wanted to or not.

By the time they reached the cemetery, it was already ablaze with a sea of flickering candles, giving it an uncharacteristically homely feeling; full of people of all ages, who had come to spend an evening with their beloved departed. Since her encounter with Tadek Lisztek, Elżbieta had found an emotional release though, deep inside, she had been dreading this day for weeks, for it would be the first All Saints Day without Jakub; the first All Saints Day when he was amongst the army of dead, and her heart hadn't fully accepted the fact; for there were times when she expected to see him running through the door, with a bunch of wildflowers in his hands, or be spotted in the branches of an old oak tree. She smiled at the memories, her heart slicing in two. Today, she knew, was going to be a tough day, for it was always Jakub who had helped her in the grieving process, and now he was no more.

As they walked slowly to the graves, Elżbieta's eyes strayed to the children decked in thick coats, hats, scarves; stamping about, grasping golden crisp leaves, and she imagined Jakub amongst them. For long minutes, they stood staring down at the graves of Krystyna, Zygmunt and Jakub. Katarzyna broke the eerie silence, "My dear, Franek and I will leave you for half an hour to visit our beloved dead. You will be all right?"

Elżbieta nodded and smiled faintly. Sitting down on an old rustic bench, huddled against the cold, she stared down at the blazing candles, her nostrils alive to the smell of chrysanthemums, intermingled with dead foliage and candle fumes, her mind drifting... *Only twelve months ago Jakub was lighting two candles to honour his grandparents. And now*—She snapped her eyes shut. The sound of rustling leaves alerted her to the fact she was not alone. "Katarzyna, I was not expecting you back so soon."

She looked around to see a figure of a man, placing a wreath of white roses onto a recently made mound. She watched as he stood back, a solitary figure lost in his own memories. He turned at the sound of her involuntary cough, and immediately she recognised him, her heart leaping to her dry throat. Abruptly, she rose to her feet and turned to go.

"Stop—please; stop." She heard a voice urge softly.

"Boże, oh dear Boże," she murmured, wishing a grave would open up and swallow her whole, as she quickened her steps.

"Wait—please—"

She stood still her feet glued to the damp cold earth, her heart beating erratically as she silently asked, *What do I do now?* She remained fixed on the spot as he approached.

"Do I know you?" he asked in a soft voice, his warm smile instantly making her feel at ease.

"No—yes—no..."

"Maybe?" He volunteered, his smile growing.

"Yes, maybe," she mumbled, her feet proceeding forward.

"Please wait, I think I may know you." Spontaneously, he grabbed her by her sleeve, his spontaneity creating an immediate flashback of Tadek Lisztek's hand on her coat sleeve.

"Get off me!" she snapped, eyes of fire flashing angrily at him, leaving a puzzled frown on the young man's face as she stormed off.

Who on earth is this woman, and what on earth is wrong with her? He wondered as he began his lonely walk home.

Chapter Twenty-Three

1962

Elżbieta gazed down at the sleeping baby in her arms, as she rocked back and forth in Zygmunt's old rocking chair, a wave of nostalgia sweeping over her as she thought back to those carefree days she spent with Zosia; her smile dying a sudden death as Wojtek, Tadek Lisztek and Lukasz crashed into her mind, and then there was Mania's revelation…

"I need to tell you something," announced Mania sipping a lemon tea, her unwavering eyes firmly fixed on her niece, making Elżbieta's heart skip a beat. The last time the older woman assumed such a grave tone was when she was announcing Wojtek's death and Zosia's illness. Elżbieta focused her eyes, her heart beating madly, wondering what on earth her auntie was about to impart.

"Wojtek knew from the very beginning that your mother was with child from another man; he knew from the very start that you were not his, and he begrudged you ever entering into the world he had mapped out for himself."

Elżbieta's eyes narrowed as a multitude of questions crashed into her mind. After long minutes of soul-searching, she muttered, "Then why did he marry Mama?" She raised her eyes to Mania as her auntie gazed into the distant past.

"She had money. He married her for the money and took you on as necessary collateral. You, Elżbieta, was a part of the deal."

The young woman's mind swam round and round as lies, greed, betrayal and disappointment added to the mix. "Oh Boże—oh Boże—Boże—Boże…" She squeezed her eyes tight, shaking her head from side to side, seeing everything clearly now. "It's no wonder he hated—despised me so much. Not only was I not his own flesh and blood; he was forced into accepting me as part of the deal. It was me or nothing. Oh Boże…" She searched Mania's clouded eyes. "But; what about the money?"

The older woman bowed her head, unable to look her niece in the eyes for fear of what she might see there. "It—it was all lost in a game of cards."

A tsunami of deathly silence consumed the two women, each desperately searching for something to say until, after torturous minutes, Mania reached out and took both her niece's trembling hands into her own, her eyes looking deep into Elżbieta's eyes. "Wojtek was a man who liked to boast. As soon as he acquired your mother's wealth, everybody knew about it. He made instant friends—and enemies. Greed feeds on greed and Wojtek was a very greedy man; he wanted more and more. He lost everything apart from the clothes he stood in."

From that moment on, Elżbieta understood everything: Wojtek's hatred of his wife, his hatred for the bastard he was now responsible for, and his attraction to wealth in the guise of Zygmunt. Everything was now crystal clear…

She rocked back and forth with her baby securely in her arms. "Krystyna, Zygmunt and I were his pawns, his collateral," she whispered. A scuffle at the door snapped her out of her dismal reverie, her glassy eyes darting to the opening door.

"Henryk!" Her eyes followed her husband, as he stooped and bestowed a soft kiss on the baby's forehead, kissing her on the cheek, making her eyes sparkle and a smile spread on her lips. *Oh, how she was learning to love this quiet, unassuming man: a doting father, a loving husband and a provider. He was her world, and she and Baby Anielka his universe.*

Nothing and nobody else mattered.

Their lives, like themselves, were quiet and modest. Henryk worked hard as a tailor while Elżbieta took on the role of full-time mother and housewife. After Wojtek's brutal treatment, Lukasz's escapades, and personal sorrows which followed, she had yearned for, and found, solace in a peaceful, secure life with Henryk. An attractive woman at twenty-four she was admired by many men, she had eyes only for her husband. They resided in Zygmunt's old house, the farmland sold long ago and the proceeds safely invested for Anielka's future, for she was their pride and joy.

Watching the light snowflakes whirling and twirling, Elżbieta's eyes flitted to the slow-moving hands of the clock. Abruptly, she dressed Anielka into suitable winter clothing, put on her own furs and headed for the door and the promise of adult company, if only in the form of passing pedestrians.

The Rynek Główny did not seem as busy today, perhaps it's the promise of bad weather, she mused, as a gust of a strong north-easterly wind swirled a bunch of dead leaves and light snowflakes into the air. She smiled. *Soon it will be Christmas; Anielka's first Christmas and their first Christmas as a family.*

The sound of the Hejnał made her heart skip a beat, the unfinished call of the trumpeter never failing to tug at her heart. She stood perfectly still listening and watching until the last note pierced the still air, adjusted the hood of Anielka's pram and turned to leave. She stood transfixed, her feet glued to the spot as her insides turned to ice, her wide eyes staring unblinkingly at the person standing before her. Instinctively, her eyes registered the identity of the person staring back at her as he tried, in vain, to pin her down to a place, a time, shaking his head from side to side unable to grasp either. Like a bird in a cage, she felt scrutinised, trapped, yearning for imminent release.

"You were the lady in the church on—on my wedding day?" He volunteered cocking an eyebrow.

She nodded silently, opening her mouth to words which failed to materialise.

"Do I know you?" He lifted a brow, a flicker of a smile playing around his mouth.

She shook her head vehemently. *For God's sake*, urged an inner voice, *just walk away, woman. What are you standing here for?* Withdrawing her eyes from him she stared down at her sleeping child and proceeded to walk away.

"Please, don't go." He urged softly, spontaneously placing his broad hand on her hand, quickly withdrawing it. "I'm sorry."

Electric shocks pulsated through her entire body, the likes of which she had not experienced since Lukasz. *This is dangerous territory*, a voice in her head boomed. *This is very dangerous territory. Go, woman. Take your baby and go—quickly—run*, the voice urged. "I have to go." She turned, her feet taking brisk steps in the opposite direction, her heart thudding.

"Meet me tomorrow. Kawiarnia Marianska. Three o'clock."

Her heart beat rapidly as she stared at her full plate of food, her mouth tightly clamped.

"Is something wrong, Elżbieta? You seem a little preoccupied this evening." Henryk raised his concerned eyes to meet those of his wife as he held a piece of roast chicken precariously on the end of his fork. "Elżbieta!"

His raised voice forced her to raise her eyes to him. "No, no there is nothing wrong. I… I was just thinking about Christmas. It will be our first with Anielka." She forced a reassuring smile.

His brow creased showing deep furrows. "But it's almost two months away."

"It will be Anielka's first Christmas," she repeated, a tinge of vexation clipping her words.

"Yes, it will be Anielka's first Christmas." He smiled, bringing his fork down to his plate as he picked up his wife's hand and kissed it softly.

Her eyes surveyed the man before her: *a good solid man; a better husband and father of their child she could not wish for*, she silently concluded as an image of the mysterious acquaintance crashed violently into her mind, the memory of his hand on her hand sending uninvited delightful shivers through her body. "I must clear up the dishes," she stated rising abruptly from the table, releasing Wojtek's hand, avoiding his eyes lest he should suspect.

Suspect what? she asked herself. *The fact she couldn't get the stranger out of her mind? The fact that she hadn't forgotten him since the day he picked up her school books so many years ago? The fact that when she had encountered him at the cemetery on All Saints Day, she couldn't get him out of her mind? Or, the fact that she secretly yearned to meet him tomorrow?*

That night two bodies lay side by side. Henryk lay brooding about the woman beside him. *Perhaps she is ill or pregnant?* A smile rushed to his lips. *How on earth could he approach either subject?* He wondered, his smile vanishing. Elżbieta lay motionless beside her husband her eyes staring starkly at the dark ceiling, as thoughts of a fair-haired man with grey eyes, warm hands, and a wife, invaded her head. By the first light of dawn, she had made her decision.

Chapter Twenty-Four

The Kawiarnia Marianska, as always, was populated with a mixture of students, middle-aged intellectuals and tourists. Her eyes scanned the smoky-filled room, her heart skipping a beat as she spotted him, alone at a table reading a newspaper, flicking ash into an ashtray already full of stubs. Her heart thudded, silently urging her to run away from this den of temptation; to run as fast as her feet would carry her to her husband and child; to run to the safety of what is, and away from the desire of what may be; to run home. Her heavy feet stuck to the floor. *Run—stay—run—stay—*Unblinking eyes fixed steadily on the *stranger* she was approaching. *Run—stay—run—*Her eyes darted to the door—*there was still time—*Her heart beat frantically.

"Come, sit down, please." His softly spoken words reverberated in her head, capturing her entire senses and turning them to jelly. Slowly, she turned back, approached the table, and sat down staring at the man before her, seeing only Henryk's kind face.

"I have to go." She stood up her cold, detached eyes staring down at him. "I must go. I… I have a husband, a—a—"

"And, I have a wife, a wife I love above all else. But why can't we be friends?"

Her eyes focused on the man she barely knew, but felt she had known all her life; a thousand logical and illogical, sorted and distorted, thoughts merging together, crashing mercilessly in her mind making her head thud. "Sit down, please."

She sat her eyes fixed firmly on the man sitting opposite, her whole body rigid, her heart and head hammering in unison. He extended his broad hand. "Paweł—Paweł Jaroszynski."

Staring unblinkingly at his hand she gingerly took it and for a delicious moment revelled in its warm, secure grasp. Roughly withdrawing her hand, she placed it on her lap as her eyes stared at the salt and pepper condiments.

"I didn't think you would come," he said. His voice was soft and friendly. Slowly raising her eyes, she met his warm gaze. "I am pleased you did come," he added, the warmth of his smile matching those of his twinkling eyes.

"I'm—I'm not sure I should be here. I don't know why I am here." Her eyes met his and dropped to the riveting salt and pepper pots. "I have a young child. I can't stay long."

"But you can stay for a little while; coffee?"

Her eyes followed him as he walked confidently towards the counter taking in his slim body, narrow shoulders and fair short cropped hair; suddenly she felt an inexplicable rush of empty loneliness. *It's not too late to go*, an inner voice whispered. *Go—go—go—*

"I have taken the liberty of ordering makowiec. I hope you like it," he smiled.

"My favourite!" she exclaimed, silently scolding herself for her spontaneous child-like enthusiasm; the dimples in his smile sending a fresh tingle through her veins. Surreptitiously, she watched him sip his black coffee as thoughts of Anielka flooded her mind.

"Please tell me something about yourself. I don't even know your name." His eyes carefully scrutinised the woman sitting opposite: her black glossy hair secured safely in a clasp, her rich brown eyes and the curve of her sensuous mouth.

"My name is Elżbieta."

"My wife has the same name."

The mention of his wife sent a fresh wave of panic surging through her body. "Look," she announced, "You have a wife; I, a husband. This liaison cannot do either of us any good."

"Liaison!" he exclaimed displaying perfect straight teeth. "I thought we were going to be just friends."

Elżbieta snapped her eyes shut tight, feeling a deep uncomfortable heat rising and suffusing her face, flooding through her entire body, silently urging her to run as fast as she could and not look back.

"Tell me about yourself." He urged his eyes steadily focused, ignoring her embarrassment.

For long seconds, she sat drowned in her own pool of humiliation. With immense effort, the words crawled out of her mouth, while her eyes remained firmly fixed on the table. "There is nothing to tell. I am married. I have a baby of three months."

"Happily married?" He raised an eyebrow.

What damned business is it of yours! She yearned to cry out, a surge of red-hot rage racing through her twisted guts. "Yes, happily married." She managed to say. "And you?" She raised her eyes to his and saw sorrow.

"My wife," he said quietly, "is ill, terminally ill. She has cancer."

"*Wife… terminally ill… cancer…*" His words crashed, dashed and swam in her still pounding head. *Then, what the hell are you doing here with me?* She so desperately wanted to blurt out.

He intercepted her jumbled, scathing thoughts. "A private nurse attends Elusia for the course of two hours each day, in which I am able to have a break." He looked steadily into Elżbieta's eyes. "I love my wife dearly but…"

Her ears were closed, her thoughts now divided into two camps: Paweł's wife and her own husband. *Both were loved, and neither deserved to be betrayed.* Neatly folding her napkin, she placed it on the table and rose to go.

"Please…" His eyes pleaded, his hand inadvertently grabbing hers, sending new electrifying shocks cursing through her veins. "Let us meet on Friday, as friends. Perhaps, we could visit Wawel."

She turned to go.

"Please…" A fresh urgency tinged his voice making her turn back. She nodded her head silently, turned, brushed past the motley gathering of young, and not so young; the open door bringing her fresh air and a sense of freedom.

Chapter Twenty-Five

Paweł Jaroszynski invaded Elżbieta's thoughts and dreams. All Anielka's needs were catered for, the furniture dusted and polished, laundry washed, the meals well prepared and ready on the table, though Henryk detected an inexplicable, intangible distance between himself and his beloved wife, and each day brought a fresh secret concern for her welfare. He intended to broach the subject, planned it all out in the tiniest detail, then ducked the subject entirely, for he knew her past and could not bear to encroach on her space. *She will tell me in her own good time*, he concluded, but still he worried.

Inwardly, Elżbieta was a bag of jangled nerves. Every little thing irritated her: Henryk's snoring, his fussing over her, the way he held his knife and fork; even little Anielka's delightful gurgling made her want to scream out loud. The time dragged, every hour seeming like ten. Her thoughts turned to her new friend: *What would he be doing now? Breakfasting? Attending to his wife's needs? Occupied in household chores? Thinking of her? Why don't you just go to work*, she silently urged her husband, wishing him to go and leave her with her secret daydreams.

When he departed for work instant, inexplicable guilt came over her in waves: guilt for betraying her husband; guilt for ever allowing a terminally ill woman's husband to invade, and take over her mind. Slumping down on to the kitchen chair she buried her head in her hands. A sudden thought brought a smile to her lips.

As he opened the door, the corner of his eyes crinkled, and a beaming smile spread on his lips.

"Father Stanisław, I hope you don't mind me coming here unannounced." Her cautious eyes took in his dark hair now speckled, here and there, with grey, the crow's feet around his eyes she hadn't seen before, causing a wave of nostalgia to sweep over her for, despite it all, there were some carefree days amidst the gloom and disharmony and, more, importantly, he was always there for her.

They sat in his parlour sharing a glass of lemonade reminiscing about old times and exchanging recent news; laughing, joking, perfectly at ease in each other's company. She saw the wave of concern covering his wise face, his smile vanishing from his lips.

"But you haven't come here solely to catch up on old times, Elżbieta?"

Her downcast eyes gave him his answer. The answer he gave to her shared secret made her world crash around her.

"You know, deep within yourself Elżbieta, you must stop seeing this—this Paweł."

"But he is just a friend. He is…"

He placed his gentle hands on hers, his soft eyes upon the girl he watched grow and mature into a beautiful woman, and his heart went out to her. "He is out of bounds, Elżbieta." She raised her eyes to meet his silently pleading eyes. "No, Elżbieta," he shook his head fervently, "he belongs to another."

With a heavy heart, she opened the door and, without looking back, walked out. She knew what she had to do.

Chapter Twenty-Six

Her heart quickened as she spotted him at the entrance to the Royal Treasury at the Castle, noticing that his eyes were looking far away into the distance. *What did he see there?* She wondered as the sound of her footsteps alerted him of her presence.

"Elżbieta." His eyes dropped.

"I have left Anielka with a neighbour. I only have an hour to spare." She stated, her heart beating with wild anticipation as he ushered her inside, her mind involuntarily drifting to Father Stanisław and his stern words. *What does he know, anyway? He's never married; probably never had a woman in his life.*

She silently consoled herself, staring at an eleventh-century chalice dating back from the abbey at Tyniec. They walked side by side in total silence, glancing fleetingly at the bejewelled golden goblets, coins and platters. She froze, her eyes fixed on the szczerbiec, a coronation sword used in the crowning ceremonies of bygone days. Since a young child, she had been mesmerised by the sword's rich Gothic design, dated back to the thirteenth century.

Now, she felt, she was thrusting the blade of finality into the essence of her married life. Deep within her heart, she knew that if she was to continue in this dangerous game, she would change the lives of the people she loved most in the world forever; life, as they knew it, would be dead. She cast a final lingering look at the szczerbiec, and all that it represented, and walked on.

In a small coffee shop, away from the bustle of the Sukiennice, they began to gradually relax in each other's company. Thoughts of Henryk and Anielka evaporated as she listened spellbound to Paweł's accounts of his childhood, his days in service and his knowledge of Kraków.

"And your wife, what is she like, Paweł?" she cautiously asked, her eyes watching his every move, as his eyes dropped to his coffee cup.

"Paweł—your wife," she urged. "What is she like?"

"She was—is very beautiful. I have known her all of my life. She is the love of my life." The words rushed out.

"Childhood sweethearts?"

"Yes."

"And—now?"

"And now she is dying—only three months left at best," he said so softly his words were barely audible.

Instinctively, Elżbieta grabbed his hand and squeezed it tightly. Their eyes locked, and she saw his pain. Abruptly, she pulled her hand away for what she felt sent shock waves cursing through her veins. His words made her guts freeze.

"Come to my apartment tomorrow, at twelve o'clock, Elżbieta. I would like you to meet my wife."

"I must go," she hastily announced rising to her feet, an invisible knife shredding her heart into pieces.

"Twenty-five Gòralska," he shouted after her.

Heavy solitary steps brought her to the brick Gothic Church of Our Lady Assumed into heaven, adjacent to the Rynek Główny. Slowly, she walked down the chancel, her eyes taking in the beauty of the stained glass windows, which dated back to the late fourteenth century. Her eyes darted to the blue star vaulting of the nave and then scanned the paintings, which blended in perfectly with the medieval architecture and the surroundings of the high altar. Inside, she was in hell; a hell of her own making *and where*, she grimly concluded, *she deserved to be.*

Sitting down in the front pew, thoughts whirling, her eyes stared unblinkingly at the wooden altarpiece. It was, she had heard, deemed to be the eighth wonder of the world by the great Pablo Picasso. Her eyes scrutinised the masterpiece. *I hate it*, she vehemently decided her eyes scanning the central panel and the two pairs of side wings, taking in its intricately carved lime wood which had been painted and gilded. She could not see the main scene as the pentaptych was closed.

The outside, she noticed, had sections depicting scenes from the life of Jesus and the Virgin Mary. Her eyes rose to the top of the altarpiece, where it portrayed the Virgin's Coronation in heaven and then dropped to both sides, where stood the statues of Saint Stanisław and Saint Adalbert, Poland's patron saints. She had remembered Zygmunt once relating to her the fact that at thirteen metres high and over ten metres wide; the pentaptych is Poland's largest and most treasured piece of medieval art; that it took ten years for its maker to complete it before its consecration in 1489.

Well, she thought shaking her head in silent disgust, *in my opinion, Veit Stoss needn't have bothered.* The crucifix at the right-hand aisle involuntarily made her eyes still as they stared at Stoss's creation. *This was what it was all about in the end, or was it?* She stared hard, her eyes riveted on the cross. Krystyna and Zygmunt seeped into her thoughts—and Father Stanisław and his damning words crashed into her head, echoing repeatedly, making her close her eyes to everything but the dark. *"You know, deep within yourself Elżbieta... you must stop seeing this... this Paweł... he belongs to another... he belongs to another... he belongs to another..."*

"He belongs to another," she stated aloud to Stoss's crucifix. She picked up her bag and made her way home to Henryk and Anielka.

Chapter Twenty-Seven

To his immense delight, Henryk saw an instant transformation in his wife's behaviour. In every way, she had come back to him, and whatever it was that had caused the temporary distance between them was forgotten. *It was*, he told himself, *nothing to worry about*, as that night he lay contently in bed, his beloved wife in his arms, their child in her cot by the side of their bed. His world was complete.

Elżbieta lay in her husband's arms, her thoughts with Paweł and his dying wife whirling around her head, giving her no mercy or much-needed sleep. Glancing at her loving husband, and Anielka sleeping soundly with her thumb in her mouth, she closed her eyes to it all. *My life is here*, she concluded. *My life is here.*

The clock on her bedside table slowly ticked away the long seconds, minutes and hours as she lay still, eyes staring starkly at the dark ceiling, her ears finely tuned to the rhythm of her husband's peaceful breathing. Thoughts of Paweł continued to occupy her tired head: *Paweł, the young handsome soldier, picking up her school books; Paweł, his grey eyes staring at her intently in the coffee shop; Paweł, walking slowly beside her in the Wawel Treasury; Paweł, silently beseeching her to come and meet his beloved wife; Paweł—Paweł—Paweł—* Carefully, placing her bed covers aside she rose and tiptoed to the window, staring out at the birth of a brand new day and, as the cool grey light of dawn spread over the oaks and fields, she knew exactly what she must do for the sake of her marriage, her security and, more importantly, her sanity.

She walked quickly, determinedly until her feet reached her destination; her heart thumping she fidgeted from foot to foot, her eyes peeled on the door willing it to open.

He peered down at two wide eyes peering from beneath a thick white woolly bobble hat. "Ah, you have brought your daughter, A…" His eyes flitted to Elżbieta where they remained fixed.

"Anielka," she prompted, chagrin in her voice for his apparent forgetfulness.

"Yes, yes, Anielka." He ushered them into the dimly lit hall, a smell of illness and waiting for death hitting Elżbieta's nostrils. She grabbed his arm forcing him to turn. "I… I have come to say goodbye, Paweł," she stuttered staring at him unflinchingly.

"Yes, yes, I know. My wife is…"

"I have come to say goodbye to you, Paweł," she stated slowly and concisely, emphasising each word lest he misunderstood, or she be misconstrued. Silence covered silence as hearts beat erratically; eyes stared at eyes; mouths unable to utter a sound. A creaking door, and slow shuffling feet, broke the deadly silence; Elżbieta's fast-beating heart rapidly turned to ice as her eyes flitted to the skeletal figure moving laboriously towards them, noticing the ghost of a smile pinned painfully on the woman's pale wan face.

A bony hand reached forth, "My name is Elżbieta, though everyone calls me by my pet name, Elusia. I am Paweł's wife. He has told me so much about you." Elżbieta opened her dry mouth and closed it, her strangled words lodged in a hard lump, as her glassy eyes stared unblinkingly at the pitiful figure stooping before her. "Don't worry, I shock myself every time I look in the mirror, but still, I look; still, I think it's going to get better one day. Come—come; let us go through to the parlour."

Elżbieta's protestations went unheeded as her feet begrudgingly followed in the steps of the dying woman. "I can only stay for half an hour," she managed to say, looking down and silently thanking Anielka for her presence. "We need to get home in time for Anielka's feed."

Elusia glanced at Anielka, a look of deep regret and loss lacing her sunken eyes as she forced a smile, her thin fingers tugging at her husband's sleeve, "Paweł, can you attend to the samovar?"

The word sliced through Elżbieta's heart, Tadek Lisztek invading her mind. "I prefer coffee," she snapped, instantly admonishing herself for her impoliteness.

Eyes flitting to Paweł, securing his brief absence, Elusia turned her frail body to Elżbieta and in a low, quavering voice said, "Thank you for coming. Paweł thinks I shall live forever. I am dying. He needs a good friend when I'm gone. Since our childhood, it has only ever been the two of us. My dear," she placed her skinny hand on her new found friend, "my Paweł, I know he seems strong, and in some ways he is, but emotionally, he is weak; he needs someone to lean on. He has spoken very fondly of your acquaintance. Please—please will you be his friend? Will you be there for him when I am gone?"

Elżbieta felt herself sinking deeper and deeper in the tsunami of the dying woman's words and her lifeline, her Henryk, was nowhere in sight. Deeper and deeper she sank until she saw nothing, heard nothing, felt nothing.

"Pani Elżbieta…"

Her eyes slowly woke up, rose and locked with the pleading desperate eyes of a loyal loving wife whose only lifeline was sitting next to her. Elżbieta's thudding heart urged her to respond to the woman's dying wish. Sighing deeply, she silently nodded her head.

The next thirty minutes were spent as relaxed as one could be in the presence of a dying woman. Elusia seemed the most relaxed, a visible amount of strain lifted from her face. Paweł sat by his wife barely touching his coffee, casting occasional glances at Elżbieta as she clock watched and silently wished the clock hand to move quicker so that she could make her escape.

At the door, out of Elusia's earshot, she turned to Paweł and stated coldly, "When the inevitable happens I will see you only as a friend, and only in the presence of Henryk, my husband." Her mouth clamped tight, Anielka firmly in her arms, she walked determinedly down the long straight street.

Chapter Twenty-Eight

The news of Elusia's demise sent a deathly chill of its own through Elżbieta's entire body, for her passing brought with it the obligation of fulfilling a dying woman's wish. She watched as Henryk placed Anielka carefully into her cot and took up his newspaper. "Henio, I have something to tell you," she softly said wiping her hands on a towel as she sat opposite him. Placing the paper on the table, he took off his glasses and looked at his wife, a tinge of puzzlement in his eyes.

"Henio..." She looked down at the table, silently fearing her feelings would overtake and betray her. "Henio, a friend of mine has just died. Her dying wish was for us to befriend her husband. He has no one else." The words rushed out before she could stop them, her heart racing as if it too would escape. Raising her eyes slowly to his, she immediately wished to God she hadn't. Opening her mouth she willed the words to come out, they failed her. Sighing deeply, she dropped her eyes to her twiddling thumbs on the table.

"Who is this friend? I wasn't aware..."

"You don't—didn't know her," she interjected. "She was an old school friend of mine." She snapped her eyes shut tight on the blatant lie she had just told her trusting husband; heavy guilt surging through her veins, washing over her, drowning her. She slowly opened her eyes and was mesmerised by her fast-moving thumbs as she hastily continued in her downward spiral. "I hadn't seen her for years then recently I bumped into her in Old Kraków. She told me her sad story. I—I didn't think to tell you."

Yes, yes, it was all coming back to him: Elżbieta's uncharacteristic behaviour, her coolness towards him. So that was what it was all about. Oh Boże... Boże... And I, in my selfishness, thought she may be pregnant. I—I couldn't spot that my own wife was living through such sorrow. Rushing to her side he took her in his arms, gently stroking her hair, "Oh my love—my love," he hushed as he gently rocked her back and forth. "Why didn't you tell me—why?"

Waves of surging bitter betrayal stilled her whole body into stone as she rocked back and forth, back and forth, in her husband's strong loving arms, feeling nothing but an aching emptiness. He gently released her and looking into her lying eyes said, "Then there is nothing more to say, Elżbieta. You must honour your friend's dying wish. We will attend the funeral. We must take this man into our circle of friends."

A final crush of finality rushed over Elżbieta, and she felt herself drowning.

Elżbieta's eyes scanned the few mourners by the graveside, her eyes avoiding Paweł lest her feelings betray her outward appearance. She dropped her eyes to the wizened corpse in the open casket. *Why, Elusia, did you bestow your dying wish on me?* Finally, she summed up her courage to raise her eyes to Paweł, and there she saw a lonely, heartbroken figure of a man, with eyes for no one except his wife's corpse. Elżbieta closed her eyes. *Elusia had been everything to this man. Now he has nothing.* She snapped out of her bleak reverie, her husband's words hitting her like a thunderbolt.

"You know, Elżbieta, we must invite Paweł over for Wigilia. Yes—yes," he went on enthusiastically, "he will be our special guest at our Christmas table."

"Wigilia is for the family." She managed to extract her strangled words.

"Don't forget, Elżbieta, we always set a place for a needy person, and I can't think of a more needy person to grace our table this year. So it's settled." Instantly, he took steps towards Paweł and, after prolonged minutes, she witnessed Paweł nodding his head. Her heart sank.

Anielka's first Christmas was proving to be Elżbieta's worst. She spent the morning of Christmas Eve preparing the twelve-course fish, cheese and mushroom dishes, her heart heavy and troubled, silently cursing Henryk for inviting Paweł to join them on this most auspicious of evenings, as knots in her stomach tightened her mind wandered into forbidden territory. Diverting her attention from the pieces of fish frying in the pan she raised her eyes to the ceiling. *For God's sake, pull yourself together, woman,* she silently scolded herself. *Paweł Jaroszynski is coming here as a friend nothing more, nothing less.* The knock on the door made her whole body jump, and a drop of fat fell off her spatula onto the floor. Rubbing her hands vigorously on her apron she made for the door. "Paweł!" she gasped. "What on earth are you…"

"I am sorry, Elżbieta, I need to see you—alone."

The familiar thumping in her heart resumed its angry march as her eyes scanned the corridor. "Come in."

Inside he shuffled from foot to foot then, as if standing to attention, he looked her directly in the eyes. "Elżbieta, I have feelings for you; I have always had feelings for you, from the first time I set eyes on you in Kraków Square all those years ago. I have to end this now for the sake of your marriage. Please make some kind of an excuse to your husband. He is a kind man, Elżbieta."

She stood still as a statue and, before she could open her mouth, he turned and was out of the door. She stood for long minutes staring at the closed door willing it to open; willing him to come back and take her in his arms. She opened the door and saw his fast-disappearing figure. Quickly, placing one foot in front of the other she began to run. She stopped, rooted to the spot. *Anielka—oh Boże—what am I thinking of? Anielka*—With equal ardour, she ran in the opposite direction.

The table was laden with an assortment of savoury dishes, bread, salads, pickles and alcoholic beverages. With Anielka securely in his arms, Henryk's eyes flitted, at regular intervals, to the clock. Elżbieta sat playing with a stray piece of straw, a symbol of Jesus' birth in a manger, which she had retrieved from beneath the white linen tablecloth, knowing full well that Paweł Jaroszynski had no intention of gracing their table. Placing a sleeping Anielka into her cot, Henryk grabbed his hat and coat and made for the door. "I am going to see what has become of our friend. Perhaps he is ill."

"No—no." Elżbieta's heart raced. "I really don't think he wants to spend Wigilia with us, Henio. Maybe he wants to be alone on this first Christmas without Elusia." Her words fell on deaf ears. She sat alone listening to the ticking of the clock, her stomach churning and eyes on her sleeping baby. "Paweł Jaroszynski has ruined everything for everyone," she stated loudly.

Turning over the naleśniki, her heart skipped a beat as she heard the clicking of the door. *Please God*, she silently prayed, *let Henryk return alone.* Turning, her heart stopped as Paweł Jaroszynski's eyes locked with hers; both were stone-cold and unforgiving.

All played their parts well. Henryk was the perfect host, making sure that his new friend was comfortable and relaxed; Elżbieta, the perfect wife, performing her kitchen duties, making sure everybody was adequately wined and dined; Paweł, the perfect guest, pleasant and outwardly grateful for his friend's hospitality. Inwardly, Elżbieta's guts wrenched and writhed, her anger soaring and targeted at both her husband and her so-called friend.

What on earth, she asked herself, *had possessed Henryk to force Paweł into coming here?* She gave a mushroom pancake a vigorous stab as it sizzled in the pan. *And, what the hell is Jaroszynski doing here anyway?* His words swirled in her head: *I have feelings for you… I have had feelings for you from the first time I set eyes on you…* Her eyes flitted to Paweł as he conversed with her husband. *How could he just sit here talking, drinking and laughing? He should be at home mourning for his wife.* She avoided the eyes of both men as she sat down and stuffed a piece of mushroom pancake into her mouth tasting nothing.

The evening wore on, the krupnik was brought out, and the two men were fast becoming *good* friends, much to Elżbieta's consternation. *This has got to stop*, she decided firmly.

"I propose a toast to Elżbieta the best wife, mother and hostess." Henryk raised his glass to his wife and watched as Elżbieta and Paweł's eyes met as their glasses touched. Feeling the heat rise to her cheeks, Elżbieta left the table to check on the state of the sucharki. The drifting words made her guts wrench in silent despair.

"You must come with us to the Sylwester," stated Henryk, his face flushed uncharacteristically with the effects of consuming too much alcohol.

Paweł cast a surreptitious eye at Elżbieta, as she adjusted the blanket over her sleeping child.

"As you can see, my friend, I have a beautiful daughter."

"Like wife, like daughter." Paweł smiled whimsically.

"Indeed—indeed." Henryk nodded his head, catching Paweł's lingering look on his wife. "So Sylwester…" Henryk resumed making Elżbieta's heart race as, with bated breath, she gently stroked her daughter's crop of black hair.

"I have a date with a friend's cousin. Well, it's not a date exactly. It's too soon—but I can't get out of it without offending my friend."

Elżbieta's breathing resumed its normal rhythm, grateful that her silent prayer was answered.

"Indeed, you shouldn't get out of it. There is no harm…"

Elżbieta did not hear the rest. In seconds, her heart had leapt for joy, then died a sudden death leaving her numb inside and out.

That night she lay beside her husband thinking what type of woman would be gracing Paweł Jaroszynski's arm on New Year's Eve.

Chapter Twenty-Nine

Eyes flitted to Elżbieta as she walked into the crowded hall of revellers in full swing, their usual mundane lives forgotten for a few hours, as they jumped about energetically to the rhythm of a lively polka, or drank until they were in a state of happy oblivion. From the midst of the crowd, one pair of eyes scanned the dark blue, full-length satin gown, rising up to the delicately plunged neckline, where sparkled a diamond and sapphire necklace given to Elżbieta by Zygmunt. The eyes rose to the rich black curls cascading around perfectly formed shoulders and stopped at the eyes. *Such happy eyes*, he thought, as his eyes lingered on the happy couple talking and laughing together. *Oblivious to others*, he concluded, *happy in their own little world.* He swallowed the hard lump lodged in his throat and turned to the woman sitting next to him. "Let's dance," he stated.

She had spotted him and secretly watched his every move. *He seemed*, she thought, *to be getting over Elusia better than expected, and seemed happy with this date of his.* Sighing deeply she scolded herself, *Elżbieta Szutka, keep your nose out of Jaroszynski's business. It's over—It never even began*, she corrected herself. *For goodness sake, you have a devoted husband and a beautiful daughter. What more do you want, woman?* She turned, placed her glass on the table, took her husband by the hand and uncharacteristically led him onto the dance floor.

Both danced their eyes on their respective partners; both shoved uninvited inappropriate thoughts out of their minds and, in the magic of Strauss's waltz, both accepted their fate.

Henryk's mind was in turmoil, for he had seen the way Paweł and Elżbieta had looked into each other's eyes at the Wigilia table; he had seen with his own eyes how they had sought each other out this very evening, for their eyes could not tell a lie. Taking a tighter hold of his wife's waist he manoeuvred towards Paweł. "May I?" He cut in holding out his hand to Paweł's date, leaving Paweł and Elżbieta in a state of momentary bemusement. Paweł took his cue holding out his hand to Elżbieta, as her heart beat wildly with a mixture of anger and excitement. She took his hand feeling the warm solid broadness, a tingling sensation cursing through her entire body, as he wrapped his strong hand around hers like a protective glove.

As he brought her slim body closer to his strong muscular mould, she felt a warmth and security she had never in her life felt before; her eyes avoiding his for fear of what she may see there, and a much greater fear of what he may witness in her own eyes. He was strong in his lead, and she abandoned herself to wherever he may take her, as they twirled around the room in each other's arms, to the rhythm of the melodious waltz. Feeling like a princess her mind was devoid of Henryk, Anielka, Jakub, Krystyna, Zygmunt, Zosia, Mania, Father Stanisław. Wojtek, Lukasz and—Tadek Lisztek. For a few precious and priceless moments, she was in the arms of this mysterious man who had haunted her since childhood, and she revelled in each invaluable second.

The dance ended. The music stopped. She heard loud clapping, cheering and the icy words, "I must get back to my date." Like an invisible dagger they thrust into the very core of her dream, making it disintegrate into fragments and vanish and, in their place, stood Henryk who shook his head in disbelief of his wandering imagination silently concluding, *I have nothing to worry about.*

Throughout the whole of the evening, Paweł Jaroszynski tortured Elżbieta's mind, giving her no respite as she could still feel his gentle but firm hand around her waist, his warm hand protectively woven around hers, his muscular body against her slender body.

Squeezing her eyes tight to obliterate every vestige of his image she opened them, a few seconds later, to see him holding his date close to his chest, as they immersed themselves in a slow tango. Grabbing a glass of wine she downed it in one go, to the horrific gasp of an elderly gossip nearby.

The air was filled with a thick aura of tension and excitement. Minutes of the old year were ticking away quickly and, with the vanishing minutes, there was a new apprehension of what was to come.

It had been a good year, reflected Elżbieta, as she sat beside Henryk with a fresh glass of wine in her hand. *Yes, a good year. She had relaxed in the security of her marriage, Anielka was born, and there were no real problems encountered until—*Her eyes flitted to Paweł, her heart thudding. *I am just a plaything to him; to amuse and flatter his ego when there is no one else, and then to cast me aside like an old rag. Why, he's no better than Lukasz; no better than Tadek Lisztek.*

He is out for all he can get and, so far, he has not got anything; nor will he. She turned her back on him, engaging her husband in trivial conversation.

Glasses were charged. Hearts beat fast. Eyes stared at the large clock above the stage as the second hand moved on its march forward, relinquishing slowly the ties of the old year.

"Ten, nine, eight…" Elżbieta joined in rapturously, "… seven, six, five, four, three, two, one… Happy New Year! Happy 1963!" boomed the Master of Ceremonies, amidst rapturous applause and excited cheering and salutations.

He watched with hooded eyes Henryk kissing his beloved wife muttering beneath his breath, "Oh, how I wish I was him."

Elżbieta succumbed to her husband's lingering kiss and all the pent-up desire she had for another she released on him. She saw Paweł out of the corner of her eye, hot anger ripping through her at his audacity for staring at her in that way. Turning her eyes to Henryk she said softly, "We must go home, Henio. I am missing Anielka." Her New Year lie reverberated louder and louder in her swimming head, as they jostled through the throng of jovial revellers to the cloakroom, where she shuffled from foot to foot, her eyes on Henryk's back, as he engaged in polite conversation with the attendant, her ears inaudible to the approaching footsteps.

"Happy New Year, Elżbieta." Paweł looked deeply into her eyes as he took her hand and kissed it softly; sending her nerve ends into shock, as he whispered in her ear, "Meet me at the Hotel Krakowianka; at midday; tomorrow. Please."

Chapter Thirty

She walked into the grand lobby of the Hotel Krakowianka, as a thousand silent commands told her to turn and run; her heart raced as her wide eyes surveyed the grandeur of the high carved white ceiling and elegantly gilded walls, lowering to the intermingled beige and white marble floor, and across to the solid mahogany reception desk which she slowly walked towards. She had seen grandeur before as Zygmunt had taken her out to many places of opulence; today, she was looking at the elegance around with illicit eyes and with a heart telling her that this was wrong: *She belonged not here, but at home her husband and child.*

Her feet walked on towards a seating area, where she sat on a plush velvet armchair her two hands in her lap, her eyes flitting erratically around willing him to appear; feeling the eyes of strangers boring into the depths of her very soul: *What are you doing here? Go home... You don't belong here... You have a husband and a child... Go home before it's too late...* they silently urged, as she remained solidly fixed in the chair.

He appeared in the doorway: tall, straight as a rod, his fair hair combed to one side, dressed in a smart dark suit, his grey eyes scanning the lobby coming to life the second he spotted Elżbieta. He approached, her heart beating wildly beneath a deceitful calm exterior, her insides turning to jelly as he smiled.

"A drink?" He cocked an eyebrow.

"I don't know why I'm here," she replied softly, averting her eyes from his potent lingering gaze.

He clicked his fingers at a passing waiter and ordered two coffees, two strawberry cheesecakes and two brandies; his eyes unwavering as he sat watching her every move. He said slowly and concisely, "You are here, Elżbieta, because you want to be here." His shrewd eyes watched her steadily as, with trembling fingers, she brushed away an imaginary piece of fluff from her coat. "You want to be here, and I want to be here," he added as an afterthought.

Momentarily, she lifted her eyes to his and felt as if she was going to crumble before him. The familiar urge of running, jumping, screaming and shouting possessed her making her place her hands on the coffee table below, and hold on to it tightly for fear of losing her very mind. "I have to go," she stated firmly.

"But you don't want to go." He placed his hands over hers and looked deeply into her wavering eyes. "Do you, Elżbieta?"

She took in a deep ragged breath and lowered her eyes to the cheesecakes. "Do you?"

Slowly, she raised her eyes to his and shook her head from side to side.

The brandy emitted a soothing warm feeling which suffused her entire body. A ghost of a smile flickered on her lips. "And, why are we here exactly?" She looked at him, puzzlement lacing her eyes.

He dangled a shiny key in front of her, making her instantly freeze in her chair. "Let's go upstairs, it's more private there, and we will be able to talk."

She followed him meekly, feeling every centimetre of the loose woman, catching imaginary *knowing* eyes, the non-existent dirty smirks and silent comments as they walked through the lobby, her heart hammering more ferociously with each step she ascended as she asked.

Oh Boże, why am I doing this? Why am I acting in the role of a tart? What on earth is wrong with me? Images of Henryk and Anielka flashed through her mind as she walked through the bedroom door; images of Tadek Lisztek possessed her mind as she saw the bed.

"Come, sit." He patted the bed, his eyes watching her every move.

She perched gingerly on the edge, her eyes staring vacantly at the seascape above the bed of a crashing ocean against rough, jagged rocks. *My marriage,* she sadly thought, *if I go through with this charade.* She sat rigid, blood rushing through her veins like the sea in the picture, her future on the pinnacle of disaster, as she stared into the depth of no return.

He had taken the liberty of ordering a bottle of wine, and this he now poured into two glasses handing one over, his eyes upon the woman he desired; the woman who was a wife and mother; the woman who was damaged goods. He broke the nauseating silence. "Elżbieta, I told you from the first time I saw you I had feelings for you. I—I think you feel something for me. Tell me I am right." Raising his hands and placing them on her upper arms he turned her to face him, bringing her chin up with his forefinger. "You do have feelings for me don't you, Elżbieta?" Her lips remained firmly clamped, her eyes riveted on his pristine white shirt. "Don't you?" he urged, gently shaking her into a response.

Slowly, she raised her eyes to him. "I do," she whispered.

He released his hold on her only to take her in his arms and, before she could protest in any way, his mouth was on hers possessive and passionate, making her feel as if she were in the crashing sea helpless and drowning as all her strength, resolve and willpower ebbed away, and she tossed all her doubts into oblivion. She was no longer a wife, a mother, an abused daughter, an abandoned lover, a raped girl; she was single, childless, adventurous and a woman in her own right. She was Elżbieta. Her body craved more—more—more as his lips became more demanding, his skilful tongue invading and probing her hungry mouth. With nimble fingers he undid the buttons on her blouse, casting it roughly aside, as he kissed her forehead, cheeks and neck; expertly unclasping her bra releasing her ample breasts and kissing each one in turn, weaving his experienced tongue around the areolae electrifying every nerve end.

"Oh please… please…" she pleaded, as he looked down on her with eyes of pure desire.

"Are you sure?"

"Yes… yes…"

He went into her as she gasped with pure ecstasy, every fibre of her body on fire as he pumped rhythmically. She responded in rhythm with him, and they flew.

He rolled over saying over and over again, "Elżbieta… oh Elżbieta…"

She was in her own heaven of heavens, fulfilled and complete as never before. *For this*, she thought, *was living; this was true, undiluted love. To hell with the consequences!*

They lay for long glorious minutes wrapped in each other's arms saying nothing, in tune with each other and themselves, as they begrudgingly allowed sounds of feet along the corridor, the distant cry of a bird outside, the closing of a door to filter through, invade their paradise and force them back into the real world. Like a thunderbolt Henryk stormed into her mind, an invisible blunt dagger jaggedly slicing through her heart. Abruptly, she rose grabbing her bra. "I must go." Finality edged her words.

Paweł propped himself on his elbow, his appreciative eyes admiring the curve of her fallen breasts as she stooped down to step into her panties. "When can I see you again, Elżbieta?"

"Next week; same time, same place." She replied without a trace of hesitation and for the first time in her life feeling free, alive; the mistress of her own fate.

Chapter Thirty-One

Happiness and guilt reigned side by side in the Szutka household. Henryk, the ever-dependable provider, husband and father was happy in his own ignorance; seeing that Elżbieta seemed much happier now and their marriage on solid ground, added to his inner bliss. Elżbieta led a double life. On the outside, she attended to Anielka and Henryk's every need, portraying the perfect mother and wife; the independent, free, adventurous spirit she had recently acquired was veiled by a niggling, torturous wrenching deep within her heart and guts, her body at war and fighting on both sides: Henryk, her loving husband and father to her child; Paweł mysterious, captivating and exciting. Both she loved.

Gently rocking Anielka in her arms, looking down at her blue eyes she whispered, "So like your father, and he adores you. What would he do without you?"

An image of Paweł flashed through her mind; closing her eyes she resumed her rocking as she stared into the far away distance: *Paweł Jaroszynski, a lonely man who needed a little bit of comfort in his life. What's wrong with that?* Her rocking took on a more vigorous rhythm. *It's all wrong: Henryk—Paweł—Paweł—Henryk—It's all so very wrong*, her confused mind told her over and over again. *It's got to stop! I am a respectable married woman with a child. This has all got to end now!* Rising abruptly, her chair rocking in her wake, she placed Anielka into her cot and, grabbing a pen and paper from the drawer, sat down at the table and wrote:

Dear Paweł,
 Our time together was wonderful, I shall never forget you.
 I am sorry, it is best that we never see each other again.
Elżbieta

The immediate sound of an opening door propelled her into stuffing the writing material back into the drawer, her heart racing as she turned her full attention to Anielka. *He is a good, hard-working man. What more does a woman want?* She asked herself as she glanced at her husband, a dull empty ache giving her a silent reply to her question. "Coffee?" she smiled.

Paweł's eyes darted from the clock on the bedside table to the firmly closed door. Thoughts of Elusia intermingled with thoughts of Elżbieta, had been his constant companions. Guilt had superseded grief and sadness which, in turn, was overtaken by a deep yearning for Elżbieta Szutka. She was fast becoming part of him: waking up with him in his thoughts each morning, the last image he put away at night; she thrived in him, and he revelled in her silent invisible companionship. He glanced at his watch a frown appearing on his forehead.

"She is going to be late," he sighed as he glanced at the mirror, adjusting his tie to form a perfect straight knot. Uninvited images of Elżbieta with her husband and baby flashed into and invaded his mind. *She will come*, he stated silently his eyes darting back to the door. Drawing the net curtains to one side, he looked out on the busy street below. "Come on, Elżbieta," he urged between clenched teeth, his eyes fixed on a frustrated chimney sweep, desperately trying to keep his paraphernalia in order.

"Come on…" His eyes flitted from one woman to another; he could see no woman with vibrant black curls rushing to the hotel. His eyes flashed back to the clock. "Twenty-five minutes to one," he mumbled. "Perhaps—perhaps there's an emergency. Maybe the child's ill; maybe—"

The gentle rapping on the door instantly made his heart leap for joy.

His heart sank.

"Room service." A young woman beamed, holding in her hands a tray with two glasses and a bottle of expensive champagne. "You ordered room service, sir."

Perched on the edge of the bed, a glass of bubbling cool liquid in his hand, his mind wandered to the same setting exactly a week ago, only now the main character was missing. *Elżbieta who, only seven days ago, had willingly slept with him, whom he'd had in his arms, his mouth on hers, possessive and passionate; his tongue exploring her mouth, her breasts, her entire body; entering her*—"Oh Boże—oh Boże—" he sighed his whole body aching, yearning, as his mind drifted… *Elusia, the beautiful vibrant woman he loved and married, the feeble, dying woman he nursed and watched die…* He placed his empty glass on the tray, grabbed his coat and opened the door.

"Elżbieta! I—I thought you were not coming. I… I…"

"Sh. Let me in," she said in a low voice.

In seconds, they were tearing violently at each other's clothes; mouth on mouth, tongue exploring tongue, hands exploring bodies they crashed on the bed, knocking the clock off the bedside table onto the floor; oblivious to everything around, conscious only of each other's needs, and their own. He entered her roughly, and she immediately rose to his rhythmic pumping as they peaked at the same time.

Reaching over he lit a cigarette. "Why did you decide to come, Elżbieta?" he asked staring at a smoke circle he had created.

"I wanted to make love to you," she replied staring at the white ceiling, a smile pinned on her lips.

"And, was it worth it?"

Her smile widened.

As Elżbieta opened the door, she smiled at the sound of Anielka's baby laughter, her smile dying a sudden death as her eyes dropped to the note in Henryk's trembling hand.

Chapter Thirty-Two

Time stood still. Elżbieta's heart turned to ice as she looked deep into her husband's eyes, where she saw herself and Paweł in bed having rough sex. Around her the beige walls, the mahogany dresser, Anielka's cot, the table, chairs and the image on the wall of the Sacred Heart of Mary were all crashing in on her, suffocating her, crushing her insides, killing her; killing all she, Henryk and Anielka had together as she stood frozen to the spot. *Adulteress... loose woman... tart... tramp...* These words, and more, pounded in her head, her eyes glued to the note in her husband's shaking hand.

"Why?" he asked his soft eyes on her.

The quietly spoken word ripped through her iced heart as if it were a sharp blade. Slowly, she raised her eyes to his, her mouth opened, closed, opened. "I... we ... you are jumping to the wrong conclusions, Henio." Her energy regained she whipped the note out of his hand and scanned the contents, turning her back on her husband as she tried desperately to formulate the right words. "Paweł and I are friends. You know that. You know his wife..."

"Liar!" roared Henryk, slamming hard his tightly clenched fist on the table, Anielka's laughter turning to cries. He snatched back the note reading each word loudly and clearly, "Dear Paweł, Our time together was wonderful, I shall never forget you. I am sorry, it is best that we never see each other again. Elżbieta."

"Henryk—please—" She took the note out of his still trembling hand and grabbed both his hands. "Please, Henio—You have misread and seen into things that are not there. *Our time together*—Didn't Paweł spend Christmas Eve with us, with me and you? And, yes, I will remember him as a friend. What's wrong with that? And, yes, I do think it's best I, we, don't see each other again. I... I think he should stand on his own two feet. I think he should have the time and space to grieve for his wife. I think it's for the best don't you, Henio?"

He sat down his shoulders hunched, breathing deeply. Slowly, he raised his eyes. "Let me see that note again." She passed the note her heart pounding, her eyes fixed on her husband's puzzled face, her mind swirling like liquid in a black cauldron, conjuring up feasible answers to further hypothetical questions, as a thousand years seemed to go by. Slowly, he raised his eyes.

"I am sorry, Elżbieta. Indeed, I think I may have jumped to the wrong conclusions; forgive me." Placing both her hands gently on her husband's face, she brought it up to hers and kissed him deeply on the mouth.

"I will take Anielka out for half an hour," he announced.

"I will start making preparations for supper," she said softly. As the door closed behind Henryk and Anielka, she headed for the cabinet and poured herself a drink.

As they sat at the supper table, Henryk stated, "I have been thinking this over, Elżbieta. I think you are wrong. In my point of view, Paweł should have all the support he can get and, I think, we are in a position to give it to him. Why, a family atmosphere may be just the right…"

She didn't hear the rest as pure, undiluted waves of anger surged through every vein in her body as she asked herself, *How can Henryk, such an intelligent man, be so utterly stupid? Oh Boże, how the hell can I get out of this mess?* Her heart swam with images of Henryk and Paweł enjoying a beer together, intermingled with images of herself and Paweł enjoying sex together. "No!" she yelled banging the table with her fist, rising and taking swift steps to the window. "No! No! No!" She repeated again and again, as Henryk's bewildered eyes stared at his wife's odd behaviour. She saw nothing through the window; could only feel Henryk's eyes drilling into the back of her head, and her heart thumping uncontrollably. *Oh Boże—oh Boże—oh Boże—*she silently sighed as her eyes stared out into the bleak January sky. *What have I done?*

"For God's sake, Elżbieta, what on earth is wrong?" Henryk approached her stiffened body and placed his gentle hands on her arms, turning her to face him. She stared deeply into his soft eyes and burst into floods of loud uncontrollable sobs, her body heaving. She stopped when her eyes were dry, her body becoming still in her husband's embrace.

That night, after they had made love, he turned his eyes on her. "Elżbieta, is there something wrong? Perhaps—perhaps you have a reason why you don't want Paweł Jaroszynski in our lives."

Her eyes closed as she tried desperately to quell the rising anger bubbling within her. "Nothing is wrong, Henio. We can all be friends." She sighed deeply and switched off the bedside light.

Chapter Thirty-Three

Elżbieta continued to live a double existence; her weekly rendezvous with Paweł becoming a necessary part of her life, a diversion she eagerly looked forward to. She was happy. Paweł was happy. Henryk lived in ignorant bliss. All was well.

The friendship between Henryk and Paweł grew; Henryk looked forward to the odd game of Tysiąc; Paweł always looked forward to seeing Elżbieta in the process. Nobody was hurt. Elżbieta grew to believe, in her heart of hearts, that all had gained from this unexpected friendship, although a frown formed on her brow as another day passed, and there was still no sign of her period. For six weeks and three days, she had shoved her negative thought to the back of her mind; now it kept resurfacing at the oddest of times: when she was eating her rye bread at breakfast time, as she was dusting furniture, in the middle of lovemaking with Henryk or Paweł until it became one overwhelming dark nightmare.

The doctor confirmed what she already knew; he could not confirm what she yearned to know, what she would never know. With a heavy heart, she slumped down on the chair and sipped the clear liquid in her glass, a thousand distorted scenarios swimming erratically in her muddled head. The potent substance tasted bitter and vile, yet it suffused her with a warm soothing feeling, like a comforting blanket, making her feel secure and that all was going to end well. Restored, and at peace with herself, she picked up her sleeping daughter and rocked her gently in her arms, as she looked out at the bare fields and skeletal trees. Her eyes looked down at the slumbering infant.

"You are going to have a brother, or maybe a sis…" The familiar thrust of the jagged blade raggedly sliced through Elżbieta's aching heart. Abruptly, she placed the child in her cot and hastened to the cabinet retrieving the bottle. *One more drop won't hurt.* She told herself, sighing deeply as the clear liquid performed its magic on her. Quickly, she restored the bottle to the depths of the cupboard and placed full bottles in front, as the door was opening.

"You look flushed, Elżbieta. Are you all right?" Henryk cast a concerned look at his wife as he pecked her on the cheek, his brow creased as he caught a faint smell. *Surely not*—Immediately, he reprimanded himself for allowing such an unsavoury thought to enter his head. *What on earth would possess my wife to drink in the middle of the day?* He shook his head in disgust at his lingering, ludicrous suspicions.

Elżbieta lay in bed her heart and head in turmoil as conflicting thoughts battled with each other. Glancing over she took in Henryk's relaxed face, the blanket covering him gently rising and falling in tune with his even breathing, his mouth slightly opened, his dark hair ruffled and askew. *Here is a good man,* she silently stated. *The best husband any woman could possibly wish for; the best father any child could want; the best choice of a father for this new life inside me and yet*—She closed her eyes, squeezing them tightly, her heart as heavy as lead. *And yet—Oh Boże, why can't I damned well be like all other women,* she cursed under her breath. *Why can't I be content?*

Like a growing cancer, Paweł Jaroszynski crept stealthily into her mind: *exciting, mysterious; everything an adventurous woman could wish for and yet—* She lay as still as a corpse, her eyes fixed and unseeing on the dark ceiling, her body cold inside and out; feeling only the fast beating of her heart, the slow ticking away of the seconds on the bedside table clock. *Time was marching on—marching on,* she reflected glumly, *and with its endless march would come new life; part of me; part of Henryk? Part of Paweł?* Her eyes snapped shut. Her thoughts raced uncontrollably: *Henryk?*

Paweł? Henryk? Paweł? Carefully casting the blanket to one side, she quietly walked out of the room and retrieved the bottle.

"Pregnant! Oh Boże, Elżbieta, you have made me feel like the luckiest man ever to walk this earth." Henryk's eyes shined as he grabbed his wife, lifted her into the air, planted her back down, and bestowed on her lips a lingering kiss. "Thank you, thank you; thank you." He kissed her lips, cheeks, forehead and hair while Elżbieta silently cursed herself for her spontaneous stupidity, regretting bitterly her premature disclosure. She pinned on a smile, closing her eyes.

Now, there is no going back, she concluded grimly. He finally pulled her away from his tight grasp, his eyes scanning her intently taking in her pale complexion, her wide big eyes and black curls. "We must tell everyone: our friends, the priest, our neighbours, Paweł…" She froze. *Paweł. Oh Boże, no—not Paweł, not Paweł—not yet—not ever. Oh Boże—I need a drink. I damned well need a drink—now!*

Paweł's smile died instantly on his lips, a sense of heavy foreboding shadowed his heart, as he opened the door to Elżbieta's drawn face, dull eyes; her lips set in a grim line. *Something*, he surmised, *was gravely wrong. She was the bearer of bad news.* Of that, he was certain.

"What is it, Elżbieta?" He sat opposite her; taking her hands into his own, he looked deep into the depths of her eyes, seeing nothing.

Slowly, withdrawing her hands, she rose and walked across to the window. "I can never see you again, Paweł," she announced, as her eyes looked uninterestingly at the grim apartment buildings around. Her words sent an electrifying shock through his entire body, propelling him into taking immediate steps towards her, grasping her arm in an attempt to turn her to face him.

"Please don't touch me," she said slowly and concisely, her body as rigid as the building she was staring at. He withdrew his hand as if it were a hot iron poker. They stood like two statues: still, gaunt, silent; the clock ticking away the minutes. She turned. "I must go," she uttered, her eyes glued to the floor beneath.

"I think you owe me an explanation, Elżbieta."

Her heart pounded though she knew exactly what she was going to say. She had rehearsed her speech a hundred times, or more: correcting, deleting, adding until she could detect no cracks, and no leeway of contesting her decision. It was final and non-negotiable.

He listened carefully to every word: *She couldn't see him anymore. Henryk and she wanted to try for another baby, a brother and sister for Anielka and while he was still in the picture, it was impossible for this to be accomplished. He had to step aside for their sake.*

Her heart was heavy-laden as she walked out into the bitter cold air. It was over.

Chapter Thirty-Four

To the outside world, Elżbieta was blooming in every sense of the word, her complexion was rosy, and she looked fit and healthy. Inwardly, she was a mess; torn between two loves, her heart was in the midst of a raging war, hoarding a deep secret neither love could know. Sighing deeply she squeezed herself out of the rocking chair and, in minutes, she was soothed by a measure of krupnik. She poured herself another, one measure was never enough these days. *Henryk's supper can wait*, she silently stated as she closed her eyes and abandoned herself to the calming effects of the amber nectar.

Rocking to and fro, she ignored Anielka's whimpers, her mind closed to the entire world and when Henryk or Paweł crashed into her consciousness she rose, poured herself another measure, carefully hiding the bottle behind a stack of old books, and returned to her rocker resuming the comforting rhythm. Somewhere she had heard or read, she couldn't remember which, that drinking alcohol was a bad thing during pregnancy. She shook her head vehemently at such a notion. "It's doing me the world of good," she said aloud taking another sip, as images of Henryk and Paweł miraculously evaporated away, replaced by a young girl being raped by a monster: *pumping—pumping—pumping—while the girl writhed beneath his bulk.*

Elżbieta's heart beat faster and faster. With trembling fingers she unscrewed the metal top and brought the bottle to her lips, swallowing mouthfuls, closing her eyes and savouring its warmth and assurance of calm and serenity. "You are my saviour," she stated, swiftly hiding her stash under her rocker. Anielka's whimpering gradually escalated into a bout of full-blown crying, as Elżbieta took her in her arms rocking to and fro drinking, thinking and eventually closing her eyes to it all.

"For God's sake, what is happening here, Elżbieta?"

The sound of her name boomed and reverberated louder and louder in her head, as she slowly opened her eyes trying desperately to focus on something, anything; her heart thumping as she caught sight of her husband bending over her, shaking her into full consciousness as he stared directly into her blurry bewildered eyes, "Elżbieta, what on earth is going on?" He demanded, releasing his grip on her arms and turning his attention to his bawling child. The rocking stopped. She sat in the chair like a frozen effigy, her eyes staring starkly at her husband and daughter, seeing and feeling nothing.

As Anielka ceased her crying, a heavy blanket of silence covered the threesome. "What is going on?" Henryk's eyes flitted to his wife. "You have been drinking alcohol, haven't you!" His cold questioning eyes penetrated into the very depths of her being. "Please do not deny that you have been drinking alcohol, Elżbieta."

Covering Anielka protectively with a blanket he stooped and grabbed Elżbieta, his fingernails digging into her flesh. "Tell me… admit to me that you have been drinking." Her lips remained firmly clamped, her eyes staring through him to some distant past. He forced her into a standing position. "Admit it!" He shook her vigorously. "God damn it, admit it!"

"I have been drinking." Her words were cold, stark, detached.

"Oh Boże… my wife… an alcoholic!" He shook his head from side to side, instantly wishing he could bite off his tongue. He released his hold on her allowing her to slump back into the rocking chair, where she rocked to and fro staring wide-eyed at the pale wall, his words echoing loudly in her aching head: "…*alcoholic… alcoholic… alcoholic…*" The worst of the worst; scum. For, in both their worlds, nobody could steep beneath the depths of an alcoholic. *And, to be a woman alcoholic*—She closed her eyes squeezing them until she could squeeze them no more obliterating her husband, her daughter, her bump, everything and anything; only in nothing could she find solace.

The sudden crashing of cupboard doors thrust her eyes to open into wide saucers. "Where is it?" His frantic eyes and hands darted in and behind cupboards, into the depths of wardrobes and inside the toilet cistern searching; frantically searching. "Where are the bottles, Elżbieta?" After half an hour of looking, he abandoned his frantic search. Grabbing her roughly by the arms he stared at her closed eyelids uncharacteristically shouting, "Where is the bottle, Elżbieta? Where is it?" His shaking grew in intensity, his voice cold and hard. Her eyes and her mouth remained firmly closed.

Finally, she heard triumph in his voice; heard the gurgling of her treasured liquid as it vanished down the plug hole and, with its disappearance, her heart sank. Crouching by his wife's side he took her cold hands into his. "Tomorrow, Elżbieta, we shall talk."

She lay motionless by his side as her whole life marched through her mind, as she tried desperately to make some sense of everything, something, anything. *Tadek Lisztek opened the first scene, starring in the main role, and remained in the play until the very last act and scene were acted out. He was the perpetrator; the reason behind every other reason and her downfall, for everything in her life started with him and finished with him. His blubbery face flashed vividly before her; his saliva-coated fleshy lips slobbering on her young skin; his rough hands mercilessly squeezing her tender young breasts; his manhood inside her pumping viciously as he ignored her pleas. Wojtek Kaminski, another monster. Zygmunt Chmielowski was a true father in every sense of the word.*

A faint smile flickered on her lips and instantly died as Lukasz Chopinski crashed into her mind. *Oh, how I loved that man,* she mused. Her eyes opened. *He didn't love me. He just used me but—but he did give me Jakub; dear sweet Jakub.* She reached out her hand to touch his curly hair and brought her empty cold hand down to rest on her swelling belly. *A new life*—A fresh nightmare began with a vengeance. *Whose life? Henryk's? Paweł's? Henryk's? Paweł's?* In a daze, she threw off the blanket and made her way to her secret hiding place. Frantically, her fingers searched: scrabbling, reaching, pushing, pulling, stretching—

"It's all gone, Elżbieta." Henryk stood behind her, his voice steady and calm.

Her guts writhing and twisting mercilessly, her heart pounding, she stated in an equally calm voice, "We will give the baby up for adoption when it is born, Henryk."

Chapter Thirty-Five

Elżbieta's stark words crashed through Henryk's consciousness; through his heart, his soul; through to the depths of his very being like some gigantic tsunami, temporarily leaving him bereft of words, feelings, dreams and ambitions as they tossed him mercilessly into a black, empty, lifeless void of his wife's making. Incredulously, he stared at the *stranger* before him his whole body numb, yet on fire with rage rushing through every fibre of his being; wanting to shake her back into a state of sanity; wishing her to deny the words she had spoken; willing the clock to turn back twenty-four hours, so they could be one happy family once more waiting for their new arrival.

He stared at his tight-lipped, pale-faced wife; this *strange* woman he did not know; did not want to know, for what kind of woman would utter such a statement? For long iced moments, they stood centimetres apart, at opposite poles, two strangers in the same room standing rigid, silent, staring, waiting. Desperately, he searched deep in the vault of his mind for the right words to say, as his thoughts swam together; mingled, intermingled and became one fuzzy mass of confusion. She broke the ice. "We will give the baby away for adoption when it is born, Henryk," she repeated her words with stark finality.

Deep within the cauldron of muddled confusion sprang vibrancy in Henryk's response, which stunned both of them to the core. "We will do nothing of the sort, Elżbieta. I think the alcohol has muddled your thinking, my dear. We will talk when you are completely sober, and thinking straight."

Days later, both sat down on opposite sides of the breakfast table; bodies tired from lack of sleep, heads aching with jumbled thoughts, hearts racing with anticipation; both on opposite sides of a war; both hoping the other would surrender.

"It was the effects of the alcohol talking, Elżbieta," he said cautiously taking her clenched fingers into his hands, as he raised his eyes to meet her eyes. There he saw no hope, only emptiness where happiness should now be residing. "Once the doctor sorts this problem we will be back on the right track, awaiting joyously for our baby to…"

"Damn you, Henryk!" She snapped as she roughly snatched her hands away from his grasp. "I don't want this baby. I can't have it. I can't cope!" The instant the last word had escaped her mouth she felt her fate had been sealed.

He recaptured her hands looking deep into her empty eyes. "No, you can't cope; not yet, Elżbieta. But—but don't you see?" He rose and took her rigid body into his arms and brought her closer to himself. "Don't you see, my darling, we are nipping your problem in the bud. You are heartbroken, perhaps you are still grieving over Jakub; after all, you never really grieved for him. We'll sort everyth…"

She slumped onto the chair listening without hearing her husband's wise, encouraging, misguided words; saw without seeing his kind face; clearly seeing a miserable, sad future full of lies and betrayals. *Oh Boże,* she silently said over and over again, *how I need that drink, then everything will be all right; then, I will cope.*

Within thirty minutes of Henryk's departure for work, a new bottle was resting in her grocery bag and her worries dissipating, providing the local gossips fresh fodder for their tongues: *"Pani Szutka has bought a new bottle, I saw it with my own eyes… Elżbieta Szutka is secretly drinking… Ah, that poor woman, still grieving with a bottle of the bad stuff for company… Pani Szutka is a good-for-nothing alcoholic who ought to be excommunicated from the church… Szutkowa is no better that Kaminski…"* Elżbieta was oblivious to the comments; the sideway looks, sneers, grins and smirks cut her to the core. In her rocker, glass in hand, her mind drifted to Tadek Lisztek's drunken face, Wojtek's drunken twisted mouth. *I am no better than Lisztek; no better than Wojtek. I am like them. I am them!* She concluded as she brought the glass to her craving mouth, knowing in her mind that she could be harming her unborn baby.

It was a short labour. The baby was born at fifteen minutes to eleven as the Sunday bells were peeling, somewhere in the distance, as if they were welcoming a new life into the world. Henryk was ecstatic pacing up and down the room, his eyes darting to the closed door, as he waited impatiently for the nursing staff to bring in his baby daughter or son. Elżbieta's heartbeat with a heavy dread, her eyes closed to the world. Abruptly, Henryk turned, his heart in his mouth, as he faced a solitary, stern-faced, middle-aged man dressed in a long white coat; his fast-beating heart fast turning into a solid block of ice, his eyes stuck on the medic.

"I am sorry," the doctor said softly as he approached Henryk, casting a concerned eye at a motionless Elżbieta. "I am sorry."

Henryk's heart stopped beating, his guts aflame twisting and turning mercilessly. The strangled words gradually came out of his mouth. "Our baby is dead?"

The doctor signalled to a chair. "Please sit down, Pan Szutka." Like an obedient pupil, Henryk sat, his eyes riveted on the man before him. "Your son is alive, however, he is very poorly."

"My son! My son!" Henryk's heart leapt with joy. "Our son—we have a son, Elżbieta!" His excited words rushed out like a raging fire which, a few minutes ago was attacking and devouring his insides. "We have a son!" He plunged his trembling fingers into the depths of his trouser pocket and, withdrawing a wooden beaded rosary, fervently kissed the crucifix. "Thank you, Boże, for the most precious gift of a son; thank you."

"Yes, you have a son," the doctor repeated his words taking on a grave tone, "but I am sorry to say, he has a weak pulse. Pan Szutka, he is, as I said, very ill. Of course, we shall do everything in our power to improve his condition. We will…"

Henryk's ears were deaf to further words. Grabbing the doctor's hand he thanked him profusely, then stooped down and took his wife's unresponsive body into his arms. "We have a son, Elżbieta. Oh Boże, we have a son!" Tears of joy streamed down his happy face, as Elżbieta's heart turned to stone feeling nothing, wanting nothing.

At six o'clock that evening, a nurse walking beside Henryk, wheeled Elżbieta into a room full of medical apparatus. As Henryk looked down at the incubator, he willed his son to gain strength; Elżbieta looked past the incubator and saw a bottle.

Chapter Thirty-Six

Henryk spent the first few weeks of his son's life at his side, willing him to live and gain strength. Elżbieta's only glimpse of her son was on the evening of his birthday, thereafter, flatly refusing to visit him or discuss any aspects of his future welfare. Henryk let her be. He visited his son whenever he could before and after work, coming home and retelling all the news of his visits, in minute detail, to deaf and unresponsive ears; to a body of stone wishing he would stop his endless prattling, willing his tired body to retire to bed, as every fibre in her body was on fire for the soothing liquid she would soon consume. The doctor came and went.

The mild tranquillisers he left were not taken. Henryk continued to find bottles some full, others partly consumed. The local gossips had enough daily material to satisfy their twisted need to shove Elżbieta deeper into the mire. Henryk cast a blind eye to his wife's drinking, for he now had a son and daughter who needed him, and they were his priority.

To Henryk's utter delight, his son had improved sufficiently to be discharged from the hospital. The news that her husband would be bringing their son home that day brought Elżbieta a desperate need to run and hide she did not know where but to stay, she knew, she could not; the thought of looking down at her son and seeing Paweł's image thrust an invisible sharp blade through her heart. She sat in her rocker vigorously rocking back and forth—back and forth—*Paweł's fair hair, his grey eyes, his exciting mouth* coming into focus*; her heart calling out for him, yearning for his firm hands on her breasts caressing, moulding, kneading them, his hands lowering to her waist, to the insides of her legs, his finger exploring deeper—deeper...* Her eyes opened wide. He was gone. There was nothing.

Quickly, she grabbed all the coins in the emergency tin snatching her coat off the hook, her ears deaf to Anielka's cries and stormed out the door. Ignoring the knowing, staring eyes she purchased a bottle of vodka and walked the streets, her stash secretly hidden in the depths of her deep pocket. Surreptitiously, her eyes scanned the periphery, seeing no one she retrieved her treasure, took a slurp and continued on her solitary walk she knew not where. Her unsteady feet brought her to the local park and, spotting an old rustic bench, she sat down, revelling in her undisturbed solitude, as she brought the bottle to her parched lips.

"He …y, l…lady, I…I th ink y…ou sh.ould share y…our sta…sh." A gruff voice bellowed.

Startled, she jumped causing some of her precious liquid to escape out of her opened mouth.

"W…e sh…sh…are th…things a…rou.nd here," he grunted his ogling eyes on her, making her feel physically sick, as she stared back at the unshaven dirty tramp, his eyes now greedily staring at her bottle. Her heart quickened as she gaped at the bearded man, now so near she could smell the stench of his heavily alcohol-laced breath. She rose secreting the bottle into her pocket. "I…I d…don't think s…so," he snarled, showing the few yellowed teeth he had left, and bestowed on her a sickly grin as he extended his grubby hand. "W…we sh…a.re."

Bloodshot eyes stared at bloodshot eyes. Begrudgingly, she handed him the bottle and saw the liquid dwindle, her heart dying as it sank further down the bottle. "Give me it back," she demanded sternly her heart racing, her whole body craving. "Give me it back!"

"Gone." He smirked giving her back the empty bottle. "Th…tha…nk y…ou." He wiped his lips with his dirty sleeve. "Y…you are i…ind…eed a l…lady." He staggered on as her heart beat frantically; her body wanting, needing; craving for the soothing balm. Cursing herself for her stupidity, she dug her trembling fingers into her pocket for spare coins and brought out her empty hand. "Oh Boże, I need a drink… I… I have to have a drink," she said aloud, for all the world to hear, as she walked on and on. For hours, she walked her body wanting, needing, craving.

She banged ferociously with both fists on a closed door, and continued to bang until it eventually opened. "Paweł," she sighed as she fell in.

Chapter Thirty-Seven

His eyes stared disdainfully at the crumpled bundle on the floor. Bending down he carefully turned his head. "Oh Boże—Elżbieta." His eyes flitted over the grubby coat, the straggly hair, the twisted mouth. "Oh Boże, it is you—it is you!"

Hastily, he unbuttoned her coat, rushing to the sink and bringing back a glass of water. Carefully, he lifted her head and eased the rim of the glass into her blistered mouth, her eyes closed to the world. "Come on drink, Elżbieta; drink!" He urged.

Laboriously, she took a sip, then another, slowly opening her eyes and closing them again. He persisted, encouraged and cajoled her into drinking more; then, taking her into his strong arms he carried her to the sofa, leaving her to sleep off her drunken stupor, his own mind in turmoil. Of all the people to have landed on his doorstep, Elżbieta Szutka was the last one he ever expected. She had made it perfectly clear their affair was over and, after much soul-searching, he begrudgingly accepted her decision and began to live without her.

Gradually, acquaintances introduced him to their friends, and now he was steadily dating a woman who lived on the other side of Kraków. He never forgot, nor did he want to forget, Elżbieta. And, here she was, in his apartment, alone with him, utterly drunk and oblivious to him and to the world.

Why? Why? Why? He asked himself as he secured a blanket around the coarse coat she was still wearing. *What on earth had brought her to his doorstep?* He let her sleep while he pondered many possible reasons, and finally rested with the one which had initially formulated in his mind: *Elżbieta and Henryk have argued. Yes, that's it.* He nodded his head as he cast a glance at the dishevelled woman sprawled out on his sofa. *But why?* He asked himself. His head stopped nodding and shook slowly from side to side. *It is not my business to know.*

She stirred in the early evening her eyes opening to the ceiling, instantly darting around the walls, onto the vase with its colourful roses on the polished table, down to the chairs and a pair of trousers. *Oh Boże, no—no—*Her heart beat frantically as if it was on the point of explosion, as ice-cold reality raced through her entire body leaving her numb. *The tramp… the bottle… Oh Boże… oh Boże…*

Slowly, she raised her tired eyes and immediately snapped them shut to the illusion in front of her, for she knew it was only the after-effect of the alcohol. Motionless, she lay in fear of opening her eyes to images she did not wish to see: Henryk… the tramp… Paweł Jaroszynski. They were all dead as far as she was concerned. Desperately, her muddled mind tried to clutch at straws and try and compose some kind of picture of what had happened, where she was and what she was doing here. Her eyelids flickered and opened. He had disappeared.

It was the alcohol, she concluded with a heavy weight of relief. Her exhausted eyes roamed around the room: the beige walls, the table and the painting on the wall, depicting a group of Cossacks on horsebacks brandishing lethal-looking sabres, seemed familiar. *I have seen all these things before*, she thought closing her eyes tightly as she willed her memory to come to her aid. With effort, she propped herself up on her elbow, stark reality hitting her with an almighty force. *Oh Boże, I have been here before*, she gasped.

"Hello, Elżbieta."

Her heart thudded, her blurry eyes transfixed on the figure before her. "P.Paweł!" She stared at the man she loved, as a thousand fragmented memories crashed through her sore head. "What… why…?"

"Not now, Elżbieta."

Her eyes followed him to the small kitchen where she could see him through the door opening, tipping black liquid out of a percolator into two small cups.

"Here, this will do you good." He sat beside her on the sofa, his closeness sending small electrifying shocks through every fibre of her body, as she yearned to edge closer to touch him, to draw him to herself. "Drink the coffee, Elżbieta. It will sober you up."

"I… I need a drink," she said softly, her pleading eyes on his face.

"You have coffee," he said curtly.

"I need alcohol, Paweł," she demanded.

"You need coffee, black coffee; drink it."

"I need alcohol… please…" Her beseeching eyes remained fixed on his. "Please let me have a drink, just one drink; please, Paweł."

His still eyes tried to grasp a grain of understanding of the woman he loved, as he surveyed the total wreck before him begging for alcohol, like a tramp. *A stranger before my eyes*, he surmised. The desperate pleading resumed.

"Please, Paweł, just one drink—please—"

He sighed deeply, picked up a cup and handed it to her, his confused head trying to make some kind of sense of her predicament. "Drink this black coffee, Elżbieta, and later we shall see about a drink."

Begrudgingly, she took the cup of coffee into her trembling hands as she looked into his eyes. "You promise?"

"I promise."

Instantly, she felt a wave of relief soothing her pent-up body, for the promise of alcohol was more than she wished for in the world.

They sat together in complete silence as the minutes ticked away, her mind fixed only on the alcohol she would later consume; his thoughts on this woman sitting next to him, the woman he had bedded and who was now a complete stranger to him. Finally, grasping the nettle, he turned to face her taking in her pale pinched face, her unruly black locks. "Elżbieta, tell me what has happened. Why are you here?"

Tense seconds matured into minutes and were eventually broken by a deep sigh, coming from somewhere in the depths of her very soul, followed by further prolonged minutes of silence. "A drink—please—you promised."

"I promised." He agreed, reluctantly rising and taking steps towards the drinks cabinet, knowing full well it was the last thing he should be giving to this woman.

She stared at the alluring glass of clear liquid in her hand, as a jeweller would stare at a rare precious diamond. Downing it in one swallow, she felt the familiar glow of warmth surging through every vein in her body. "I need another," she demanded.

He brought the bottle for he well recognised her need; he had seen it in his brother. He sat by her side as the slow minutes ticked away.

"I have had a baby," she stated, and taking another generous gulp, she looked him straight in the eyes. "I don't know whether Henryk, or you are the biological father." She refilled her glass.

He snatched the glass and drank the contents, his body shaking involuntarily at the potency of the liquid. "What did you just say?" He glared at her incredulously.

"You heard."

As he continued to stare in total disbelief, he could feel his whole world come crashing down around him, *and here she was calmly gulping down his vodka!*

"Are you out of your mind, Elżbieta?" The words escaped his mouth before he could stop them, and immediately he regretted his damnable mistake. Abruptly, he rose, sat down, poured himself another drink and downed it. Grabbing her roughly by the arms he turned her to face him, waiting a moment for her glazed eyes to focus on him. "Elżbieta, you have got to tell me everything—everything."

He tried desperately to take it all in; to digest and accept the words she was telling him; the overwhelming information that would change all their lives. When the words ceased to come out he looked at her long and hard, his whole body in turmoil, for he knew what he had just heard was undoubtedly the truth. "Does Henryk know the whole truth, Elżbieta?"

Silently, she shook her head from side to side.

"Then, he must know."

"It will break him." She sobbed between gulps of vodka.

"He has a right to know," stated Paweł. "We must tell him the whole truth."

Chapter Thirty-Eight

The words ripped through Henryk like a devastating tornado, destroying in their wake everything he held precious: his marriage, trust, role as a provider and, more than anything else, the question of parental identity. He sat motionless, his eyes stark and still, as he stared at the woman he loved; his guts grinding as his whole world came down on him crushing him, suffocating him, killing him inside. Everything was a confused mass of lies and betrayal, and he was staring at the cause of it all. His lips formed into a thin, firmly clamped line, his knuckles clenched so tightly they became white, as he asked himself over and over again: *How can this woman destroy us all like this?*

Shaking his head in miserable incredulity his sad eyes darted to Paweł, his so-called friend; the lonely, widowed man he had so wanted to help; his enemy. "When did the affair start?" he asked in a cold detached voice. The clock ticked away in ominous silence as three mouths remained firmly closed. Henryk rose crashing his tight fist on the table. "God damn you both! When did it start?" he shouted, his wild unblinking eyes glued on his betrayers. Elżbieta opened her mouth to immediately close it again.

"Henryk, my friend…" started Paweł.

"Don't you dare call me, friend!" Henryk turned his eyes of blazing fire from Paweł to his wife and waved a dismissive hand. "Forget it, Elżbieta. I don't want to know." He slumped onto the rocking chair and rocked in a steady rhythm, his eyes staring starkly at the wall. After torturous minutes of deathly silence, he stated in a calm, collected tone, "What I would like you to do, Elżbieta, is to pack your things and leave with Pan Jaroszynski."

Like iced water, the words stirred Elżbieta into an immediate response. "W.what do you mean to leave, Henio?"

"Leave, take your possessions and go." His eyes remained fixed on the wall.

Unbelieving, stark eyes stared at Henryk as he continued to rock in a calm, steady rhythm. "It's my house," she stated in a low voice, hoping her trump card would give her some leeway.

"Yes, it is your house, and your home and you are entitled to live here. However, I have to stay here until I find suitable accommodation for the children and myself. You can return as soon as we have departed your house." His lips returned to a firm clamp, his eyes unmoving while his words sliced, with a bitter thrust, through the fibre of her being, making her reel and reach for a nearby chair where she sat rigid, horrified, dumbstruck staring at her husband rocking calmly. Paweł stepped in.

"Henio—Henryk, I think you must take time to reconsider."

"Get out! Get out of my sight, Jaroszynski. Now!" roared Henryk, his eyes ablaze with fire.

Paweł stared at Henryk's red face, his eyes flitting to Elżbieta who gave him a silent nod.

The door firmly closed behind Paweł, leaving Henryk and his wife sitting at opposite sides of a bare table; his eyes unwavering upon Elżbieta; her eyes on the scuffed wood as her heart pounded. "I cannot leave the children," she finally said, her eyes riveted on an ancient black coffee stain, as the seconds ticked loudly away in her ears.

Deep sadness, mixed with regret, entered his accusing eyes as he coldly stated. "You left Anielka weeks ago to the mercy of neighbours when you rushed to get your pants off for Jaroszynski; as for your baby son, well, you never even acknowledged him. You are no mother, no wife, Elżbieta. You are a tart; a tart whose only interest is a good fuck and the damned bottle."

Abruptly, he rose and left the table, his words thrusting deeper and deeper into her heart, mind and soul as she acknowledged them to be the bitter truth. *Wojtek had been right all along. She was a good-for-nothing tart.*

"Where do you expect me to go?" she asked in a low trembling voice.

"I don't know." He shrugged his shoulders nonchalantly. "Maybe your lover will take pity on you and take you in."

Within the hour she had packed her belongings and silently, without a backward glance, she walked out of the apartment, closing the door firmly behind her.

Chapter Thirty-Nine

There was a silent distance between Elżbieta and Paweł; things were not the same, and she knew not how to remedy the awkward situation. The welcome she had expected she did not receive. He was cool; detached. He provided her with a roof over her head; gave her food and money for clothing and shared his bed with her but he was not there for her. His mind, head and heart were elsewhere, and Elżbieta secretly surmised they lay with the woman who lived somewhere on the other side of Kraków.

They never discussed the baby, Anielka, Henryk or their own relationship as they lived their day-to-day existence of civility, indulging in consensual sex and tolerating each other's circumstances; she was all too aware that without his charity she would be on the streets; he was fully aware of her alcohol need and cast a blind eye to it all, frequently leaving her alone in the evenings to go and see his lover on the other side of Kraków. On those evenings, Elżbieta revelled in her freedom and drank to her heart's content.

The days were long and hard. While Paweł was at work she would drink whatever supplies she had, take any money of his she could find, beg on the streets and return to his apartment for a fresh bout of undisturbed drinking. Whatever thoughts she had of Henryk, the children and Paweł soon vanished into obscurity.

One morning, she roamed the streets begging from anyone she thought might be merciful; ignoring dirty looks and abusive comments, she held out her shaking hand and pleaded, "A grosz if you have any to spare, sir." She had already acquired enough money for a bottle, when she heard laughter coming from an approaching couple and decided to try her luck as they turned the corner. "A grosz plea…"

Eyes locked. The young woman ceased her laughter, her brow furrowing as she looked askance at her man. "Do you know this tramp?" she giggled staring disdainfully at the unkempt woman before her.

Closing her fingers protectively around the coins the man had given her, Elżbieta pulled up her skirt, turned and ran as fast as her legs would carry her; she knew not where, neither did she care. Her heart raced faster and faster as she ran, not daring to glance back running—running—running—

"You know that woman don't you, Paweł?" The woman asked softly.

"No." He fervently shook his head. "No, I do not know the tramp," he stated as his stark eyes stared ahead, his ears deaf to the full-blown account of the latest trend in millinery, the elegant woman clinging to his arm was describing.

Her treasure now secure, her eyes establishing she was free of uninvited tramps who would steal her stash, Elżbieta slumped onto the damp ground obscured on three sides by coarse bushes. Swallowing gulps of vodka she wished with all her heart the image of Paweł, and the beautiful woman he was escorting, to vanish. She took another generous gulp coughing, spilling a mouthful out, cursing for the waste and bringing the bottle up to her mouth again; already her body was beginning to loosen and relax. Sudden stark images of Henryk, Anielka and the baby propelled her into taking another gulp—and another—and another.

A scruffy black dog found her, circling around her, sniffing and whimpering and eventually alerting nearby pedestrians with his loud, consistent barking. Within the hour she was securely locked away in a room with a bed, a bare bedside table and four white walls surrounding her. As her eyes slowly flickered and opened, raw panic overtook her body making her sit up straight and scream and scream, until a sharp needle in her arm forced her to slump down and clamp her mouth shut tight. Within seconds she was oblivious to the world and everything in it.

For weeks, her existence followed the same routine. She would wake, feed and lay rigid on the bed. Any slight sign of protest would immediately result in the now familiar sharp needle in her arm, resulting in instant silence. No visitors came. No thoughts entered her head.

She neither cared for anything nor wanted anything. Men and women in white coats came, talked in serious subdued tones, stared, shook their heads and exited the room. Bits of apparatus were attached to her head and shocks given, injections inserted; ice-cold baths became an unconscious routine; different people in white coats and suits came, their faces grave as they shook their heads, puzzled frowns etched on their faces; more electric shocks, more ice-cold baths as Elżbieta Szutka, wife and mother of two children, withdrew further and further from this world and into her own private and silent hell.

Paweł Jaroszynski was fully aware of the entire situation, for she had his address in her coat pocket on the entrance to the Kraków mental institution, and they had informed Paweł about the matter; he, in turn, had formally written to Henryk. Both were forbidden any contact with Elżbieta until her intense treatment was completed, and she showed signs of improvement; neither man desired any contact with her.

Henryk fell into a settled role of provider and carer for the children. By day, while he worked, the children were well cared for by his sister and her husband, and when he was not working, he spent his time doting on Anielka and Marek; they became his life. He had put Elżbieta firmly into the back of his mind. *The children*, he determined, *would never again be hurt in any way by their unfaithful, alcoholic mother*.

Silence reigned between Paweł and Ewa, as he desperately searched for the appropriate words to her statement, while she picked at her chocolate gateau waiting for an answer. "What do you mean, Ewa?" He finally retorted, his puzzled eyes staring at her.

"I mean…" She raised a pastry fork of cake and slid it into her mouth. "I mean, we should help Elżbieta Szutka. She was once your love; wasn't she? You did care for her once upon a time?"

He stared at her in silence.

"Didn't you?" She cocked a shapely eyebrow.

Finally, he nodded. "Yes, I cared."

She popped another piece of gateau into her mouth, pushing the plate to one side. "Then it's up to you and me to help this unfortunate woman," she announced with determined finality. He continued to stare at the woman he loved, as she picked up her coffee cup and brought it up to her lips, her large brown eyes on him, waiting.

Placing her cup on its flower-patterned saucer, she placed her hand softly on his hand making his eyes blink, and a hundred thousand distorted feelings and thoughts stirred within him: thoughts of his beloved dead wife; thoughts of Elżbieta and her children; thoughts of Henryk; thoughts of the woman sitting opposite him now were interwoven with conflicting feelings of love, hate and uncertainty, until all whirled uncontrollably and became one big mass of tangled confusion. "We have got to help her, Paweł, she has got nobody else."

Her words echoed and reverberated in his muddled head until finally the spinning stopped, and his thoughts and feelings began to unravel and the mist began to lift. Slowly, he nodded his head. "Yes, I suppose we have got to help," he said in such a low voice it was barely audible. "Yes," he stated determinedly, his thoughts coming together, "we will help Elżbieta," and taking Ewa's hand, he kissed it softly.

They stared at her long, hard and silently as she lay rigid on the bed, her stark eyes pinned to the ceiling. Finally, Paweł turned to Ewa. "I do not think there is anything we can do for her," he silently stated.

Ewa sighed deeply, her eyes glued on the still figure of a woman on the bed, raising them to Paweł she said, "I agree, there is nothing we can specifically do, but I think, Tato may be able to suggest something; he has a close friend in the medical profession. I will discuss the matter with him tonight." As they turned to leave, he grabbed her by the arm and turned her to face him.

"Why do you want to help this woman you do not know, Ewa?"

"Because I had misjudged her—because I… I wanted you all to myself and that is not the right thing to do; because—you loved this woman once and, because I love you, Paweł."

He gathered her into his arms and gave her a lingering kiss. "I love you, Ewa Kowalska."

The meeting with her father went well and by the end of the week plans, which would ultimately affect Elżbieta's life, were placed in motion.

"But a sanatorium in Gdansk?" questioned Paweł.

"She needs peace, relaxation and tranquillity, and to be away from familiar faces and surroundings; she needs to totally empty herself to become herself," insisted Doctor Makowski, Edek Kowalski's close friend, and so it was settled.

Chapter Forty

The sanatorium was an old sprawling building of grey stone and leaded windows, looking out on acres of beautifully landscaped lawns, colourful flower beds and interesting water features; a sanctuary for troubled hearts and souls.

For days, her lips remained firmly clamped as she resided in her own private world. Gradually, her eyes began to wander, flitting from one resident to another, lingering on artistically created bouquets of colourful flowers in sparkling crystal vases, staring at the nurses in their smart blue uniforms and caps, darting to the ancient oak trees that shaded the main dining room. She felt nothing and thought nothing. She began to pick less and eat a little more of the delicious mouth-watering food that was placed in front of her.

With the aid of a nurse, she began to take walks in the spacious grounds. With each passing day, she saw a little more, ate a little more, walked a little further and soon her nights became a little more restful. And, then, something stirred within, she knew not what, enabling her to see a little clearer, to feel the warmth of the sun on her face, to see the different shades of colour around her; the progress was slow, taking little physical and mental steps, but it was a start and, on this foundation, she started to grow and mature. The one-to-one sessions bore no fruit. As she faced her personal mentor, her lips and mind were firmly sealed and so too was withheld the key to her freedom.

On a dull damp morning, as she sat opposite her mentor, she tried to focus her eyes on the soft blue eyes and the greying mentor that smiledhair of her middle-aged counsellor. Unable to hold her gaze, her eyes darted to the window and stared unblinkingly at a couple of russet-coloured swirling leaves, her eyes following their slow swaying death dance to the ground. "Jakub," she whispered, staring at the dull overcast sky.

"Jakub," repeated the mentor her steady eyes firmly fixed on Elżbieta, waiting.

Elżbieta's eyes darted back to the woman and dropped to her lap, her lips tightly and stubbornly compressed into a thin line. The session had come to an end, *but* smiled the mentor, *it was a start.*

The weeks rolled into months and eased into the New Year. On a crisp day, as Elżbieta strolled in the grounds, her eyes flitted to clusters of white, orange and lilac crocuses sprinkled randomly about. Stooping, she plucked a lilac specimen out of the damp ground and held it gently between her fingers, marvelling at its cup-shaped flower, her forefinger tracing the grass-like ensiform leaf with its white stripe along the central leaf axis. She brought the flower up to her lips and kissed it softly.

"Would you like some to brighten your room?" asked a young nurse.

Elżbieta smiled.

The colourful crocuses stood in a small glass on her bedside table, making her heart flutter with a feeling she could not explain, a smile dancing on her lips every time her eyes strayed to the colourful first signs of spring. One evening as she lay on her bed, her mind a blank, her eyes on the colourful flowers, images began to form in her mind; at first, distorted and disjointed they were small masses of grey blotches, then slowly they began to formulate into a bigger mass and a picture began to emerge: *flowers—boys—a hand—a boy—*"Jakub!" she screamed at the top of her voice, grasping out her hand and clutching at an invisible bunch of red poppies intermingled with white daisies. "Jakub!"

The middle-aged counsellor stood at the open door while Elżbieta screamed out again and again and again, until her voice became hoarse, and she could scream no more, and, burying her head in her pillow, she sobbed bitterly.

Taking the exhausted body, drained of all tears and screams, into her arms Ola gently rocked her patient stroking her hair. "Let it go, my dear," she soothed. "Let it go."

Elżbieta began to talk. At first, the counselling sessions were short talking only about generalities: the new buds formulating on the trees, the improving weather. Gradually, the sessions lengthened and Elżbieta began to express her likes and dislikes regarding fashion, food, movies and music; her mind began to visit the distant past when she was at her happiest: *Zosia's wedding—her work at the museum—her day out in Kraków with her mother—*"The Krakowianka doll..." she smiled, her eyes sparkling.

"And—why was this Krakowianka doll special, Elżbieta?"

She looked into the far away distance. "Mama bought it for me on our special day out together." Her smile vanished, the shine in her eyes replaced by a dull sheen. "Tato destroyed it like—like—he destroyed everything else in our lives—like he destroyed Zosia's life."

"Zosia?" Ola probed looking deep into her patient's empty eyes and her drawn face and noticed her lips were tightly clamped.

"You mentioned someone called Zosia in our last ses…"

"She is my cousin," intercepted Elżbieta her eyes darting to Ola, now her trusted counsellor and friend. "She was raped by my father. He—he ruined her life, just like Lisztek ruined…" Abruptly, she rose to her feet.

"Tell me about your cousin, Zosia, Elżbieta. What is she like?"

Memories flashed into the forefront of Elżbieta's mind: *Good, happy memories of her cousin's wedding day—happy times spent in each other's company—and now, they were more like strangers corresponding only by letter and, as time went by, the letters were becoming more shorter, more formal and fewer in number.* Her words came out slow and full of meaning, "She was a rare beauty both inside and out, admired by many—raped by Wojtek Kaminski, my so-called father. He raped her and ruined her life." She raised her glassy eyes to Ola where they stared unblinkingly.

"And; Lisztek?" Immediately Ola witnessed the trembling of Elżbieta's lips, the ice in her eyes.

"He raped me."

Inwardly, Ola rejoiced for she knew that Elżbieta was on the road to recovery; there was no going back. It was going to be a long process, but they had already taken the first step of the arduous journey.

Prompted by Ola's gentle and discreet probing, Elżbieta started to give more of herself and, at the end of each session, Ola felt that her patient had left fragments of her past in the room as she walked out. But, this particular evening, Elżbieta felt a heavy trepidation eating away at her, and she put the blame firmly at Ola's door for it was Ola, her closest friend and confidante, who had asked her to perform a task which was causing her untold misery and dread. She could only pick at her chicken and vegetables at the supper table, her stomach-wrenching at the mere thought of putting the tiniest morsel into her mouth; sleep avoided her that night as she tossed and turned, unsuccessfully trying to banish gross images of Lisztek's bulk on top of her; scenes of a drunken Wojtek hitting her *mother and giving her a lashing in the process; Lukasz making sweet love to her, abandoning her and their baby; Jakub, wildflowers in his hand—days later, his casket lowered deeper and deeper into the dark, black earth; Zygmunt, dear sweet Zygmunt; Henio—Paweł—Anielka—her baby son who she had abandoned.*

She rose, roughly tossing her blanket to one side, took out a pen and writing pad and began her arduous assignment.

The dawn light filtered through her curtains as she closed her pad, her mind and body exhausted as her wobbly legs walked her to her bed. There she lay drained and devoid of any feelings, yearning only to sleep.

"Have you done what I have asked you to do?" Ola cocked an enquiring eyebrow as Elżbieta silently nodded her head. "Do you feel you are ready to do this?"

Elżbieta raised her tired eyes to her trusted mentor and dear friend and, with shaking fingers, picked up the pad and opened the cover. "Yes, I am ready," she replied softly and, with a trembling voice began: "Dear Future, I am writing this letter to you because, to possess you, I must tell you about my past." She paused, took a deep breath and resumed. "My father was a cruel man who drank, was violent and treated my mother, and I like unpaid servants; treated all women like dishcloths to be used, then to be looked down on with disgust and thrown away. It was he who introduced me to his best friend, Tadek Lisztek, the man who raped me when I was a child of twelve.

"I feel it was because of these two men, but primarily Lisztek, that I lost all faith and trust in men and, eventually even in God. I loved Lukasz. He did not love me. He used me for his own amusement, but gave me my beloved son, Jakub; the love of my life, who God thought fit to snatch away from me. When I thought I could love and trust Zygmunt, it turned out that he was my biological father.

"So who could I trust, my mother; Lukasz; Zosia; Zygmunt? I thought I could trust Paweł though it turned out I couldn't trust him. Henio was trustworthy, but in the end, he couldn't cope with me, banning me from the house and forbidding me to see my children. The only true and real friend I ever had in my life, dependable at all times, was alcohol. To this trusted friend I could turn to at any time; never to be turned away or tossed aside like an old sock, and from whom I always found a source of comfort; my only source of comfort for I had nothing else.

"I have nothing, but I have slowly come to realise I am something; I am a person with feelings, hopes and aspirations and someday, with help, I look forward to accomplishing these hopes and dreams of mine; I am a person in my own right. I am Elżbieta Szutka."

They sat in silence Elżbieta looking down at the tear-blotched ink on the trembling page in her hand. Ola spoke softly. "How do you feel, Elżbieta?"

Elżbieta smiled faintly. "Like a weight has been lifted."

"Good—good." Ola nodded, smiling encouragingly. "Now it is time to take part in the Farewell Ceremony."

"The Farewell Ceremony?"

"The ceremony of release; come."

Elżbieta meekly followed Ola to a blazing fire in an open fireplace.

"The past needs to be released and only you can let go of it, Elżbieta; only then will you be allowed to grasp the future."

Elżbieta's eyes dropped and lingered on the open pad in her hand, roughly she tore out the page and tossed it into the fire and watched entranced as the consuming flames curled the edges of the paper; drew the page, with its murky past, into its hungry furnace until it was gone.

She was free.

Chapter Forty-One

Elżbieta had come a long way in terms of her recovery though there was one delicate, important aspect of her life which needed to be sorted out; her role of mother. In recent sessions, Ola had noticed a deep sadness and remorse come over Elżbieta whenever her children were mentioned; she had noticed the way her patient's lips clamped tightly, the shine in her eyes disappearing, her whole body reverting into a clearly visible state of tension and silent despair; her mind closed and unresponsive to any gentle probing.

On one such day, Elżbieta's eyes strayed to the watery sunshine, as it tried to filter some of its weak rays through the window, and mumbled, "I think of Marek on days like these."

"Marek?"

"My son—he was weak too, like the sun in the sky this morning."

"Would you like to tell me about him, Elżbieta?"

She stared down at her hands her fingers clenched tightly in her lap. "I didn't—don't know him."

"And, your daughter?"

A faint smile wavered on Elżbieta's lips, her eyes distant. "Anielka, my little girl, she—she is so beautiful." She raised her glassy eyes to Ola, her smile widening. "She was such a good baby—such a good baby—" She nodded her head as if to reinforce her statement.

Ola raised her eyes to Elżbieta and asked in clear words, "Would you like to see your children, Elżbieta?"

The words struck Elżbieta like a thunderbolt, as fragmented images of Anielka and Marek crashed into her mind. One clear image emerged; *Marek cooing in his cot, beside which Henryk stood with a sleeping Anielka in his strong, secure arms.* She nodded her head, her eyes closing to the image, and there was darkness once more.

The loud knocks on the door made Henryk jump. Peering at the clock, adjusting Marek's blanket, he strode to the door wondering who on earth it could be calling on him at eight o'clock in the evening. His disbelieving eyes stared at the two people standing before him. He began to close the door on his uninvited visitors.

"Please, Pan Szutka, we need to speak."

"I have nothing to say to you; please go." Once again he proceeded to close the door.

"We have to talk," insisted the intruder.

"I have nothing to say to you," Henryk stated coldly.

"Please, Pan Szutka, this is extremely important," insisted a softly spoken voice. "This is a matter of grave urgency."

His eyes switched to the woman and scanned her kind brown eyes; her fair hair tied back in a neat bun and slowly opened the door as he glared at her companion. "Not you; you are not welcome here." Henryk lashed eyes of fire and venom at his nemesis.

"Paweł, go and sit in the car—please—" implored his companion.

Henryk scrutinised the woman as she took off her black leather gloves, placing them tidily on the table before she turned to face him.

"Pan Szutka, you don't know me, but I have heard a lot about you. I know you are a good man; a man of respect and honour; a pillar of the community."

He shuffled from foot to foot his eyes on the beauty before him, wondering where all this was going, good manners preventing him from interrupting.

"I am here concerning the welfare of Elżbieta, your wife."

"I know who my wife is, Pani… Pani…?" He stopped silently, admonishing himself for his uncharacteristic sharp tongue.

"Kowalska. My name is Ewa Kowalska. Your wife is currently residing at the sanatorium in Gdansk." She started taking a surreptitious glance at Henryk's bland expression. "She is progressing very well. In fact, she will be…"

He abandoned his manners altogether as he cut into her flow of words. "I am sorry to be blunt, Pani Kowalska, but I do not wish to know any more about Elżbieta. As far as I am concerned, she is no wife of mine; no mother to her children."

"But—but—"

"No buts, Pani Kowalska. The simple fact is that the children and I want nothing more to do with Elżbieta. As far as we are concerned, she has made her bed and now…"

"And now she is paying the price. Pan Szutka, it seems to me you are speaking for your children; surely you will allow Elżbieta to see the children; after all, they are her flesh and blood."

Henryk looked long and hard at the woman standing confidently before him. "Pani Kowalska, let me put it to you this way. I will not allow an adulteress, an alcoholic mother, who incidentally abandoned her children in one way or another, to venture through this door."

"Pan Szutka…"

"Good evening to you, Pani Kowalska." His icy eyes locked with her eyes. "Please do not call here again."

With heavy heart Ewa Kowalska walked away, her eyes uncharacteristically downcast as she approached Paweł. "He won't have anything to do with her," she said softly, in a voice he barely heard.

He sighed deeply as he started the car.

Chapter Forty-Two

A seriously faced Ola sat beside her patient. Taking her hands into her own, looking deep into her friend's eyes she said softly, "Your friends, Paweł and Ewa, have been in touch with your husband, Henryk. I am afraid…"

Elżbieta did not hear the rest as she watched Ola's mouth open and close, stared at her concerned kind eyes upon her, her thumping heart slowly turning into a block of ice. *There was no hope, and it was all of her own making. She had been the perpetrator of her own destiny, and now she must live with the consequences. Henryk's word was his bond.* She was oblivious to Ola's exit as she sat alone, staring unseeingly at the mature oaks lining the drive, as she contemplated life without Henryk and the children; life without Paweł Jaroszynski; life without alcohol.

Closing her eyes, she shook her head from side to side. *It was going to be near impossible. The thought of turning to the bottle seemed enticing and,* she concluded, *there would be no one to stop me now.* As she dwelt on the matter, she could almost smell its raw sting, and feel the strong potency turning into soothing warmth deep inside her.

Her thought grew and matured. *She could see herself slowly unscrewing the top, hearing the sound of metal against the glass, as the open bottle stared at her willing her, urging her, welcoming her back into its magic world; she could see herself pouring the clear liquid into a glass, bringing it to her mouth and tasting its sweet rawness, its welcoming release. Yes,* she thought, *yes—yes—*The gentle knocking on the door made her jump, her eyes darting to the opening door.

"A visitor for you, Elżbieta."

"I don't want to see anybody," she snapped, turning her eyes away from the door.

"This visitor has come here especially to see you, Elżbieta."

Butterflies fluttered in her stomach, her heart racing. "It's Henio; he has changed his mind!" she exclaimed turning her expectant eyes back to the door, feeling she was about to burst with sheer happiness. "Father Stanisław!" Her heart stopped its erratic beating. "What on earth are you doing here?" she asked, hoping against hope he was bringing news of Henryk and the children. She stood up extending her arms wide to greet her old friend.

"Well, this is a fine welcome, I must say." He extended his arms, a wide smile beaming on his face, as she buried her head in the cool smooth fabric of his soutane. For long seconds, she stayed in his arms: secure, calm, protected; years peeling away like the skin of an onion, until she was a young girl again… *listening to his wise words in Saint Adalbert's Church. If only she had listened to him then and in later years. If only…*

For a while, they sat opposite each other in silent contemplation reminiscing about past days, innocent days. *He had aged*, she noticed, *lots more grey in his hair, more lines etching his lively eyes; he had put weight on, but it suited him*, she silently surmised. He broke their secret reveries. "I have come to take you home, Elżbieta," he announced.

"Home—but—" Her thoughts wandered as her heart danced. *Henio wants his wife back, the mother of their children.*

"It's all been arranged. Don't you worry your head about anything?"

"Has—has Henio sent you here?" The words escaped her mouth as butterflies fluttered wildly in her fast-beating heart.

Silently, he shook his head. The butterflies ceased their dance of joy. "You are going to stay with my sister."

"But; what about Henio? What about my children?" Her eyes clouded over as they rested on her friend.

His grim face told her it would be futile to ask any more questions.

Bronia was ten years younger than her brother, Stanisław; a gentle, hard-working woman with three small children. Her husband worked at a local bottling plant, and it was clear to see that, although Bronia was extremely capable, she would appreciate any help. On her arrival, Elżbieta stared at the children in turn: Franciszekek was the oldest, a boy of eight with black hair and a gentle face like his Wujek Stanisław; Bartek was a boy of six and the lively one of the bunch. Elżbieta's eyes strayed and fixed on the baby, instantly yearning to run as fast as her legs would carry her. Father Stanisław, watching her carefully, fully understood where her thoughts were leading and placed his gentle hand on her arm.

"Give it a chance, Elżbieta," he urged softly, his reassuring eyes on the friend he had always looked out for. Her eyes flitting to him saw the gentleness and softness in his eyes, which eased the pounding in her heart. She nodded silently.

In exchange for board and food, her duties were light: washing, cleaning, lighting the fire, helping out in the kitchen and, as she helped out with the chores, she wondered why she was asked to come for she could see that Bronia was quite capable of doing the extra few tasks. Deep within her heart, she knew Father Stanisław always had good reasons behind his acts of kindness, and she knew only time would give her answers.

The days eased into weeks. One morning, as she was washing the breakfast dishes, her heart skipped a beat for surely, she thought, she must have imagined what she had just heard. Shaking her head, she picked up a plate and proceeded to wash away the preserve.

"I wouldn't ask you, Elżbieta, but I have a doctor's appointment, and it would be a great help to me." Bronia stood waiting patiently for a response, her eyes seeing undiluted pain in Elżbieta's eyes as she turned to face her. She quickly tried to amend her grave mistake. "Oh, I am being silly. I'll manage. Don't worry, I'll manage."

"I will look after the children for you, Bronia." The second she uttered the words she regretted deeply opening her foolish mouth. *Oh Boże, Elżbieta, you are such a cholerna idiot. What the hell are you thinking?* She cursed herself over and over again. Opening her mouth, about to retract her hasty, thoughtless words, she saw the delighted relief in Bronia's face. "Do you trust me with your children?" Elżbieta asked quietly, her heart thudding, her eyes focused starkly on Bronia as her friend smiled warmly.

"Of course, I trust you, Elżbieta and, before you ask, yes, Stanisław has told me everything."

The familiar butterflies returned, fluttering in her stomach and in her heart. *She trusts me with her children,* she silently rejoiced. *She trusts me with her children!*

Her heart sank as Bronia left the kitchen to get ready for her appointment, and she stared out the window, her eyes somewhere in the distant past. *Can I be trusted, though? Can I trust myself*, she pondered as uninvited ghoulish scenarios crashed into her head: *Franciszek had split his head open, a gush of blood flowing uncontrollably; Bartek was screaming at the top of his voice, his hand burnt raw on the stove; baby Mania in her cot supervised by her own drunken self, as she took generous swigs out the bottle. You can't do it—you can't do it!* An inner voice tormented her mercilessly. *You can't do it—you're a drunk—you're useless.* "You can't do it!" she exclaimed.

"Yes, you can do it," Bronia said softly. "I trust you." She swiftly said her goodbyes and was out the door before Elżbieta could utter another word of protest.

The door firmly closed, Franciszek and Bartek at school and pre-school, her heart beat wildly in her chest as she took cautious steps towards baby Mania. For long, long minutes, she stood staring down, not able to move a muscle, her chest heaving as she continued to stare. She blinked hard chasing away the bitter hot tears welling up in her eyes and, sighing deeply, she stooped and gently picked up the sleeping baby. Catching a glimpse of her reflection in the mirror, she stood transfixed. "Mother and child," she whispered, as thoughts of her own baby and Anielka rushed into her head.

Snapping out of her trance-like state, she quickly placed Mania back into her cot and sat in a rocking chair rocking back and forth, back and forth. She looked down at her hands, and there was no glass containing soothing liquid; just herself and her fast-beating heart. She listened to its rhythm, her eyes on the slight rising and falling of the baby's blanket. "I don't need a drink," she said aloud. "Bronia trusts me; Baby Mania trusts me; I trust me."

Rising she picked up the baby once more and sat back down in the rocker, humming a soft lullaby her eyes, thoughts and attention wholly fixed on the baby in her secure arms as a warm feeling, like a protective blanket, enveloped her as she continued the rhythmic rocking.

The following weeks brought more responsibilities involving the children, and Elżbieta's confidence grew daily. Bronia and her husband had noticed that she was talking more and smiling more; Father Stanisław noticed a total transformation. He knew his plan would work and was inwardly confident that it was now coming to fruition; he also knew there was one major missing link, and there he knew he had to tread very carefully and with extreme caution. *One wrong move*, he silently surmised, *and it could all go so drastically and irrevocably wrong.*

Deep inside Elżbieta knew her thoughts and feelings were changing. The need for alcohol-induced release was lessening each day, as she found fulfilment and satisfaction in taking care of the children and menial daily chores; undertaking each task diligently, and looking forward to the next with added zest and vigour. But there was, deep within her, a niggling feeling that would not go away and could not be filled by anything else. Every day her thoughts drifted back to her own children, the void in her heart growing deeper and deeper, and no amount of substitution could alleviate the need and love for her own flesh and blood; the children she was banned from seeing and thus the blade in her heart grew sharper, and thrust deeper, with each passing day.

It was Bronia who finally broached the subject as she sat opposite her brother, a glass of lemon tea poised in her hand. "What are we going to do, Stanisław? Elżbieta needs her children; the children need their mother. We have seen how good she is with Franciszek, Bartek and Mania; I don't see any reason why Henryk cannot be approached."

He took a sip of his strong coffee and, placing the cup gently back onto its saucer, looked lovingly into his sister's kind eyes. "It is not so easy, Bronia. Elżbieta has had a past which has not been altogether savoury. In her husband's eyes, she has rejected the children. We must tread carefully, very carefully."

"You must go and see Henryk Szutka," insisted Bronia. "It is your duty, Stanisław, as his priest and as his friend."

He nodded secretly wondering if his visit would do any good or, indeed, if it would stir up a whole lot of unwanted resentment.

Chapter Forty-Three

Henryk Szutka listened to everything his priest, confidante and friend told him. His mind was made up before Father Stanisław had uttered his last word and his resolute face, and determined eyes, had given his visitor the silent answer he did not want to acknowledge. Father Stanisław looked appealingly at his old friend.

"Henryk, your wife has changed. My sister, Bronia, has ultimate trust in Elżbieta when it comes to child care, and your wife has proved herself time and time again. She is to be trusted, my friend." He was hoping against hope that his words were sinking in; that his friend would relent and give his wife one last chance.

Henryk shook his head from side to side a grim, determined line on his mouth gave a silent and irrevocable answer.

There was one last straw to be grasped, and Father Stanisław grabbed it like a drowning man reaching out for a lifeline. "Will you, at least, think about it, Henryk?"

He closed the door on a stubborn-faced, resolute man.

In the days following, Father Stanisław's visit, thoughts of Elżbieta invaded Henryk's mind both at work and when he was at home with his children. *Things were not always bad. In fact, we were very happy at the start of our marriage*, he mused as he used his shears skilfully on a length of cloth, following carefully his previously made chalk markings. *Yes, things were very good until—until—Jaroszynski came onto the scene. Elżbieta had been a good wife; a good mother to Anielka until that bastard came into our lives and ruined it all.*

Damn him. Damn her. "Oh, damn! Damn! Damn!" He cursed loudly and uncharacteristically as he cut out the line. "Damn!" He sat down on a stool, laying his shears on the long, broad, cloth-covered table, his shaking head in his hands. *Why did she have to befriend him? Why did I take him into our home? How long did she know him?* A multitude of questions whirled around in his head, and to them, more unanswerable questions were added. Staring into space, after long minutes, he muttered aloud, "Perhaps, it was not all Elżbieta's fault;

perhaps—I did not give my wife the attention she needed. Perhaps—perhaps—I should give her another chance."

No! No! No! An inner voice admonished. *Don't you dare! She betrayed you; she slept with your so-called friend; she is an alcoholic; she is no fit wife or mother.* But his conscience argued, *Father Stanislaw, my old trusted friend, tells me she has changed; tells me she can be trusted and that she deserves a second chance. Doesn't everyone deserve a second chance in life?* These thoughts stayed with him throughout his working day, and well into the evening. When the children were sleeping securely, and he was in the rocker, a small glass of krupnik in his hand, he wondered, *Maybe her drinking started out innocently; maybe events took over, over which she had no control and, if she couldn't talk to me—Maybe, I should give her one last chance.*

The grim face told Elżbieta all she needed to know. *She was to be denied access to her children; her fate was sealed.*

"I think there is hope, Elżbieta," Father Stanisław added, hoping his words would lighten her heavy load.

Rigidly, she sat, her guts writhing and craving for the only medicine she knew would ease her raw anguish. *Just go, Stanislaw*, she silently commanded. *Just go, now!*

"There is always hope, my dear Elżbieta." His departing words reverberated loudly in her head, as she grabbed her coat and stormed out the door. "There is no hope," she stated loudly, running down the long corridor and down the street to her destination; her heart racing in eager anticipation, need and want.

As she stuffed the bottle into the depths of her deep pocket, a pair of eyes saw it all.

"There is no hope," Henryk Szutka stated aloud to himself on his way to work. "No hope at all!"

With her fingers protectively clutched around the cool bottle, her heart decreased its rapid beating; already a veil of calm was shrouding her. *Soon*, she told herself, *nothing will really matter; very soon.*

She entered the apartment, immediately feeling an eeriness surrounding her for usually, by now, it was full of chatter, baby gurgling and soft background music. Clad in her heavy coat she sat and retrieved her treasure, placing it on the table, her eyes glued to the clear potent liquid inside, so inviting. Hastily, with trembling fingers, she unscrewed the metal top and poured out a gurgling generous measure into a coffee cup, her body silently crying out for the liquid, urging her to quickly hurl it down her throat; to taste and feel its magic. Her fingers curled round the cup, her eyes on the still liquid. *For God's sake, drink it, woman*, an inner voice exhorted.

Stop; don't drink it, another voice protested.

Drink it, now!
No—no, don't do it, think about what you may lose.
There is nothing to lose; nothing!

She brought the cup up to her trembling lips.

Drink it! Drink it! Drink it!

Opening her lips she paused as uninvited images of Henryk, Anielka and her baby crashed into the forefront of her mind. Hastily, she withdrew the cup from her craving mouth and lashed it, and its precious contents, against the wall, causing the cup to shatter into two pieces, and the vodka to splatter on the walls and the linoleum below. "Never! Never! Never!" she screamed with all of her might stumbling, in her eagerness to get away, as she rose from the chair. "Never again will you ruin my life; never!" She didn't hear the door open as she stared at the liquid gurgling down the plug hole.

"Elżbieta! Elżbieta!" cried Bronia, hugging her friend as she witnessed the last of the vodka disappear out of sight. "Elżbieta," she whispered over and over again, as both women hugged and sobbed in each other's tight embrace.

With a heavy heart, Henryk sat down to his solitary supper that evening, his hopes and dreams dashed as he questioned his own judgement and those of others. Chewing his rye bread with kielbasa, he tasted nothing but bitter anguish. *How on earth*, he asked himself, *could I have been so wrong? What possessed me to ever think that Elżbieta could be cured of her alcoholism? How could I let myself think that she could be the wife and mother she once was? What was Father Stanisław thinking of when he referred to Elżbieta's positive progress? Both of us have been deluded; in our own little dream worlds. But, more importantly, has Bronia lost her mind completely, placing her children in the care of a hopeless alcoholic? Oh Boże, how Elżbieta has made a fool of us all;*

how blind we all were. He shook his head in total despondency, pushing his plate roughly to one side.

In bed, he tossed and turned, his mind whirling with images of Elżbieta: *staggering, drinking, begging for alcohol; children in her care.* As the dawn light began to filter into his gloomy room, he determined to pay his wife a visit, for this needed to be settled once and for all.

Chapter Forty-Four

Father Stanisław handed Elżbieta the sealed envelope. "It's from Henryk," he stated, oblivious to its contents, as he waited to see a positive reaction on his friend's face. His eyes scrutinised her carefully as, with trembling fingers, she ripped open the envelope, her impatient eyes scanning the copperplate words on the page, her hopeful eyes shining as her heart jumped for joy. A chuckle escaped his lips as she spontaneously wrapped her arms around his neck and pecked him on the cheek. "Oh, Father Stanisław, this truly is beyond a dream. Henryk wants to see me. You were right all along. There is hope, after all!"

Sleep eluded Elżbieta that night for she was in the company of Henryk, Anielka and baby Marek: *She was secure in the bosom of her family, and they had their wife and mother back at home with them. She saw herself rocking baby Marek, pushing Anielka on the swing and making love with her husband. They were going to be so happy; so very, very happy.* As the first morning light squeezed through the curtains, she was spreading butter on pieces of rye bread for Bronia's brood. Glancing at the clock she silently sighed. *Thirteen long hours to go before her fate was sealed before she was on her way home to her family; thirteen long hours…*

She was left to look after baby Mania for the day. In recent days, this was such an honour and delight. For now, she was trusted implicitly, and this sent a warm, happy feeling through her entire body. Today, as she eased the bottle teat into baby Mania's small mouth, she saw only her own baby; a deep yearning taking over her whole body. *Eleven hours*, she exhaled another deep sigh.

She squeezed her eyes tight to obliterate the sudden image of the vodka bottle standing before her eyes. *Oh Boże*, she silently prayed, *make it go away please—please—*A soft cough snapped her out of her reverie, and the bottle disappeared, her eyes seeing only baby Mania. "Sh," she soothed, softly patting Mania's back. "Never again will I forsake my family; never!"

Seconds dragged into minutes; minutes into hours as Elżbieta dusted, washed, made beds and prepared the evening meal. As she stared down at the bubbling pan of rosòł, her thoughts drifted to Henryk and their marriage: *It was good, to begin with sharing a loving, trusting, caring relationship and then came Paweł Jaroszynski.*

Closing her eyes to the bubbling liquid, Paweł's image loomed large and clear in her mind: *tall, fair-haired, grey eyes. There was,* she mused, *something mysterious and exciting about him; something Henio did not, and would never be able to, possess or acquire for it was a charm,* she surmised, *a man was born with; it could never be earned. He had sent shivers up and down her spine with his mere presence and when he had touched her, caressed her, loved her she had reached the very pinnacle of heaven. And yet,* she thought as she opened her eyes and resumed her stirring, *there was a vital component missing in him; loyalty to one woman.* She cast her mind further back to their very first encounter in Kraków Square, so many years ago—*He had stooped to pick up her school books, their eyes locking*—yet, *those eyes should have been reserved for the woman walking by his side.*

He claimed to love Elusia with all of his heart yet he loved me, or claimed to love me. And now, he has tossed me aside for this so-called new love. An exciting man, yes; reliable, no. Never; not like Henio. Henio had proved himself to be there when it mattered: dependable, reliable, honest, a shining example; my husband and the father of my children, the head of our family. And now, he is giving me a second chance.

A smile broke on her lips. "A chance," she quietly said, "I am not worthy of." She gave the rosòł a more vigorous stir as she stared unseeingly at the bits of chicken, and small strips of pasta, swirling round and round. "I am going to prove to Henio that I can be the best wife and mother any man could desire."

The gentle knocking on the door sent her heart racing.

"I'll go," Bronia stated. "Go and make yourself comfortable in the sitting room. I will make sure the children don't disturb you."

She sat rigidly in the armchair, her hands clasped tightly together, her heart pounding, as her expectant eyes waited impatiently for her husband to appear. His quietly spoken voice seemed to penetrate the whole apartment as, in her ears, it seemed to become louder and clearer with each passing moment.

"Elżbieta."

Slowly, she raised her eyes to his, her hand to his extended hand as if they were mere acquaintances; as he took her hand in his firm, warm grasp her heart danced. She smiled cautiously. "Hello, Henio."

They sat opposite each other united in marriage. Her eyes stared at Henio this quiet, unassuming man she once loved, straying to his dark hair and soft blue eyes, feeling as if she was staring at a complete stranger. *This was not as she had imagined it would be.* Her body tense, eyes firmly glued on her husband, fingers tightly clenched into a tight ball, she waited as her heart pumped furiously, for him to break the ice, as the intruding clock on the mantelpiece ticked loudly in her head.

Henryk looked at his rigid wife, feeling her tension, and blinked hard. *This was not going* to be easy, he grimly concluded. *Not easy at all. But* he sighed inwardly, *it had to be done.* "Elżbieta."

Her heart skipped a thousand beats.

"What I have to say, Elżbieta, is not easy." He met her eyes and held her gaze.

Her heart pounded as she told herself severely: *I have to hear this through. I have failed both as a wife and a mother and now I have to listen patiently, and politely, if I want a chance.* She braced herself, feeling as if her heart was about to jump out of her chest. "I am ready to listen, Henio," she said quietly.

He coughed lightly, focusing again his serious eyes on his wife. "Elżbieta, as I have said, there is no easy way of saying what I have to say." He paused, trying desperately to find the right words. "I saw you buying a bottle of vodka the other day, therefore, I cannot; I will not allow you to have any contact with the children, whatsoever."

He saw in her eyes her whole world crashing down and collapsing around her; his heart aching for the woman he loved, still loved, but could never have while there was a threesome in their marriage *and the third* party, he sadly concluded, *had totally possessed her body and soul.* "I am very sorry, Elżbieta." He shook his head regretfully from side to side, his lips set in a firm determined line. "It is over, Elżbieta. I am deeply sorry."

All her thoughts, dreams, ambitions and feelings were swimming round and round in her head; a distorted, jumbled-up mass of shattered aspirations and heavy regrets swirling around and around, until they all broke up and disintegrated into nothing and all were dead. Her stark eyes stared at the man, she thought, she knew; the husband who could have given her a final chance; the man on whom she had pinned all her hopes who, in a space of a few words, had killed her entire future and left her with nothing. Her guts ceased their ruthless twisting and her heart no longer thudded. She opened her mouth; no words came out for they too were dead.

"I am sorry." He picked up his cap his heart heavy and, without casting her a second glance, walked purposefully towards the door.

It was over. Her world was over and her life might as well be, Elżbieta concluded. *For this was it.* She sat, like a solid block, unable to move a muscle, staring unseeingly into space for everything was dead.

"I am sorry for your trouble Bronia—Tomek." Henryk opened up his squashed cap and placed it firmly onto his head, looking seriously at the kind couple. "I cannot—I cannot have an alcoholic looking after my children. I understand you may feel differently about your own children." He reached for the door handle.

Bronia hastily caught the handle before him. "What do you mean, Henryk? Elżbieta has not had one single drop since the sanatorium."

He turned to his hostess smiling wryly as he took on a formal tone. "She may have fooled you both, but I have seen her with my own eyes, only the other day purchasing alcohol."

Bronia placed her hand on his arm. "Come and sit down, Henio."

Henryk took a deep exasperated sigh. "No one can deny what I saw," he said, a touch of impatience laced in his words.

"Please—please, sit down." Bronia patted the top of the chair encouragingly.

Obediently, he sat down, his eyes following Bronia's every move as she sat opposite and placed both her hands on the table. "What you saw was the truth. Elżbieta did buy a bottle of vodka. And, yes, she brought it home and, yes, she was about to drink the contents." He stirred in his chair as she watched his every move, placing a gentle hand on his hand. "Please, you need to hear this." She steadied her eyes until they were level with his and, with a calm voice, continued. "Your wife had a craving and, in those desperate moments, she wanted alcohol more than…"

"More than the children," cut in Henryk.

"Yes, perhaps more than the children, but Henio, the important fact is; that, at the point of succumbing, she threw it down the sink. I walked into the room and saw it with my very eyes, just as surely as you saw her buying the alcohol."

Desperately, he tried to take it all in; to digest and make some kind of sense of it all. "But why buy it in the first place?" he asked his eyes firmly on Bronia. "Why not just walk past the liquor store?"

"Because," she looked steadily into his eyes, "she was still not strong enough."

"And, what if you hadn't walked in—she could have drank it then?"

"Yes, she could have consumed it then and since then she has had plenty of opportunities of doing so, Henio, and not once has she succumbed."

They sat in sombre silence, each milling over what the other had said; Elżbieta's future hanging precariously in the balance as the minutes ticked laboriously on.

"And, what if she is tempted in the future?"

Bronia desperately searched for the right words for she knew this could be a possibility in the future. She held her gaze as she ventured on. "And Henio what if you or I are tempted? There, but for the grace of God."

He looked away into the distance of possibilities; silently he nodded his head and rose from his chair.

"Will you stay for a drink of tea, Henio?"

"No thank you. I need time to think."

Bronia took slow steps into the living room and found Elżbieta sitting rigidly staring into space. Taking her friend into her arms she stroked her black curls. "He said he needs time to think."

Elżbieta's heart had already turned to stone.

Chapter Forty-Five

Elżbieta withdrew back into herself immersing herself in a shroud of regret for, she concluded, *whatever good she may do now, would be of no consequence at all. Henryk's mind was made up, and he was a man of his word. She would never ever see her children again, and she herself was to blame.* As she lay in her bed, the darkness surrounding her, dark thoughts invaded her tortured mind: *What was the use of carrying on? What was the point of it all; to only ever look after somebody else's children, and never to hold her own; to live in somebody else home, and never again live in the security of her own home?* She closed her eyes squeezing them tightly. *Death would surely be a welcome release for then*, she thought, *I would feel nothing at all. There would be no more hurt—no more pain.*

Tangled, distorted, fragmented thoughts weaved, turned and twisted formulating into a dark mass, maturing into an ever darker idea which was becoming very clear. *It was the only way out; the very best solution for all concerned, especially the children, because who would want to own up to having an alcoholic for a mother?*

As the days grew longer and warmer, her world grew smaller and darker. One thought invaded and took permanent residency in her mind. *Death*. It remained constant and became her sole companion. With it would come freedom; a release from guilt, betrayal, lies, mistrust, disappointment and regret.

Each time she opened the door into her world of release, death's dark seed grew larger and larger until it took over all her thoughts. Robotically, she made the beds, washed the dishes and ironed clothes thinking only of one thing until slowly a date, time and method weaved into a plan of execution. *Alcohol and pills*, she decided, *would be the means. There would be no letter.* A faint smile played on her lips. *Tomorrow, I shall be free.*

The morning brought with it its usual busy routine in the Szymnak household: breakfast to be made, children prepared and taken to school and household chores to be done. With a steely determination, Elżbieta remained inwardly detached, pinning a smile onto her lips, as she said her usual farewells to the children, to Bronia and Tomek as they set off for school. Breakfast dishes were washed and put away, the day shopping done with one extra item in her basket; her one true *friend* which had never let her down.

She placed the bottle with its clear, potent liquid on the table and, from the depths of a drawer, brought out the pills she had saved from the sanatorium and placed them beside the bottle. Retrieving a glass, she sat on the rocking chair and began to pour. The knock on the door made her jump, drops of vodka spilling onto her hand. "Cholera jasna!" she cursed loudly at the closed door her body rigid, the bottle poised in her hand. "Who the hell can that be?" Quickly, she shoved the bottle, glass and pills into a cupboard, rinsed her hands and made for the door, a multitude of silent curses on her lips. Pinning a smile on her face, opening the door, her eyes became stark and wide. For long moments, she stood… frozen.

"Aren't you going to let me in?"

"Z-Zosia!" She managed to squeeze the strangled name out.

Zosia dropped her canvas bag onto the floor and took her cousin into her arms, hugging and squeezing her, standing back and taking her in, then hugging her again once more.

"Zosia, I can't believe it! I can't believe it!" Elżbieta stared incredulously at her beloved cousin and friend, as tears streamed down her face. "Zosia—Oh Zosia, how good it is to see you but how…"

"Henio gave me your address," she intercepted.

"Henio!" gasped Elżbieta. "But how… why—?"

"Because you are his wife, you silly goose," chuckled Zosia showing her white even teeth. "But what is this I hear…?"

Elżbieta didn't hear the rest as the familiar claws were clutching her heart, squeezing it tighter, and tighter still. She gasped for breath, grabbing hold of a chair.

"What on earth is it? What has happened?" Zosia placed a gentle arm around her cousin and helped her onto a chair as she sat opposite, her puzzled eyes on Elżbieta.

Slowly, laboriously Elżbieta related the entire facts to the one beloved person she could trust omitting nothing, adding nothing, speaking the whole truth in its raw intensity, after which she closed her eyes feeling as if all of her blood had been drained away from every vein in her body. They sat in silence wrapped in their own thoughts of regret each wishing life had dealt them a better hand, each accepting their lot as the clock ticked ponderously on. Finally, Zosia smiled. "All is not lost, Elżbieta. You know the saying: Where there is life, there is hope. Well, it is very true." She watched her cousin shake her head from side to side.

"Not in my case, Zosia."

"Yes, in your case, in my case and in everyone's case."

Elżbieta continued to shake her head, lost in her own thoughts, as Zosia watched her cousin in her despair; the cousin who long ago had helped her had saved her. *Now it is my turn*, she silently stated. *I have to help Elżbieta.* Abruptly, she rose from her chair and disposed of the pills and alcohol. "Nobody will ever know," she smiled. "We start living now, Elżbieta."

An inexplicable warm feeling enveloped Elżbieta as she studied her cousin's kind face. *So like Ciocia Mania*, she thought. *Maybe there is hope; maybe—*

Somewhere from the depths of her being, like a dark serpent, a familiar yearning wove into her heart and emptiness entered her eyes, for it was a yearning not for Henryk and her children. It was a yearning for Paweł Jaroszynski.

Chapter Forty-Six

Paweł Jaroszynski's engagement to Ewa Kowalska was announced in the local newspaper, the Banns of Marriage displayed at Saint Adalbert's entrance for all to see and comment upon. Henryk glanced at the announcement, a knife slicing through his heart and reopening an old wound. *If it wasn't for that man—If I had not let him into my home—*he mused.

The news had not reached Elżbieta, leaving her to live in her dreams. As she vigorously scrubbed the kitchen floor, she mused on Zosia's words: *We start living now, Elżbieta... We start living now...* "Yes, we do start living now, Elżbieta," she stated loudly dropping her scrubbing brush into the metal pail, allowing drops of soapy water to spill onto the floor; throwing her apron on to a chair and extracting a pen and pad from the drawer, she sat down at the table and wrote:

My dear Paweł,
   I need to see you at the Kawiarnia Marianska. Two o'clock.
   Tomorrow.
Elżbieta

   Do not bring Ewa.

In the afternoon, she handed the envelope, with a few coins, to Franciszek saying in a quiet voice, "Take this to the address on the envelope. This is our secret, Franciszek."

The door opened to his vigorous knocking, his young eyes widened as they rose to a pair of mysterious eyes and a sweet smile. Hastily, his eyes dropped to the name on the envelope, his lips forming into a boyish grimace. "Mm... this is not for you, Pani. Its—it's for a Pan Jaroszynski."

Ewa's smile grew as she extended her slim hand. "I will make sure Pan Jaroszynski gets it."

For a moment, Franciszek held on tightly to the envelope, and slowly, his mouth turned into a grin. "I suppose it doesn't matter if I give it to you, as long as Pan Jaroszynski gets it in the end."

"He will," she nodded closing the door.

The sealed envelope burned in her hand as she twisted it this way and that, surmising that the neat copperplate address was probably written by a female hand. Finally, she popped it onto the mantelpiece and resumed reading her latest fashion magazine, her thoughts immediately returning to the mysterious envelope and the sender. Abruptly, she rose to her feet and retracted the envelope, her heart was racing. *No—no—*she firmly told herself, as she placed it back only to snatch it back, tear the seal open and take out the page her heart racing; anger rising within her like a wild tsunami as she read and reread the words over and over again and stopped at the words: *Do not bring Ewa.*

Silent rage replaced anger, seething and bubbling through every vein, her teeth clenched, her eyes stuck on the last sentence as she paced up and down the room. Finally, the note still in her hand, she stared into space seeing only Elżbieta and, for the first time in her life, she felt a deep sense of betrayal. "How could she?" she asked aloud. "How could she betray me in this way when all I wanted to do was to help her? Oh Boże, how could she?" She closed her eyes tightly and tried to rein in her runaway thoughts. The door opened as she hastily stuffed the envelope into her dress pocket.

Sleep evaded Elżbieta as mixed thoughts rushed in and out of her mind throughout the long, torturous night. Tadek Lisztek, Zygmunt, Łukasz, Wojtek and her mother weaved distorted patterns in her head. One image loomed large and clear, Paweł Jaroszynski; the mysterious man she had loved since the day he had picked up her school book. *There was*, she surmised, *an inexplicable connection between them which could never be broken, not even by Ewa.*

She sat in the cosy kawiarnia her fingers clutched tightly around a coffee cup, her eyes flitting from a bunch of talkative students to an elderly couple, to a professor whose nose was in a thick tome. *This place has not changed much,* she decided a whimsical smile breaking on her lips, as her mind drifted back to the day she had introduced Łukasz to Zygmunt. *If only I had listened to him— but then*, her smile widened, *there would have been no Jakub, the sunshine of my life. And Henio, he was a good husband, a good father and yet—and yet—I wanted more—more—more—*Looking down at the black liquid in her cup she grimly concluded, *I have ended up with nothing but empty futile dreams.*

She grabbed her coat and pushed her way through pensioners and students and rushed out the door and down the street as fast as her legs would carry her, her mind in a cauldron of bitter regret and—a glimmer of hope. *Father Stanisław was right. Ola was right. Zosia was right. There is hope—there is hope—there is hope*—Breathless, she opened the door and stated to a wide-eyed Bronia, "There is hope!"

Bronia wiped her hands on her apron and hugged her friend. "Of course, there is hope, kochanie, but we must not rush into things. We must give Henio time."

"But—but I haven't got time. I have to see my children. I have to be with them; now!"

Taking a deep sigh searching for the appropriate words, Bronia took her friend's hands into her own trying to quell her rising excitement and premature expectations, as she looked steadily into her eyes. "You must give Henio time. It is important, Elżbieta." She took another deep inward breath and continued. "He has been hurt, betrayed. You…"

"I have hurt him. I have betrayed him, I know," cut in Elżbieta, "but I must…"

"Time," Bronia stated softly but firmly.

Elżbieta's glassy eyes betrayed her restless spirit, her gnawing heart and wrenching guts as her inner defiance fought a desperate war with Bronia's sensible, wise words.

Bronia waited patiently, her steady warm eyes trying silently to still her friend's inner anguish for, she knew Elżbieta well; knew her stubborn will and knew her deep yearning to see her children for, she too, was a mother.

Throughout the day Elżbieta's mind was in turmoil although something had changed. For, as the sun lifts the mists from the valleys, she too had experienced the mist of delusion starting to lift. She noticed, for the first time in many years, the lilac trees around and bringing a flowering lilac to her nose inhaled deeply, savouring its sweet heady fragrance, her eyes dropping to the green grass verge where they lingered on a cluster of red, white and purple tulips as she felt the comforting warmth of the May sun on her face. *It is spring*, she mused, smiling. *Everything is coming to life. I am coming to life!*

Chapter Forty-Seven

From the corner of his eye, pushed into the side of the sofa, Paweł caught a glimpse of a crumpled-up paper, and thinking it was rubbish to be discarded, he screwed it up into a tighter ball and threw it into the waste paper bin. Minutes later, about to walk out the door, his eyes darted back to the bin. Taking the crumpled paper out, he unfolded it, his eyes widening as they recognised the copperplate. Hastily, his impatient fingers straightened the paper out, his heart sinking.

"I will be late tonight, Paweł. I told Tato I'd look in." Ewa's sweet voice sliced through his heart, like an invisible blade of betrayal, as he quickly stuffed the note into his trouser pocket, pinning on a genial smile.

"I have a few things to attend to myself," he replied, hoping she would not notice the hurt and anger in his voice. Inside, his blood bubbled and seethed for, *how could this woman he was about to marry be so deceitful? Somehow*, he grimly concluded, *Ewa had acquired Elżbieta's note and had taken it upon herself to deny him any knowledge of its existence; but why? And, why did Elżbieta want to see me?* He asked himself repeatedly. *Whatever it was they had had between them was finished long ago* or, so he thought.

As the door closed after Ewa, he withdrew his note and reread each word slowly. "Damn!" he cursed. "Damn! Damn! It's too late." Sitting down he stared at the beautiful copperplate as images of Elżbieta seeped into his mind, the veils of time lifting as he remembered her... *a young girl of about twelve or so, her brown eyes staring into his as he handed over her school book. So innocent,* he thought, *and yet so knowing; the married woman helping him in his time of need; the sexy vamp in his bed; the mother who had abandoned her children for him...*

A sudden inexplicable urge to see her rushed through his veins, his head; through every living cell and fibre of his body. "I have to see her," he stated loudly, glaring at the note and grabbing his coat he stormed out the door into the warmth of the midday sun.

She gasped as she opened the door, her heart thudding.

"Elżbieta."

His soft voice penetrated her racing heart, her feet feeling like jelly. She took a tighter grip on the door, the knuckles of her hand white, as she stared at the man before her; the man, up until a few days ago, she had yearned for, would have given her life for and now fervently wishing that he would disappear. "P.Paweł," she finally managed to mumble, her eyes unblinking and glassy.

He smiled, his grey eyes twinkling sending an involuntary shiver through her entire body. "May I come in?" He cocked an eyebrow in question.

Waking up from her spell, she glanced back at the children in her care. "No—no—I am sorry. No." She closed the door to a small opening.

Through the crack, he heard Franciszekek reading aloud a story in his *Elementarz*. "You are looking after Bronia's children, I understand. But I need to see you. I have to see you, Elżbieta. Your note, I have only just…"

"It was a mistake," she interjected, staring at the man she once loved. "It is over, Paweł."

His eyes took in the woman before him: calm, cool, collected and totally in control of her life. Without thinking he reached out his hand and touched her face, feeling a thousand sparks rush through his body for the woman, and the girl, he knew he had to finally release.

"I am sorry, Paweł." She closed the door further.

"Please—" he urged.

Something in his plea made her stop. "All right; I will get the children ready."

"The children?"

"Yes, the children; they are in my care, Paweł," she stated coldly.

Walking down the avenue of lime trees they sat down on a rustic bench looking out onto a large pond. As she took off Mania's bonnet, he surreptitiously glanced down at her and silently cursed his stupidity at letting this woman go, repeatedly asking himself the same question. *Yes*, he admitted; *she had a husband and children, she was an alcoholic; she had many issues and hang-ups, but she was warm, caring and loving, and there was something mysterious; something he could not explain; something Ewa did not possess.*

She avoided his eyes, staring at the family of ducks waddling into the pond, as she sat rigid feeling every centimetre of his manly presence. *Oh, what she would have done for this man only a week ago.* She sighed deeply. *It was all false, unreal; a dream which had spent itself and almost ruined her in the process. It was no more.*

"Elżbieta." He turned to face her. "Elżbieta, I have made a grave mistake. I love you."

Without moving a millimetre she stated coldly, "I do not love you, Paweł."

"But… but you wanted to see me secretly. Why?"

Inwardly, a war was raging as she stared unseeingly into the distance. *Should I tell him the truth? Should I lie? Should I reveal everything? Should I reveal nothing?* Blinking hard she desperately tried to get a hold of her emotions. "Paweł, I am not going to lie to you." Slowly, she turned to face him and dared to open her eyes to him. "I thought I still loved you; I thought we may have a future together. But…"

"But you knew I was engaged," he interrupted her flow of words.

Her heart froze. "Engaged?" Her eyes widened, *surely she must have misheard.*

"Yes engaged, Elżbieta. It was in all the newspapers, our Banns are displayed openly in Saint Adalbert's Church." He stared at her incredulous face as the colour vanished before his eyes, and an invisible vice gripped her heart. "You didn't know." He shook his head in utter disbelief. "You didn't know—"

"I didn't know," she stated silently adding, *and nobody bothered to tell me*, as a rush of undiluted bitterness coursed through her veins. She snapped her eyes shut, trying to get her swirling thoughts into some kind of order; to take a grip of her silent anger at Bronia for making her feel so fragile, as if the news would somehow break her. She forced a smile. "Then, Paweł, I wish you and Ewa the very best for the future." She rose to go, calling Bartek who was chatting away to the ducks.

"I love you," Paweł stated clearly.

Her smile widened making his heart flutter with hope. "And I love Henio and my children." Immediately, she saw his eyes cloud over, the smile vanish from his face. "Perhaps, we can all be friends." *Perhaps only then*, she silently concluded, *they could all move on. It was a tall order to ask on all sides*, she thought meditatively.

"Perhaps," he whispered.

Chapter Forty-Eight

Warm days slid into long, hot days, and still, there was no word from Henryk.

"My dear, Elżbieta, you have to be patient," smiled Zosia.

"Time; Henio still needs time. He will be in contact with you when the time is right." Bronia wisely stated.

"It is in God's will." Father Stanisław declared. "In the meantime, Elżbieta, why don't you soothe your mind and soul by coming to our Majòwka?"

Elżbieta grimaced at Father Stanisław's suggestion, for she had felt that God had abandoned her to her fate long ago, and she had almost forgotten Him.

That evening she watched as Bronia adjusted a flyaway wisp of hair into a hair grip and picked up her handbag turning. "Elżbieta, why don't you join me? You never know, it might do you the world of good."

Elżbieta laughed softly. "And, when has God ever done anything for me?"

Her friend looked her steadily in the eyes while easing her fingers into a pair of white gloves. "You'd be surprised what He can do."

On the point of casting a derisive comment, Elżbieta closed her mouth staring unblinkingly at her friend for a few moments before she rose from the sofa. "Actually, I think I will join you, Bronia; if only to prove you wrong."

Bronia smiled.

As they sauntered, with a group of Bronia's friends, towards the statue of Our Lady of Lourdes on the open green, a warm inexplicable feeling of belonging was enveloping Elżbieta making her feel at one with the group. Standing in a circle, facing the statue with vases of tulips and lilac beneath, her eyes flitted from a grey-haired doubled-up woman leaning on her wobbly walking stick, to a young bright-eyed girl of about eleven or twelve, to a middle-aged man, to a student, her thoughts wondering: *What are all these people doing here? What are they praying for; hoping for? Who are they praying to?*

She cast her eyes to the statue of a lady dressed in a white robe with a blue sash around her waist, her hands together in prayer, her eyes turned Heavenwards. *What can She do for them? And yet*—Her eyes darted again across the faithful, resting on the young girl and seeing herself. *What is she praying for? What on earth is she hoping for?* She snapped her eyes shut tight, her feet itching to run.

"In the name of the Father, and of…"

Trapped, she stared at her long-time friend as he continued his opening prayer, feeling empty inside as she stared—listened—stared at the assortment of mouths opening and closing, the army of colourful rosary beads dangling from fingers, each bead symbolising a prayer of hope. *Would their prayers be answered?*

And, still, they opened and closed their mouths, and still she stared. And now they sang that old familiar hymn she hadn't heard in years, her mother's favourite, "Zdrowaś Maryjo." They sang in unison, their voices loud and clear as if they were directed to the very pinnacle of heaven. Her thoughts turned to her mother. *She had hoped. She had prayed. And look where it got her. And yet—*Something was starting to stir in the depths of her soul; something she could not explain, and she found herself involuntarily opening her mouth and joining in the joyful hymn.

She saw him from afar; a distant image coming nearer and nearer, carrying a child in one arm and pushing a pushchair with his free hand. Her heart stopped. She froze, her eyes fixed on the growing image. "Henio and my children," she whispered, her heart thudding, her eyes dropping to the youngsters. Her ears were deaf to further prayers and readings, her eyes only on her beloved family. *They were here before her very eyes! This was*, she concluded, *truly a prayer answered.* The praying stopped, the singing ceased and her old friend was by her side.

"It's so very good to see you here, Elżbieta."

Reluctantly, she tore her eyes away from her family to acknowledge Father Stanisław. When she turned round Henryk and the children had disappeared.

Bronia placed her gentle hand on her friend's arm. "All in good time, my dear."

Chapter Forty-Nine

Elżbieta was counting down the hours to Majòwka that evening. Against Bronia's advice, she was formulating her own plan. She would, at the end of the service, go up to Henio and reintroduce herself to her own children. That evening her plan was thwarted. Henryk and the children did not appear; neither did they appear for the next consecutive evenings, leaving Elżbieta in a state of perplexity and silent despair.

Bronia placed her tea glass onto its saucer. "You know, Elżbieta," she glanced at her friend's drawn face, "it is no good fretting about it. He will come when he is ready. He needs time and space."

"Time! Time! Time! That's all I hear. Well, he's had plenty of time; he has had all the time in the world, and now it's my time!" Elżbieta exclaimed.

Bronia looked steadily into her friend's fiery eyes. "If you don't give him time, you may lose him and the children forever. Remember, it is you who walked out on them."

Elżbieta listened to her friend's harsh words, something in them told her Bronia was right; something inexplicable told her it was in God's hands and, despite Henryk's absence, she continued to attend the Majòwka each evening and, at the end of each service, her heart was lightened, and she walked home with a little more hope.

For weeks, Henryk had been building a case to allow Elżbieta back into his life, and the life of their children. He was hearing positive snippets of information from neighbours and friends, and now he had seen it with his own eyes. *She was*, he decided, *a changed woman: calmer, more subdued. Soon it would be time but—not yet.*

On the last day of May, Elżbieta attended the Majòwka for the last time, her heart full of heavy trepidation for *what if Henryk did not appear?* Her heart leapt as she approached the crowd and spotted the unmistakable bold patch on the back of his head. Muddled-up words crashed into her mind whirling and weaving, making no sense at all; her venture of formulating an opening sentence failed miserably. She prayed urgently to her invisible God, feeling nothing but deep hollow despair. *This is my chance*, she told herself, *and I am going to lose it.*

She closed her eyes tightly, her heart racing, her ears hearing jumbled words coming forth from the mouths of the faithful. Everything seemed distorted, nothing seemed to make sense at all, and she was about to lose everything. She attempted to move one foot in front of the other, and found her feet firmly glued to the spot; she attempted to flit her eyes to her children, and they were riveted to the statue; her body felt like stone. She was a living statue. She didn't see as he took slow measured steps towards her; didn't see him until he was almost upon her.

"Elżbieta." His voice was like a soothing balm, melting her until she was free to turn her body towards him, her eyes dropping to her children, her heart full to bursting. She opened her mouth to dry words. "How are you, Elżbieta?" Her eyes rose to him as she nodded her head in silence, a faint smile managing to dance on her lips, her heart racing wildly. "You are looking well," he smiled.

Her eyes switched to Anielka; a bitter wave of regret swept over her as she noticed the change in her daughter, for now, she had fine curls and the sweetest smile to melt any heart. "She has grown," she managed to say.

"And, she is missing her mother."

Elżbieta's dark eyes darted back to her husband, for she was sure she had misheard his last words, her heart stopped, waiting for reassurance.

"The children are missing you, Elżbieta. I am missing you."

Her eyes flitted to the child in the pushchair; the child she had abandoned as a baby, she now craved to hold more than anything else in the world. Bronia's words crashed loudly in her ears. *He has to make the first move.*

"We shall make arrangements, Elżbieta, in the near future."

She nodded her head in silent consent, smiled at the two children in turn, and then at her husband, and walked back home arm in arm with Bronia, her heart dancing.

Chapter Fifty

In the very depths of his heart, from his first sighting of the very young Elżbieta in Kraków Square, Paweł Jaroszynski knew that it was never to be. *And now*, he pondered in the silence of his own company, *he was right.*

His mind drifted back in time as he peeled away the years… *At the very beginning, she was but a child and then she grew up with a husband, children and emotional baggage. Their worlds*, he mused as he drew hard on a cigarette, *crossed mysteriously but never were they to unite permanently.* But there was something—something unique about her he could not get out of his mind, and he could not fathom out this something. *Perhaps, I will never know*, he grimly concluded. *Perhaps, she will always remain an enigma…*

Ewa had departed to her parents, telling him she needed to think things over. In reality, her body had turned into a cauldron of bubbling jealousy and seething bitterness. *How could Paweł betray her so? And, as far as Elżbieta*—She closed her eyes and squeezed them tightly, wishing to obliterate every vestige of her image from her mind. *As far as she was concerned, they were welcome to each other. It was over!*

Elżbieta walked around with a smile on her face for she knew her nightmare was over, and it was only a matter of time until she was with her family again. She no longer asked: *When; why; how?* She was at peace. However, there was one little niggle that would not go away; the fate of Paweł. She could not get out of her mind the thought that her note may have somehow rocked the boat between him and Ewa, the two people who had been instrumental in her recovery. The thought infiltrated her mind, and became a permanent fixture in her head, casting a shadow over her own happiness. *It was,* she thought, *her duty to set things right, but how?*

One evening, Henryk came by unannounced. As she opened the door, her smile diminished as she saw a solitary figure standing on the threshold.

He intercepted her thoughts. "My sister is looking after the children."

Over a glass of lemon tea and sernik, they finalised the details of Elżbieta's move back home. Henryk departed leaving a thousand fluttering butterflies in his wife's tummy, preventing her from any sleep that night as she tossed and turned, got up, lay down and looked out of the window into the dark empty street. Finally, grabbing a coat and wrapping it over her nightgown, slipping on a pair of socks and sturdy shoes, she crept out the door. As she walked the streets, a solitary figure wrapped in a blanket of her own happiness and excitement, one thought still gave her no peace; *Paweł and Ewa.* For an hour, she walked, her feet taking her through the wrought iron gate entrance of the park, her whole body shivering as she wandered amongst the shadowy silhouettes of gnarled trunks and intertwined branches.

Sitting down on a damp wooden bench she wrapped the coat more snuggly around her shivering frame and stared into the silent spooky darkness. Uninvited black thoughts seeped into her mind: *She lay quivering beneath his heavy weight... deafening blasts of thunder drowning out her muffled screams and, with them, her hope of an imminent release... his blubbery face as he forced his twisted fleshy lips on hers... the stench of garlic intermingled with vodka making her stomach churn... her whole body wrenching with revulsion for the despicable monster on top of her as he pumped... pumped... pumped mercilessly on... the shiny samovar... the minuscule reflection of a girl being raped...* Rapidly, opening her eyes she announced to the black distorted silhouettes around her, "I have the solution!"

As soon as she walked through the door, she rushed to the drawer, withdrew a pen and writing pad and began to write her invitations. *Henryk,* she thought as she bit her bottom lip, *will be another bridge to cross when I get to it.*

Chapter Fifty-One

Elżbieta settled into her former life with remarkable ease due to Henryk's patience, forgiveness and understanding, and the children's innocent acceptance. She felt at home from the moment she walked over the threshold, and was ready for her role as mother and wife. She played both roles to perfection. Her love for Henryk was growing by the day for, she had come to realise, he had always been a pillar on which she could lean. He would never let her down. One evening, when they had settled the children for the night, she cautiously broached the subject that had been constantly playing on her mind.

"Henio, I have been thinking, I ought to thank all the people who were involved in my recovery."

He smiled nodding his head. "Yes, yes I think that is a very good idea. What are you thinking of doing?"

"Perhaps we could have a small tea party. We could have a little bigos, maybe some cakes; nothing formal, just a small Thanksgiving get-together."

"Yes, that sounds like a splendid idea. Who are you thinking of inviting?"

"Well, there's Father Stanisław, Ola from the sanatorium, Bronia, Tomek, Zosia and…" She raised her eyes to his smiling face.

"And?" He cocked one eyebrow, his eyes intently focused on his wife's eyes.

"And Ewa and—Paweł." She watched as his eyes clouded over, the smile instantly disappearing from his face.

"Paweł?" His heart thundered.

"Yes, and Ewa."

"Why Paweł?" His voice had become icy cold. "Why him?"

"Because without Ewa and Paweł, I would never have recovered. It was Ewa who made things possible regarding the sanatorium."

"But why Paweł?" His eyes remained locked with Elżbieta's eyes as a heavy, overbearing blanket of silence enveloped them both. After long minutes, he persisted, "Why Paweł, Elżbieta?"

She felt the lump lodged in her throat, her eyes glazing over. "Because I—I feel that, because of my foolishness, he and Ewa have split up; because the Thanksgiving celebration might be a way of getting them back together, and—" She stopped, her eyes dropping to the table.

"And?"

"And for letting bygones be bygones, Henio." She said in a quiet voice, her eyes fixed on the table, her guts churning ruthlessly as she waited for his response.

He rose from the chair and walked towards the window, looking out. "All right, if that is what you wish, Elżbieta."

Chapter Fifty-Two

Within the week seven pairs of eyes stared down at the same worded invitation:

Elżbieta and Henryk Szutka, Cordially invite you to an evening of celebration on Friday, 8th August. Eight o'clock.
Your presence is of the greatest importance.

As soon as the envelope landed on the floor, Zosia tore it open and eagerly wrote her acceptance.

Father Stanisław looked at the envelope long and hard. He recognised the copperplate. His wise eyes scanned the written words and stopped at the word, *celebration. Celebrating what?* He wondered. *Giving their marriage another chance? Perhaps they are expecting another baby? But,* he asked himself, *why should my presence be of any importance?* "Of course, I'll be there," he stated loudly putting pen to paper, a smile dancing on his lips.

Ola's heart leapt. She had no intention of letting her friend down, no matter what distance she may have to travel.

Bronia showed the invitation to Tomek, and they both hugged, crying silent tears of joy.

Ewa and Paweł felt the same as they stood with their respective invitations in their hands, eyes glued to the words, lips set in a determined line, their minds resolute.

Henryk watched as the sparkle in Elżbieta's eyes clouded over, and the smile died on her lips. Her eyes flitted to Henryk. "They're not coming."

"Who?" he asked, hoping his voice did not betray what he was secretly hoping.

"Ewa."

"Ewa?" His heart skipped a beat.

"And Paweł. I… I wanted this celebration to be one of unity, as well as one of thanksgiving; a time in which to heal old wounds."

His heart danced, though only for a brief moment, as his eyes witnessed the deep disappointment in his wife's eyes. *Could it be*, he asked himself, *she still cares for him; still has feelings for him?* He sighed deeply searching for the right words to comfort the woman he loved so desperately and to somehow put an end to all this nonsense.

She slumped down onto a chair, Paweł's brief note still clutched in her hand, her eyes on the words but reading something very different.

Henryk's eyes stayed on his wife, his heart yearning for her love and, realising that she was out of reach.

The long dark night would not allow Henryk that indulgence. Elżbieta's words haunted and possessed his mind… *I wanted this celebration to be one of unity… to heal old wounds.*

Her poignant words rattled around in his head throughout the entire day forcing him, after work, to walk in the opposite direction to his usual route home. His feet standing outside Paweł Jaroszynski's door, his tight knuckles rapped on the door as he took in a deep breath. For long torturous seconds, they stood face to face, each man thinking the same thought, *If it wasn't for this man*—Finally, Paweł inclined his head, his words softly spoken. "You wish to see me, Henryk? Please, come inside."

The older man stepped inside, instantly taken aback by the mound of unwashed pots he could see in the sink, opened beer bottles on the stained coffee table and jumpers and coats strewn carelessly over armchairs. *And this,* he thought, *was once a military man.*

"Please sit down." Paweł indicated a chair, swiftly snatching a jumper away.

Henryk remained standing looking his adversary straight in the eyes. "Pan Jaroszynski, I shall come straight to the point." He coughed lightly and resumed. "We both know full well what happened in the past. We don't need to dwell on that. The fact is that Elżbieta and I are now together again in every sense of the word. We would like you and Ewa to join us, to—to help us heal the past, so to say."

Paweł shook his head from side to side. "No," he said vehemently.

"Pan Jaroszynski—Paweł, it would mean a great deal to Elżbieta."

For long seconds they stood, time ticking ponderously on; both men going over the potential consequences this get-together could create.

Finally, Paweł nodded his head. "All right," he quietly said. "I shall be there." Henryk found no such resistance from Ewa.

Joy, intermingled with trepidation, beat in Elżbieta's heart. Finally, Paweł and Ewa accepted her invitation, but with each acceptance, uninvited doubts crashed into her head. She busied herself from early morning to dusk each day cleaning the apartment and preparing a mountain of food, her mind whirling uncontrollably with thoughts of Paweł and the feelings she once had for this man she had loved; thoughts of Ewa, the woman she had betrayed and the amends she would need to make.

Her guts churned relentlessly. *This was the first gathering she was holding since—since—*she couldn't remember, *and it had to be a success. Would her cleaning come up to scratch? And—what about the bigos? Would the variety of kiełbaski, she had stirred into the mix, be of sufficient taste and quality? Had she soaked the śledzie for an adequate amount of time? If only Mama was here, she would know. Does the yeast cake have enough flavourings?*

She had prepared these foodstuffs hundreds of times before and yet—She bit her lip dipping her wooden spoon into the big pan of simmering bigos, and bringing a spoonful up to her lips, shook her head and added extra chunks of Krakowska into the mix. Her head was buzzing, her feet ached while her heart and guts continued to churn with inexplicable excitement and dread.

The first guest to arrive was Ola who stood at the door, with her small case by her side, eagerly waiting for the door to open. As it opened, her eyes widened and twinkled, a delightful smile spread on her lips. "My dear, Elżbieta, how wonderful you look!" she exclaimed joyously.

Elżbieta stood and stared transfixed at her saviour. "You've made it!"

"What's five hundred, or so, kilometres between friends? I wouldn't have missed this for the world." She dropped her case unceremoniously onto the threshold and took Elżbieta into her arms, hugging her tightly. "Thanks, be to God." She raised her tear-filled eyes Heavenwards. "Thanks, be to the Almighty Lord!"

The next guests to simultaneously arrive were Zosia and Father Stanisław, with a fresh round of hugs and kisses, followed by Bronia and Tomek. The guests soon mingled and fussed over the children, while Elżbieta made final food preparations her eyes flitting, at regular intervals, to the closed door. The gentle knock on the door brought an uncontrollable attack of merciless thudding to her heart, her eyes darting nervously to the door as Ewa made her entrance.

The door closed, and Elżbieta's guts resumed their ruthless churning and twisting. She heard the knocking loud and clear and her heart stopped as she held her baby close to her chest, her eyes glued on the door. She watched as one potential father to her youngest child opened the door, and the other walked in; her heartbreaking and, at that very moment in time, accepting the fact her child would never know the true identity of his father, for the answer would never be known.

Inner fears gradually subsided as, on the surface, etiquette was preserved and all behaved civilly towards each other though there was a distinct coolness between Ewa and Paweł.

The most important item to grace the celebration had been carefully taken out of its layers of soft cloth and polished repeatedly until it gleamed. It was the most precious item Elżbieta owned for, not only had dear Zygmunt bequeathed it to her in his will, it represented all that she was, and is now. Carefully, she stood it on an elaborately embroidered cloth on top of a small table in the corner of the room, ready for the right moment.

Henryk's eyes flitted around the room, full of chatter and charged with tension. *Ewa and Paweł,* he sadly concluded, *were worlds apart, neither engaging in conversation and clearly avoiding eye contact.* Ola and Bronia were in deep conversation which, from his vantage point, looked deep and meaningful. Father Stanisław, Elżbieta and Zosia were reminiscing about old times and old friends who had passed from this earth but never forgotten. Tomek was blissfully engaged with the children.

Paweł, nursing a glass of vodka in his hand, darted his eyes to Elżbieta, brought the glass up to his lips and swallowed hard the liquor in one gulp, shuddering and squeezing his eyes tightly. Henryk clinked a glass with a teaspoon and smiled broadly. "I think, my friends, it is time to sit down at the table." Spontaneously, Paweł brought his empty glass to his lips as he saw the loving looks exchanged between Elżbieta and Henryk. *To hell with them all! He cursed silently.*

The table was laden with a variety of salads: small plates of chopped tomatoes and onions with cucumber and sour cream, others with small pieces of mixed vegetables; a mixture of breads jostled with each other as well as plates of a variety of spicy sausages. Henryk's eyes strayed to the carefully prepared śledzie and a smile broke out on his lips as he remembered... *Anielka crying, pointing at the offending fish soaking in the bowl of fresh water saying accusingly, "Tatuś, I don't like them. They're—they're staring at me…"*

His eyes flitted to his daughter now sitting on a pile of cushions, switching to his son secured in his high chair happily banging his spoon, and he felt a wave of ultimate joy in his heart as he felt his wife's presence by his side. He looked around the table; at each individual who, in their own way, had helped to save Elżbieta from herself and gave her back to him. Raising a glass of wine he stated, "My dear friends, this evening is important to us all. It is an evening to forgive and forget." His eyes flitted across to Paweł where they lingered. "To forget, my friends, and to thank Our Lord for the chance of a new beginning." His eyes switched to his old friend. "Father Stanisław, please could you say grace?"

Grace was said, glasses clinked, a hot tureen of mushroom soup was brought out and the meal commenced. Elżbieta beamed at her guests tucking into her homemade food. *Yes, I am a good cook*, she smiled to herself. *And, I am going to be a first-class mother and wife.* She looked across at Henryk, and they exchanged a secret smile, Henryk's smile extending as he witnessed an exchanged look between Ewa and Paweł. *There is hope*, he said to himself. *There is always hope!*

The meal was over, the children were put to bed, the grown-ups relaxed in the sitting room with charged glasses in their hands chatting, reminiscing and laughing. Paweł's glassy eyes strayed to Henryk and Elżbieta. *They are happy; yes, they are happy.* His unhappy eyes wandered to Ewa. Eyes locked. She smiled. He smiled back.

Elżbieta rose, her heart racing. *It was time! All the years of her life had been leading up to this moment and now it was here.* Taking slow steps she approached the shiny samovar, her heart thudding uncontrollably, her mind with a purpose of its own. She filled the container with water, securing the smoke stack on the top to ensure enough draft. Henryk, rushing to her side, helped his wife to bring the table, with its symbolic cargo, to the guests, amidst much admiration of the traditional Russian tea maker, as Elżbieta ignited the small coals to heat the water.

Waiting for the water to boil, she brought out a multi-layered chocolate sponge cake, amidst more sighs, and extinguished the fire, while Henryk deftly removed the smoke stack and placed a teapot on top, to be gradually heated by the rising hot air.

Elżbieta sat opposite the precious samovar waiting for the zavarka to be brewed, thoughts of long ago crashing into her head... *Intermittent spikes of jagged lightning quivered in the semi-darkened room as the young girl, pinned down to her bed, lay quivering beneath the heavy weight on top of her. Deafening blasts of thunder drowned out her muffled screams and, with them, her hope of an imminent release. She squeezed her eyes tight to obliterate his blubbery face as he forced his fleshy lips on hers, the stench of garlic and vodka made her stomach churn, her whole body wrench with revulsion for this monster on top of her as he pumped on mercilessly. Her hot prickly eyes strayed to the shiny samovar where they witnessed...* a crowd of people. She looked around at the happy smiling faces around her; her family and friends; the people who had saved her. Her eyes flitted back to the shiny samovar. Tadek Lisztek was gone.

Carefully, she diluted the zavarka with the boiling water from the main container and handed the tea glasses, one by one, to her husband and her friends. She was happy. She was complete.